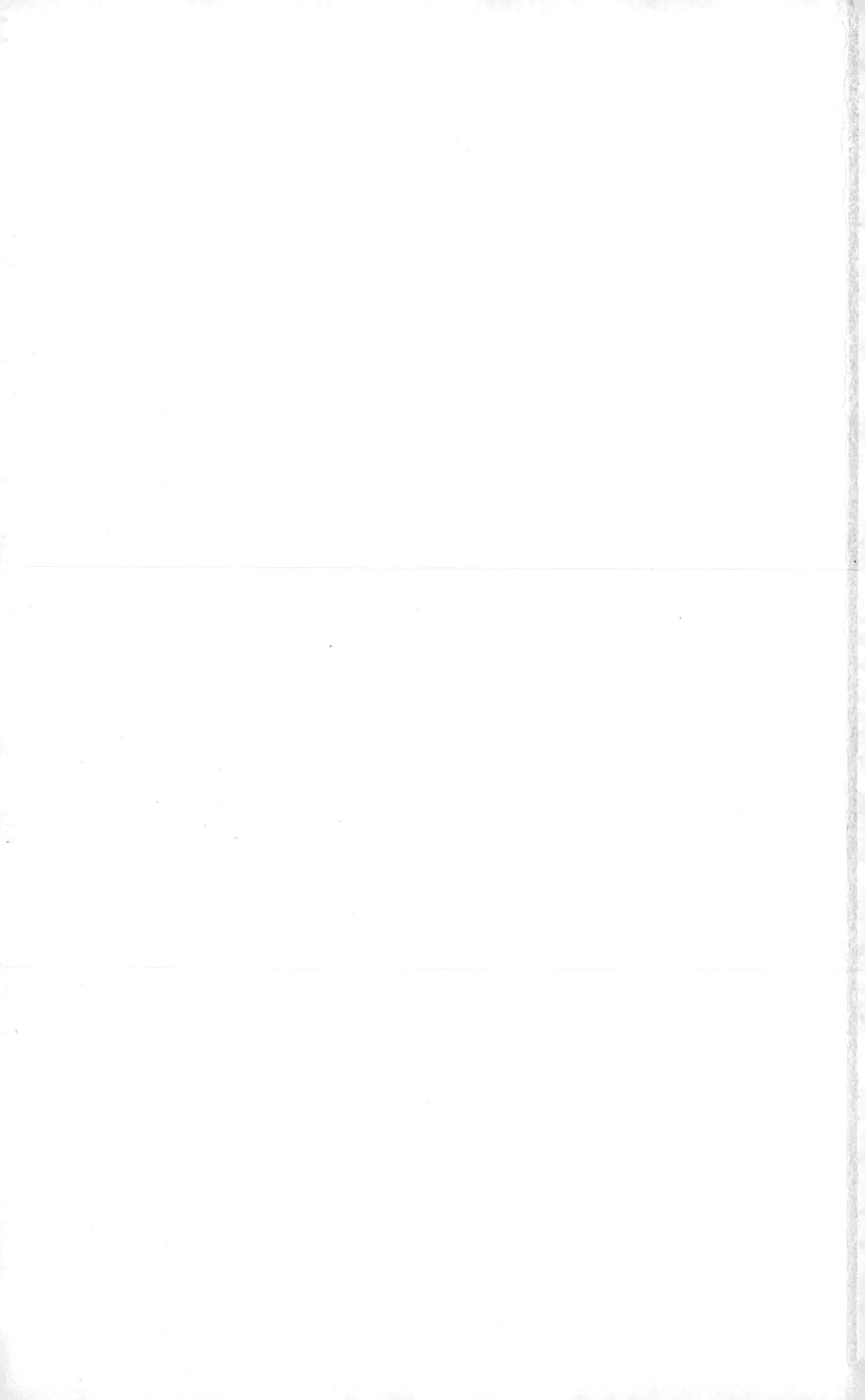

Praise for
THE UNBINDING OF MARY READE

"*The Unbinding of Mary Reade* is a rollicking, breathtaking adventure full of heart, passion, wit, and intelligence. I was turning pages fast as a wind fills a sail, marveling at the talent that is Miriam McNamara."

—An Na, Printz Award Winner and National Book Award Finalist for *A Step from Heaven*

"A captivating account of gender, feminism, agency, and all manner of desire—most importantly, the desire to be free. Badass, through and through."

—M-E Girard, Lambda Literary Award Winner and William C. Morris Award Finalist for *Girl Mans Up*

"Issues of gender identity and who and how to love make *The Unbinding of Mary Reade* resonate as strongly in the present as in the past. Action-packed, this romantic tale is bound to entice teen and adult readers alike."

—Cordelia Jensen, author of *Skyscraping* and *The Way the Light Bends*

"*The Unbinding of Mary Reade* is a stunning debut—intense and unforgettable, thrilling to the very last page!"

—Melanie Crowder, author of *Audacity* and *An Uninterrupted View of the Sky*

"I dare you not to yell *huzzah!* at least ten times while reading *The Unbinding of Mary Reade*, a swashbuckling girl-power adventure about owning who you are and loving who you want. Mary is an unforgettable heroine who is tough yet tender, a survivor who's got swagger and courage. I'd join her pirate crew any day!"

—Heather Demetrios, author of *Bad Romance* and *Exquisite Captive*

"This is the pirate novel we've been waiting for. Epic and confident, with a plot that sizzles and then ignites like a powder keg. Longing and love tangle in nuanced, powerful combinations as Mary takes to the high seas and meets her match in Anne Bonny. An unstoppable romance, an unforgettable adventure."

—Amy Rose Capetta, author of *Echo after Echo*

"Fantastic, unique, and inclusively diverse young adult fiction . . . You had me at 'queer pirates.' *grabby hands*"

—Tor.com

"Canonically queer pirate girls? Yes, please."

—Barnes & Noble Teen Blog

MIRIAM McNAMARA

Sky Pony Press
New York

Sky Pony Press books may be purchased in bulk at special discounts for sales promotion, corporate gifts, fund-raising, or educational purposes. Special editions can also be created to specifications. For details, contact the Special Sales Department, Sky Pony Press, 307 West 36th Street, 11th Floor, New York, NY 10018 or info@skyhorsepublishing.com.

Sky Pony® is a registered trademark of Skyhorse Publishing, Inc.®, a Delaware corporation.

www.skyponypress.com

www.MiriamMcNamara.com

10 9 8 7 6 5 4 3 2 1

Library of Congress Cataloging-in-Publication Data is available on file.

Cover design by Sammy Yuen
Cover image credit iStockphoto

Print ISBN: 978-1-5107-2705-2
E-book ISBN: 978-1-5107-2711-3

Printed in the United States of America

For Al
We have shaken loose from our moorings
We could go anywhere from here

"Now we are to begin a History full of surprising Turns and Adventures; I mean, that of Mary Read . . . the odd Incidents of their rambling Lives are such that some may be tempted to think the whole Story no better than a Novel or Romance . . ."

—*A General History of the Robberies and Murders of the Most Notorious Pyrates*

The Unbinding of Mary Reade

CHAPTER ONE

Caribbean Sea—1719

Mary dove into the jolly boat, flattened herself between the benches, and prayed no one noticed it swinging from its goose-necked davits. She struggled to catch her breath, her gasps almost drowning out the smattering of gunfire, the desperate shouts of the crew, and the cries and moans of the injured littering the deck.

She squeezed her eyes shut and again saw the wild, screaming men with gold earrings, brightly patterned bandanas, and cutlasses in their teeth, crawling up the grappling lines—rogues clearing the path before them with their bullets, firing flintlocks with both hands—swordsmen slinging themselves on board from the taffrail carrying swirling blades—men barefoot and naked to the waist, all shades of sunburned, brown, and even the darkest black—all men—

But one?

Mary was sure she had imagined it.

She squinted over the side of the jolly boat, the thick smoke a steel-colored curtain. There she was. A *girl* pirate. There was no mistaking it. Unlike Mary, the girl wore a red velvet dress and had long, auburn hair, everything about her curving and feminine—except for the way Mary had just watched her cut down one man and shoot another.

Mary guessed the man fighting by her side was the pirate captain. He wore a coat, unlike the other pirates, one made of chintz swirling with red, cream, and green, and britches to match. His face was handsome, soft at the mouth and eye, framed by thick brown curls that hung to his shoulders.

Movement beside the jolly boat caught Mary's attention. Paddy's thinning blond hair appeared as he peered over a tarpaulin-covered crate, then his eyes, staring at the pirates with a fierce expression. The red-haired girl pointed up to the poop deck, where *Kapitein* Baas was playing sniper with a few of his best men. The pirate captain looked up and narrowed his eyes. He cocked his head, aimed his pistol through the fog, and fired, but the angle of the poop from the quarterdeck blocked his shot.

From Mary's vantage she had a clear view of *Kapitein* Baas, no ladders or masts to hinder her gaze. She had a clear view of Paddy, hunched behind the tarpaulin with murder in his eyes. She looked back at the girl who stood like a man in her skirts, and the handsome pirate reloading his pistol.

Paddy wanted to kill the pirates.

The pirates wanted to kill *Kapitein* Baas.

Mary only wanted to escape this fight alive, make her way to Nassau, and be reunited with Nat—but as her eyes caught the girl pirate again, she paused.

The girl looked in her direction, and Mary's insides knotted up. Then the girl shouted something and pointed to the forecastle. The two pirates erupted into the melee surrounding them, and in seconds they'd hacked their way through the worst of the fighting. Mary barely scrunched down in time to keep out of their sight as they approached. Her breath rasped heavily on the wood of the bench beneath her cheek, and she forced herself to quiet the sound. She remembered the outline of Paddy's hunched back and prayed he wasn't seen.

"Quick, see if you've got a clear shot," the pirate girl panted. Mary peeked above the gunwale again. She could have reached out and touched them. The girl whipped left and right, pistol raised, but no one approached.

"I'm still blocked, damn it." The gentleman pointed his pistol at the poop deck, then dropped the weapon and pulled himself up on the foremast shrouds with one arm to aim again. The girl let her weapon lower slightly as she turned to gauge his angle.

Paddy's musket bobbed over the tarpaulin while the pirates' backs were turned. Mary's stomach tightened as he slowly brought the barrel of his musket to bear on the gentleman. The click when Paddy cocked the hammer seemed a little thing, but Mary saw the girl's shoulders tense, her head tilting slightly.

Mary didn't dare breathe or move. The pirate captain squinted back up at the poop, trying to perfect his angle.

Mary imagined Paddy's trigger finger tightening ever so carefully.

The girl whirled around, roaring as she slammed a fist into the barrel of Paddy's musket as it fired. The shot ripped into the forecastle wall and Paddy stumbled onto the deck on his hands and knees. The girl kicked the musket out of Paddy's reach and leveled her flintlock at his head, her teeth bared and chest heaving.

"No!" Mary yelled, standing and pointing her musket at the girl's head at the same moment that the pirate captain whirled and brought his weapon to bear on her chest. The jolly boat rocked wildly beneath her feet, and she struggled to keep her balance. Her breath caught in her throat, but she held her ground. Now was her chance to *earn* her freedom, instead of sneaking off and hoping no one shot her.

Mary deliberately shifted her weapon away from the girl and pointed it up, toward the poop deck. She saw the pirate captain's expression shift slightly, and he put up a hand to stay the girl. Mary crouched until she was in the same position she'd been in before. *Kapitein* Baas came into view, as clear as he'd been earlier.

Mary had watched sailors shoot at seagulls from the quarter-gallery balconies, squinting down the musket's length at their targets. She imitated their position now, cocking the hammer fully as Paddy and the pirates watched her in disbelief. The *kapitein*'s inhumanity had earned her hatred many times over as they'd crossed the ocean, and it was easy enough to imagine him an animal now.

Mary pulled the trigger, the recoil knocking her to the bottom of the jolly boat as it jerked beneath her. She dropped the musket and scrambled to the gunwale to see what she'd done.

Up on the poop a few men rushed to bend over the prostrate form of *Kapitein* Baas.

The pirate gentleman hopped from the shrouds, smiling broadly. "Well, young man! Looks like you hit your mark."

She nodded curtly, clutching the gunwale to steady her shaking hands.

The pirate captain sprinted for the sterncastle steps. The pirate girl stayed, her pistol still held to Paddy's head. Mary stood awkwardly as the girl's gaze flicked over the skinny length of her and up to her face. The girl had eyes so brown they were nearly black. Deep-set, but not in an unattractive way. Like a hawk.

"Don't shoot him," Mary said, her eyes darting to Paddy.

Mary's pulse sped up as the girl smiled lasciviously, lowering her weapon. "Anything for you, young marksman." Then she whirled, skirts swishing, and followed her man.

CHAPTER TWO

London, England—1704

Mum told Mary over and over, as their feet stumbled across the cobblestones, that once they got to Granny's Mary must be quiet.

"Don't say a word, Mary. Not one word."

Mary didn't know what *Granny's* was, or why they were going there. That morning, after days of lying slumped against the wall, oblivious to Mary's cries of cold and hunger, Mum had finally staggered to her feet and dressed Mary in Mark's old frock and pudding cap. Mum had told her, with feverish intensity, that if Mary was good there'd be a pasty in it for her, and Mary had promised she'd do whatever she was told.

They walked forever. Mary was so tired she could barely get up the whitewashed steps of the big house Mum led her to. Mum knocked on the door, then clutched Mary to her chest as she begged to come in. A man in a crisp coat and black shoes with bright silver buckles brought them to a dark, wide room stuffed with soft and shiny things, the oily smell of burning lamps making Mary feel dizzy and sick. The yellow of Mum's hair caught the light as she set Mary down and pushed her forward, toward a frowning, gray-haired woman seated on a beautiful chair.

"Mark, I'm sure you remember your Granny?"

Mum's hand tightened on Mary's shoulder. *Don't say anything*, Mary remembered, so she didn't, even though Mark was dead and she certainly didn't remember this strange woman. Mum continued talking, her voice growing tearful. Mary focused on the woman's fingers kneading a green velvet cushion. Little strips of color lifted beneath her nails, then settled as she stroked the fabric smooth.

"There's no one else but you." Mum's tears caught the light of the lamps, spotting her skirts as they fell. "You're all the family we have left."

"Family indeed, whether I like it or not." But when Granny looked at Mary her face seemed to soften. "He does have eyes just like his father's."

A glint of silver appeared in Granny's palm. She held out a pretty, shiny coin, and both Mary and Mum reached for it. Granny hesitated, then leaned down and pressed it into Mary's palm. "You're a Reade, even if your father died before I made peace with it," she said. "Come see your Granny once a month, and each time I'll give you a coin just like this one."

On the walk back to Wapping Mum bought them a meat pasty and small beer, and that night they slept in a room of their own.

Things were better after that. They had enough food to eat, enough kindling for a fire to warm the little room they had to themselves. Mum wasn't so sad. She was even happy sometimes, when there was enough left over for a bottle of gin.

All Mary had to do for it was change her name, and that was an easy thing to do.

CHAPTER THREE

Caribbean Sea—1719

The pirate captain easily convinced the sailors left alive, being exhausted and liking life, to drop their weapons in exchange for the promise of safe passage.

The sun sweltered as the day went on. The brigands slapped each other's backs and paid the captives scant attention; they were busy passing the rum around, throwing things around in the captain's quarters, and breaking into the hold.

Sailors fidgeted and picked at their skin as they waited. They'd all heard stories about pirates eating the beating hearts out of captains' chests while they were still alive, or forcing entire crews overboard into the sea. Mary had heard those stories told countless times by boys on the docks when she was young. But she'd also heard that pirates were just as likely to offer goodwill to their captured crews. They might even find certain enterprising men a place on their crew and a share of the prize money. Equal share, almost, to that of the captain. That's what the stories said.

Mary forced herself to calm her breathing. She had nothing to fear from children's stories. She'd taken charge, gotten herself noticed. Baas was vanquished, all of his officers deposed by the pirates. There was nothing between her and Nassau now.

"Hello, lad."

Mary turned, and the pirate captain was there. He wasn't tall but he was striking, with broad shoulders and brilliant green eyes. He flipped the lace cuffs off his wrists and leaned against the barrel next to Mary. "Allow me to introduce myself. The name's Calico Jack Rackham. Captain Jack to you buggers."

Mary nodded, trying to look hard.

"And you would be . . ."

She cleared her throat. "Mark Reade, sir." There, she didn't sound too intimidated.

Fabric rustled at Mary's other side, and she jumped when the pirate girl leaned over the gunwale just beside her.

"And this fair lady is Anne Bonny," said Captain Jack, turning to the girl. "You were right! He speaks English."

Anne nudged her, eyes sparkling. "The boy who shot his own captain, to join the pirate band!" She made Mary's crime sound like one of the stories the boys on the Wapping docks had told. The pirate tales that had enthralled her so. Mary sounded like someone else, someone grand and fearless.

Jack continued. "Well, I must say, you made quite the impression with that bit of marksmanship. Our crew needs boys like you. Boys ready to seize a moment before it passes. Boys clever enough to be sure they're on the winning side."

Mary looked over the gunwale at the nearby shore of Curaçao. The beaches and trees were clearly visible off the port bow, with the promise of Willemstad just beyond. But that promise hadn't ever been for her. The *kapitein* had been planning to lock his sailors in the hold overnight to make sure they couldn't disappear and leave him crewless for his journey back to Rotterdam. The pirates, on the other hand, would surely let her go free, head to shore if she wanted to. She could take a jolly boat to Willemstad and find passage from there to Nassau. She was so close to finding Nat now.

"You look near starving," Anne added. She leaned in as if to whisper a secret in confidence. "Don't you think, whatever you was looking forward to there, it can wait till you've a little meat on your bones and a bit of treasure in your pocket?" The bare skin of the pirate girl's neck was smudged with gunpowder, where she might have run her fingers to push her hair back in battle. She'd bird-nested her tresses into a mass of windblown curls, frizzled and festooned with bits of ribbon and a tiny gold chain. The pirates let this girl sail with them—just like this, undisguised.

Of course they wouldn't accept a skinny boy-girl like Mary in the same way. She'd have to be more careful than ever in the company of such ruffians. She didn't have a captain protecting her pretty arse, if her secret were discovered.

"Well?" asked Anne. She seemed amused by Mary's open-mouthed staring.

Mary dropped her gaze and looked over at Paddy sitting hunched on a crate, looking despondent. It had been a godsend having someone look out for her these past few months, and she was loath to give him up. "Me friend there, he speaks English as well." She met Jack's eyes boldly. "If I'm coming, he's coming, too. He'll make a loyal and brave crewmate. Despite some, ah, understandable mistakes that were made in the heat of battle."

Jack raised his brows. "That old Irish bloke that tried to kill me?" he asked, amused.

"Absolutely not," said Anne. "It's enough that I didn't kill him."

"Give him a chance, miss," said Mary. "You'll be glad to have his loyalty. There's no one I trust more."

"I like loyalty," said Jack, glancing at Anne. "He can come, so long as he knows what side he's on. Remember, *I'm* the one who chose to take you on."

"Of course," said Mary, heart accelerating. "You won't regret it."

"Look at this!" a pirate crowed, running up and holding out his arms. Dozens of gold and silver pocket watches hung from his hands on glistening chains. From what Mary had gathered, they were part of a huge parcel of metal luxury items the *Zilveren Vissen* had carried from Rotterdam—letter openers, candlesticks, paperweights, compasses. "This might be as good a haul as the *Kingston*!"

"See?" said Anne to Jack. "If you'd gone seeking pardon when you first started going on about it, you'd be this much poorer!"

Jack smiled ruefully. "That's why a good captain always listens to his crew."

The man handed Jack a fistful of chains. "Aye, and that's why *you're* captain now, not Vane."

Gold flashed as the trinkets swung in the sun. Mary was mesmerized by their glint.

"Here *you* are." Jack picked off a watch and tossed it to her, offhand. "That's for joining the account."

Solid gold it was, she was sure of it. The weight of it in her hand made her breathless. Scrolling gleamed around the edge. The image of a ship and a dark-haired girl waving a handkerchief from the shore shone brightly at the center, painted with a fine hand. Mary looked up, searching for Paddy. If something like this was put in his hand, surely it would convince him.

The pirates, growing wilder from the rum, whooped as they dragged bits of treasure up from the hold—a bale of lace, a trunkful of ladies' underthings. They'd found bottles of wine and were waving them about. One man was running about with a pair of lady's beribboned stockings rolled up to his elbows, walking them up others' arms like an obscene pair of legs.

The *Zilveren Vissen* was beginning to list portside from damage dealt by the pirate ship's cannon, and surely wouldn't last the night. Off the port side of the brig, a jolly boat full of sailors still bound for Curaçao was ready to lower into the shadow cast by the setting sun.

Paddy was standing beside the boat, waving her over. "Come on, lad!" he shouted.

She ran over and he turned to board, but she grabbed his arm and pulled him away. "I'm joining the pirates," she said quickly, "and you should come with me." Mary swung the pocket watch in front of him as Jack had done to her. "You see this?" He watched it in disapproval or admiration, she couldn't tell. "How might Katie feel if you brought back a few of these to her?"

"It's beautiful," he said slowly. "Katie'd be sure to love it."

Mary waved dismissively at the jolly boat. "If you go into port with that lot, you'll be back where you started, without any payment for the journey. But if you come with *us*, your share will surely be enough to make an honest woman out of Katie!"

Paddy looked around, tight-lipped. She could tell he didn't like the pirates' wildness. But his eyes came to rest on the riches strewn across the deck, all the wealth that had been locked away this entire journey suddenly spread out before them. Opulent fabric spilled everywhere, florid and peacocked damasks shimmering in blues and deep wine colors. Raw silks crumpled into earth-toned valleys among heaps of familiar navy and cream linens. The tilt of evening light shaded the men to gray and gold as they clambered up from the hold, tossing compasses and candlesticks onto the rainbow drifts while the sky deepened to indigo in the east.

He hesitated—Mary could tell he was tempted—but his hands worried a tear in his shirt. "You know better than me about the king's proclamation!" he whispered. "You leave here with them, and you're worth a pretty penny if you're captured. There's men who'll track you down, make no mistake."

That promise of reward, Mary knew, was what had brought Nat to the islands. It wasn't just the Navy hunting pirates now—anyone with a ship and a couple of cannons was gathering a crew, and Nat had been eager to join up. "They may try to, but what are the chances?" she argued. "Probably less than those of being killed by a whipping under another captain like Baas. Join up and you'll likely be home after a few voyages, with a pocketful of gold, a ruby or two, and nobody the wiser."

"They know I tried to kill him," Paddy said in a low voice, his eyes flicking to Jack.

"And they know I shot the *kapitein*," Mary said. "Since I vouch for you, they'll trust you. I'm sure of it."

Paddy groaned and put his head in his hands. "Jaysus, I hope God forgives me. Lord knows the king won't."

"You're coming!" Mary crowed.

"I might as well forget Katie if I stay. I'll never have the means to woo her otherwise." Paddy sighed. "What convinced you to join up? I thought you was dead set on getting to dry land soon as possible."

Mary looked at the girl, who stood for all the world like a captain herself in her caramel boots, ordering her men about. She saw the way every man on the ship was staring at Anne. It wasn't her body that did it, or her hair or face—it was something else.

She wanted Nat to stare at her like all those men were staring at Anne. She wanted him to never look away from her again.

"You're going for that girl, ain't you," Paddy said. "I can see it on your face."

She'd be daft to admit what she was after. "I'm going for this," she said instead, dangling the pocket watch in front of him. "And the promise of more like it."

Paddy laughed and shook his head. "She's the captain's girl, son. You'd be wise to remember that."

CHAPTER FOUR

Wapping, London—1707

Muffled crying drew Mary out of her tenement room. She hesitated on the landing, listening to the sniffles and whimpers of someone clearly trying not to sob. Slowly, she followed the sounds down the cold, dark steps and found the boy from the kip next to hers hunched under the stair. His split lip bled into the dust, tears streaking his dirty cheeks.

"Nat?" Mary put a hand on his shoulder, but he smacked it away.

"Bugger off, Mark!" he mumbled, wiping snot from his face as he curled into the wall.

Mary recalled that Nat's da had gotten back from the sea just days ago. Nat had shared some sugar mice with her, a gift from his mum before his da drank up the rest of the money. She'd been jealous that Nat's mum was nice enough to spend extra money on treats instead of gin, but then she'd heard his da come home late the next night. The sounds of his raging, the pleading and crashes of things breaking, had made her think she was better off after all.

Nat was always so happy down on the docks when they played sailors and pirates, his big grin gapped by missing teeth. Too bad it was so cold outside, or she would have asked him if he wanted to race her to the river. Instead, Mary sat down and began dragging her finger through the dirt, tracing the outline of a grand ship with lots of masts. "This is our ship," she said. "We'll sail it far away and find our fortune."

His sniffling quieted as he watched her add waves and a shining sun. Then he shifted onto his knees next to her and started tracing, too. "This is the island we'll sail to," he said, the tears gone from his voice. "And this is the castle we'll live in, with locks on all the doors so Da can't get in."

"Me granny lives in a place like that!" Mary thought of another way to cheer him up. "When I'm big Mum says it's going to be my house. There's plenty of rooms for you and your mum too."

Nat made a dismissive noise. "In the new world folks don't have to have a rich granny. Anyone can live in a big house and do whatever they want."

Imagine being free of pleasing Granny! Mum browbeat Mary any chance she got with threats of transportation or worse if anyone figured out she was a girl. Meanwhile, life in a house like Granny's felt as far off as Nat's castle on an island. Mary traced two figures on her ship, both brandishing swords. "This is us, striking terror into the hearts of anyone who tells us what to do!"

Nat leaned in to survey her work. He nodded, then added a smudge to her picture. "And that's me parrot. He sits on me shoulder."

Mary laughed and added a smudge for herself to match.

"I can't wait," Nat said. The blood on his gums looked dreadful, but his smile was bright. "I can't wait till the two of us sail far away from here."

CHAPTER FIVE

Caribbean Sea—1719

Mary woke with a start to the tap of ropes knocking against a mast in a gray morning breeze. The pirates' brigantine, the *Ranger*, creaked and sloshed in a steady rhythm. Material crinkled underneath her as she stretched. A bale of lace had come undone in the night, its drape forming a flimsy blanket. If it hadn't been for the sounds of the ship she might have thought she was back at Granny's house in Westminster, waking up beneath the covers—the smell of clean, fine fabric and its bright white color brought to mind her little bed in the garret.

Her head bumped against something solid as she curled to her side, and she reached out to find Paddy's grubby feet were inches from her face. Mary felt a thrill, remembering he'd come. Ever since Paddy had found her in the dark hold of the *Vissen*, cornered by a particularly foul tar who'd had one too many rums, he'd kept an eye out for her. She'd been grateful for his vigilance after learning that passing as a boy was not always enough to protect her.

Mary curled away from him, blinking to clear her eyes, and pushed the lace back.

Across the deck and amid a tumble of damask, the rumpled top of Jack's head and one bare arm were clearly visible. Mary tried to imagine *Kapitein* Baas sprawled in the same position, tickled at the thought of him snoring away in the company of his sailors.

The two captains couldn't be more different. Baas treated the poor tars who worked for him as if they were barely human. The past three months Mary's stomach had screamed with hunger, and her limbs had ached with cold worse than the days right after Mark had died. Baas had given his sailors only enough food and rest to keep them alive, and sometimes not even that. She'd watched sailors get tied to the mainmast and lashed for minor infractions at his command. Men had died from those beatings, or the infections that always followed.

Jack, in contrast, had given her a pocket watch. A *gold* pocket watch. She touched the chain she'd looped around her neck. She'd never had anything so fine belong to her—and it was just a tiny piece of the cargo that had been distributed among the entire crew.

Mary lifted herself further, looking for the red of Anne's dress, but if she was there the fabric hid her. Mary stood, piled the lace on top of Paddy, and looked around. Damp, cool air skimmed across her skin; the sky was a delicate pre-dawn slate. Nothing but rocking water in all directions—but Nassau was out there. Nassau was *so* close.

She wondered how close, exactly. The cabin door was slightly ajar. Captains kept maps in their cabins, and a captain like Jack wouldn't keelhaul her for looking at one. Mary hopped lightly to her feet and picked her way around the bales to the cabin door. It was dark and still within. With one last glance over her shoulder to make sure Jack hadn't moved, she slipped inside.

"You're up early, Mark."

Mary stopped dead when she saw Anne in the shadows, Her hair was even bigger than the night before, curling wildly around her face. "Come here," Anne whispered loudly. She held her hand out, something round and soft in it. "You've *got* to try this."

Looking at a map was one thing—lingering in a room with the captain's girl while he slept was another. But Anne didn't seem concerned. With one last nervous glance behind her, Mary crept inside.

"I woke up starving." Anne's cheek bore the marks of sleep still fading across it. "I thought there was one of them left, and I wanted to get to it before Jack did." *Taught dair*, not *thought there*. She spoke like the poor girls back in Wapping, just off the boat from Ireland, but her accent was muddled and hard to catch. She held a curious, pale-pink fruit, her face glowing with delight. It glistened strangely, a diamond-shaped network of grooves on its surface.

Anne pulled a knife out of her boot and sliced clean through the fruit, revealing a cream-colored flesh studded with black seeds. Placing one half in her mouth, she scraped a bit of pulp from the skin and handed over the other piece. The fruit was knobby against Mary's palm, giving off an intoxicating scent.

"Mmm." Anne held the fruit in her mouth for a moment, spat a seed on the floor, and swallowed. "Custard apple. I'll bet you've never had anything like it before. I know I never had, not till Jack gave me one." Mary imitated her, running her teeth against the skin to pull the flesh off. It really tasted like custard, eggy and sweet. Mary closed her eyes. This was what she'd imagined the New World would be like, all those times she and Nat had told their stories back in Wapping. Fruit like this, handed to her like it was nothing. Like there was more than enough for everyone.

Anne took another bite. "Since you're here, tell me—how'd a British chap like you end up on a boat full of Dutchmen, and do you have a sweetheart what was the cause of it?"

Mary started at her bluntness. "A sweetheart, miss?" She turned away from Anne, looking around the cabin. "I suppose so." The cabin was lit by a few smoking candles perched on the chandelier. "Ah, I have reason to believe me sweetheart is in Nassau. I came in here to look at a map, actually. To see if I was getting close."

Anne clapped her hands. "I knew it! There's *always* a good story, as long as you ask."

Mary made a noncommittal noise and walked over to the great, dark table in the center of the room that was covered in parchments and clutter.

"Go on, then," Anne urged, following her. "Tell me about her. I've tried to get good stories out of the others, but they're all disgusting. I can tell you're different. A *romantic*."

Mary couldn't begin to think of how to tell her story without giving herself away. She leaned over the table and flipped up a corner of parchment, revealing something that looked promising. "Would you be able to point out where we are on a map?"

Anne winked, circling the table. "Playing hard to crack, are you? Never mind, I'll get the tale out of you soon enough."

Mary uncovered the parchment and, sure enough, it was a map of the islands. "I'd rather hear how someone like *you* ended up on this ship," she said. "That seems more like a tale worth telling."

Anne brushed aside crusts and a compass and helped Mary spread out the map. "Here, I'll show you." Anne bent over the parchment with great interest, pushing curls off her forehead.

Mary couldn't see the map very well, so she inched closer. They were almost touching. Her heart was beating hard and she kept glancing at the door, but no one appeared.

The center of the map represented water, decorated by swirling mermaids and taloned sea monsters. The outer edges were ringed with shapes, what must have been islands and landforms. Most of them were colored red, with bunches of tiny words crammed into every corner. "It's gorgeous," Mary murmured. And mostly illegible—she couldn't begin to make sense of it.

"Let's see, I got off the boat from Ireland in Charleston." Anne's hand settled on the top righthand corner of the map. "With me da. Then I landed, let's see—here." Her finger landed on an island not far from the same corner. "With James. And now I'm here—" her finger slid to around the middle-left of the map, over open water. "With Jack."

Mary thought about questions she could ask, but all of them felt wildly intimate. "So that's where we are now. Do you know where we're headed?" she asked, keeping her gaze fixed on the map. *Say Nassau. Show me Nassau.*

Anne's fingers inched over to a tiny red blob off of a large red island's southwest shore. "Isla de Cotorras. Isle of Parrots. We're going to lay low there, until all the disagreement among the crew gets settled and we decide what to do next. It's deserted, although the Spanish lay claim to it. That's why it's red. Cuba's the island just beside it, also Spanish. As you can see, they own most everything." Her fingers walked down the map to a small island in blue. "That's Jamaica. The blue color means it's a British crown colony—we'll be passing that shortly, but giving it wide berth. And Curaçao is way down here, just off Terra Firma—that's where we picked you up." The island she poked at, one of three beside the swath of red on the left side of the map, was picked out in white—the Dutch color, Mary imagined.

"Where's Nassau, then?"

Anne nudged her delightedly. "Oh, yes!" She pointed to a small blue dot among a cluster of them. "If I have me way we'll be headed there next," she added. "Don't you worry. You'll be reunited with your sweetheart soon."

Mary stared. She was almost there, a fact that was exhilarating—and terrifying. "It'll be thrilling to hide out on Isla for a bit," Anne continued. Mary smelled the briny tang of her hair as she turned her head. "Rumor has it that Edward Teach buried some of his treasure there. Blackbeard's treasure! Wish we had a map for *that*." She nudged Mary with her hip, and Mary felt her cheeks color. "Might be worth doing a little searching anyway, while we're there, eh? You up for a bit of treasure hunting?"

"I—ah—" There was something elastic about Anne's skin, something round and smooth that seemed so young, up this close, for all her confidence and posturing. The barest hint of freckles dotted her cheeks. *She can't be much older than my seventeen years,* Mary thought.

Anne tilted her head and turned to face Mary. They were almost the same height. The table's edge dug into Mary's buttocks as she leaned away. "There's something about you that's familiar," Anne said, tapping her filthy fingernails on the table. *Tap, tap, tap.* Her breath was sweet, an echo of the fruity taste on Mary's tongue.

Mary attempted a careless, masculine stance, but her pulse quickened. "Oh?"

Tap, tap, tap. "Hmmm. Not sure what it is . . ." Anne trailed off as she smiled. "But I'm quite sure I like it."

Mary's exhale sounded loud in the still cabin.

Louder still was the bang as the cabin door was thrust open. They both jumped and spun around. "What's this?" Jack stood in the doorway, the beginnings of sunrise silhouetting him so that his face was dark in shadow.

"Oh, Jack!" Anne whirled around the table and flounced toward him. "Sure I was just showing the new lad the route we're on." She placed a coy hand on his arm. Jack didn't take his eyes off Mary.

She began to sweat. "Morning, captain," she said, dipping her head nervously.

"The boy that shot his captain for you," Anne reminded him. "Mark, remember?"

"Mark." Jack narrowed his eyes. "Ah, yes. I like the looks of you. You remind me of me, when I was joining the account." He put his arm around Anne but kept his eyes on Mary. "Which makes me think I need to give you something to do, to keep you out of trouble."

Mary didn't like the way he said *trouble*. "Have you need of some mending?" she asked quickly. "Paddy was the sail maker on the *Vissen*, and I apprenticed under him. I noticed yours could use some work."

"Perfect. I'll lash you to the mainmast till you finish mending all our buggered sailcloth."

"Now, Jack," Anne giggled. "You ought to give this boy some gold and let him lie about, else Bill will get the votes he needs to maroon the two of us on some deserted island."

"I had a good talk with Bill last night," Jack said tightly. "He knows I'm only trying to do what's best for the crew."

"Oh, I know," said Anne softly. "Sure, I was only joking. Besides, it wouldn't be *so* bad to be marooned with me, would it?"

Jack's demeanor cracked when he looked down at her. "That's enough out of you," he said severely, but he was smiling. "Mind you make yourself useful as well, or I'll see you walk the plank."

Anne placed her palms against Jack's chest. Mary's face grew warm as he pulled Anne in for a kiss, but she couldn't look away. Anne's dress crushed against Jack's body as his grip tightened, heat flaring between them. Mary knew what it was like to want to kiss someone no matter who was watching. How nice it must be, to be able to just pull that person close.

She looked down at the map in front of her as Anne murmured against Jack's lips. All that water, bits of land—so many places she could be in this new world. But for all of Anne's geography lessons, Mary was still hopeless at figuring out where exactly she might fit in it.

CHAPTER SIX

WAPPING, LONDON—1717

BY THE DISTANT ROARING THAT WAS GROWING EVER CLOSER, MARY WAS sure the cart would be rolling past on its way to Tyburn from the Old Bailey at any moment. The crowd was hot and surly, and she was glad she hadn't tried to get any closer to the gallows, opting instead to find a spot for her and Nat in the tight streets near the rookeries of Saint Giles. Several people had died in the crush at the last hanging.

The condemned would be completely drunk by now, promising a good show. She craned to see over the crowd and thought she could make out the city marshal on horseback, surrounded by a thicket of staves carried by those charged with beating back the crowd. Almost here!

She twisted around, trying to spot Nat, but the crowd was so thick that Mary doubted he'd make it back. He'd heard someone hawking the Old Bailey handbill and pushed his way after the sound, insisting he get one so Mary could read him all the wretched details of the condemned.

She was grateful to get away from Mum for the day, whether Nat kept her company or not. Granny's gout had finally gotten bad enough that she'd asked Mary to come be her footboy, and Mum had been crowing about it for days. *This is it, Mark! Next thing you know, she'll be leaving everything to you!* Then she'd look up from her bottle, as though remembering who her child really was, and her mood would start to darken. She'd begin to wonder why God left her with her bastard daughter, instead of the golden son who would have let her live such a life honestly.

If anyone finds you out we're done for. We'll both be sent straight to Newgate, to be hanged or transported.

You are impulsive, thoughtless. You don't take enough care.

You'll be found out, one way or another.

Mum was right. Mary was impulsive and thoughtless and—worse—a girl, not the boy she pretended to be. It was ridiculous to think she could live in a house full of servants and her shrewd grandmother and fool them all.

She took a deep gulp of air, trying to calm her breath, but her ribs were constricted by her new binding. Mum had bound Mary's slight curves up tight with a strip of linen, and she eyed her suspiciously every time she saw her now, as if trying to discern any visible hint of their secret.

"Got it!" panted Nat, pushing through a narrow opening in the crowd next to her and brandishing a small pamphlet. "You owe me a ha'penny."

"Do I, now?" she said, grinning. "It wasn't my idea for you to go after it!"

"The chap selling it told me the gist," Nat said, handing her the pamphlet and settling into the press just behind her. "Wait till you hear this! Sodomites, all of them. Apprehended near Saint James wearing women's togs. Apparently they fooled crowds of fellows into thinking they was ladies, until one clever chap tipped off the Society!"

"Disgusting," spat a woman next to Mary. "Did you hear that?" she asked the man next to her. "They're hanging mollies today."

Mary's stomach turned over as she trained her eyes on the pamphlet. She was jostled so much by the crowd she could hardly focus on the words. "'A full and true account of the discovery and apprehending of a notorious gang of sodomites in Saint James,'" she read aloud slowly. "'Taken in for wearing the dress and affecting the mannerisms of women.' They're being *hanged* for that?" She felt sick.

"That ain't the worst of it," Nat said over her shoulder. "A man dressed in women's clothing—he's fooling men for one reason only, as you might imagine. Keep reading, would you? I want to hear all of it."

Mary flipped through the pages of cramped print, the words blurring before her eyes. Lurid details jumped out: COQUETTISH LAUGH, BRANDISHED FAN, LIFTED SKIRTS . . .

"Go on, what else does it say?"

A roar drowned Nat out as the throng surged around them so tightly, it lifted Mary off her feet. The city marshal was just passing now, the crowd tightening like a vise as people were beaten back off the street. There was no way out. Everyone was screaming, even people leaning out of the windows above.

"Hanging's too good for sinners like you!"

"The likes of you condemn us all to Hell—"

"Disgusting, evil, immoral—"

Though Mum fretted about what would happen if anyone found out, she always insisted that Mary dressing as her brother had God's blessing. But it sounded like He'd send Mary to Hell for it, from what these people were screaming.

"Would you look at that cheek!" Nat's voice was right in her ear, his chest pressed against her back. "Some of them wore *dresses* to be hanged in!"

Not all the men who rode the coffins stacked on the cart wore dresses, but many of them did, their faces painted too, red lips blowing kisses as they hung off the cart drunkenly. Others were catatonic, their lips moving slightly, eyelids occasionally flickering. All of them were skin and bones from their time at Newgate. People flung rotting vegetables, mud, a dead cat. One of the condemned took a flask someone in the crush of bodies held up and drank from it. "Thank you, lovey!" he sang. "I'll pay for it on me way back!" The crowd laughed uproariously at the joke, but the insults kept coming. The man flinched as an apple struck his cheek and left behind a streak of rotten pulp, but then he was back to winking and waving, ducking the thrown filth, swaying with every jolt of the cart.

Mary couldn't breathe; she had to get away, she had to—she fumbled against the crowd, trying to find a way to escape. She pushed in all directions, a frantic sob escaping her—

"Here now, it's all right," Nat said in her ear. She'd turned herself around and her face was mashed into his shoulder, her newly bound chest pressed against his. She struggled to push away but it was no use, the crowd was too tight—she let her body sag against him, her tears soaking into his shirt. If he didn't figure out her secret right this instant, he'd at the very least never let her hear the end of how she cried over a bunch of mollies. "It's all right," he said again, his hands coming up to her shoulders. "I know. Sometimes it hits you, how wrong it is. But there's nothing you can do."

Mary took a few gulping breaths of air.

"They're completely soused," he soothed. "They won't feel a thing. They're blacked out drunk already."

"I didn't know you could be hanged for wearing the wrong clothes," Mary murmured.

"I don't think it's right either," Nat said quietly. "You'd think a stint in the pillory would be punishment enough. It's not like they killed anyone."

Mary breathed in the smell of him, slowly becoming aware of the breadth of his shoulders, how he'd filled out in the past few months, all of a sudden standing half a head taller than her. The feeling of his hands resting on her shoulders. The curl of his hair that tickled her cheek. They were both sweaty from the crush of the crowd. It was useless to try to move away, so she didn't, and he didn't move either, until the cart had passed, trailing men with javelins who threatened those who came too close.

The cart turned a corner up ahead, and the pressure around them abruptly softened.

She didn't want to let go.

"All right, there's enough of that," said Nat, a teasing note in his voice as he squeezed her shoulder. "Else they think we're sodomites, and throw us up on that cart along with the others."

She looked up sharply as she pulled back—but when her eyes met his he smiled. His face was so close. That freckle on his lip, like a smudge of dirt she always wanted to wipe off—she felt as though she couldn't stop herself from reaching out and pressing a finger to it.

She stepped back suddenly, her heart pounding.

He dropped his gaze. "Seems like we're both losing our taste for this sort of sport," he said, taking the crumpled pamphlet from her fist and tossing it in the mud. "Come on, let's find something better to get into."

She watched him push through the crowd and disappear. She didn't want to move from where he'd held her. She could still feel the echo of his chest against hers.

Impulsive, thoughtless. You don't take enough care.

If anyone *finds you out . . .*

Nat reappeared, straining over the crowd to look for her. She shivered, then ducked and pushed toward him before he could see how long she'd lingered, staring after him.

CHAPTER SEVEN

CARIBBEAN SEA—1719

MARY GAZED DOWN, FROM A SWAYING PERCH ATOP THE FOREMAST, AT the mottled pirate crew below her, all readying the ship to drop anchor without a single order from the captain. *Votes*, Anne had said. Everyone on the crew had one, even Mary. After sailing from Rotterdam on a merchant vessel it sounded too good to be true.

Why have a captain at all, if that was the case?

There was Jack, with his flashy britches and genteel air, near the helm with Anne draped across him. It was hard to believe the pirates had mutinied against their last captain to follow him. What lay beneath his sleek surface that would command respect from such a band of rogues? Mary had been observing the crew all day as she climbed the masts and inspected the damage done to the sails in the battle, but from up here everyone looked perfectly amiable. No conspiratorial meetings, no dirty looks. What had Anne meant by "disagreements among the crew," and her joke about marooning?

A thin strip of beach holding back a riot of jungle materialized against the dusky natural harbor the *Ranger* was maneuvering into. A cluster of sailcloth tents and awnings dotted the sand, along with a couple of overturned canoes and the burned remains of fire pits. A plundered brig and a couple of piraguas stood in the harbor.

Mary gave the gaskets one last pat and monkeyed down the shrouds. The brisk wind felt wonderful on her skin. After being separated from Nat, it had been much easier to appreciate what her disguise allowed. Even Anne, despite her unusual liberty, would never have been able to climb up the rigging in all those skirts. She would never feel the breeze up here.

The *Ranger* rolled forward and turned toward the wind, slowing considerably. Mary alit on the deck just as Anne sprang up from the hold, almost bowling her over. The shiny new ruffles of a baby blue petticoat were conspicuous beneath Anne's soiled skirts. "You! Take these—" She shoved a few wine bottles into Mary's hands, then plunged back down below deck. A passing pirate swiped one and began to work the stopper out with his teeth.

The crew, some of them already soused by the looks of it, ran about like madmen collecting wine, sails, rope, machetes, and knives. Jolly boats swung over the sides of the *Ranger*. Mary followed Paddy onto the closest one, noticing that his arms were full of wine bottles as well.

The little boat lurched as it lowered to the water, rocking with the weight of men jammed in on every side. Mary hauled an oar with Paddy, making sure to brush him only with bony elbows and knees. She could see the sea floor clear through the surf, though it must have been forty feet below. Rocks shaped like the heads and fingers of drowning giants reached up, swarmed by fish and seaweed. She put her hand to the water. The sea was cool and smooth, softer than silk stockings. Petticoats and lace hats floated like pale, beribboned jellyfish in their wake.

When she looked up her eyes met those of the dark-skinned man with locks in his hair who had manned the helm as they'd dropped anchor. "So you're the new boy," he said. He had a gritty, steady voice.

"Mark," she said. "And this is the new old man, Paddy." Paddy chuckled and gave her an elbow to the ribs as the man nodded.

"Bill," the man said, introducing himself. "I'm the quarter-master."

A commotion erupted in the boat ahead, men shouting as the vessel rocked crazily. Jack stood with Anne shrieking in his arms and chucked her into the shallows. She flailed around and came up howling. He hopped out after her into waist-high water and pulled her to her feet, shouting, "I told you I'd make you walk the plank if you didn't mind yourself!" She kissed him on the mouth, water streaming from her hair. Mary cracked a smile as the others laughed or ignored their captain's antics. She glanced back at Bill, still grinning. He had an unreadable expression on his face as he watched Jack and Anne kiss.

Mary's boat ground onto sand and she pitched out into sea-foam warm as bathwater. She resurfaced whooping, blowing water out her nose as men sloshed the boats to shore. The waves were mild, bare ripples that swelled before breaking softly on the sand, but Mary's sea legs were unbalanced by them. She sank to her knees, and little silvery fish swirled around and nipped at her legs. She had made it to land at last! Putting her head under, she scrubbed hard at her scalp and shouted into the water, gibberish bubbling up around her face.

She flipped her head up to suck in air just in time to hear Jack ask about the wine. "It's here!" Mary called, and turned to pull the bottles out of the boat. When she turned back the captain was beside her, his dark curls haloing his face. Mary's stomach tight-ened, and she tugged her shirt away from the contours of her skin with one hand as she handed him a couple of bottles with the other. The others had left her alone with the boat and the wine, already dragging driftwood into a pile next to a fire pit on shore, chatting and laughing as kindling ignited.

"Thanks, mate."

His green eyes were bright as crystal, his shirt open to the waist. There was no chance he felt threatened by her this morning—he was a man of five-and-twenty at least, and so handsome, despite the wild look in his eyes. Still, he hadn't seemed happy to find her and Anne alone.

"Don't eye me so nervously," he said, a large onion-shaped bottle in each hand. "I do like you, you know."

She started pulling the jolly boat to shore, where the rest of them were already beached. "That's good to hear, sir."

He set one of the bottles back in the boat and began working the cork of the other. "I was only a bit younger than you when pirates took the ship I was traveling on—thirteen years old. I loved pirate stories. I was excited when I realized we'd be facing real buccaneers."

"I think we all dreamed of being pirates when we was young," she offered, giving the jolly boat another hard tug. "The stories about Henry Avery and the like are hard to ignore, especially when you're poor and stuck in some filthy tenement."

"Well, it didn't go quite how I imagined it. The pirates that took me on was a nasty lot. Once they captured our brig, they went about killing every last captive. They killed my nurse right in front of me, while I cowered. My father must have died during the fighting—I found him with his throat slit." Jack stared at the cork he'd pulled free of the bottleneck. "When I saw him dead—this raging desire to live came over me. I stomped up and down the deck brandishing a cutlass, screaming about how I was going to be the most infamous freebooter that ever lived. That they'd be sorry if they didn't take me on. I'd hunt them all down and make them walk the plank. They were charmed, I think. I was very convincing." The cork came loose with a popping sound. "I put on the show of my life—just like you did back there."

Survival by performance—that did sound like her. "I can't imagine standing up to monsters like that."

"I wasn't a child for long." He paused to take a long drink, then wiped his mouth with the back of his hand. "But it worked out for the best. Here I am, still a gentleman of fortune, though I could have found a way off the account long ago." There was a note of bitterness in his voice as he tossed the cork in the water and offered the bottle to her. "Here you are, son. I think making safe harbor after a caper like that deserves a celebration, don't you?"

Mary took the wine. "Sounds like a cracking idea, sir."

Jack dipped his hands in the sea and wiped the grime from his face. "Anne says that you're keen to get to Nassau," he said casually, as he left the swash and put a hand on the jolly boat's prow.

Mary was embarrassed to think Anne had told the captain about her *sweetheart*—although it might have helped convince Jack she wasn't keen on his mistress. "Oh, aye. That's where I'm aiming to end up eventually." She got behind the boat and braced herself to push.

"That's grand," Jack said in a satisfied tone. He lifted the front end with two hands. "You seem like a trustworthy chap. I'm going to tell you something in confidence. The king's offering pardon to pirates who turn themselves in. You've heard about this?"

"Aye," Mary grunted, pushing with her free hand as Jack lifted, until most of the boat was out of the water. It was part of the same proclamation that had brought Nat to the new world to hunt pirates. Along with the promise of pardon, the king was offering hefty rewards for bringing in those pirates that didn't turn themselves in—and it was all coordinated in Nassau, where the new governor was intent on stamping out the pirate nuisance that had lingered after the war with the Spanish.

Jack waited as she set her bottle down in the sand. She lifted her end, and they began walking the boat onto the beach. "Our crew has been lucky of late. With the haul we just took in from the *Vissen*, I'm thinking I might have enough shine to merit taking that pardon and exchanging the account for a comfortable life. It might be high time to go to Nassau to claim the pardon."

"That's brilliant!" Who would have imagined it would be so easy to get where she was going?

"I was hoping you'd say that. Sadly, not everyone on the crew feels that way, and I can't just waltz off and leave my crew behind. Some consensus needs to be reached. Even Anne has been hard to persuade." They set the boat down out of danger of the tide. "She can be very hard to please, as you might imagine."

"But she told me she wanted to go to Nassau—" Mary huffed, catching her breath.

"Aye, and it would be what's best for her. She likes you, Mark. I think she might listen to you, if you were to tell her your reasons for wanting a peaceful return to Nassau, so that we might keep our treasure and our lives." Jack picked up the bottle she had set down. "And if you happened to talk to some of the other men who didn't seem inclined to take the pardon—you might tell them your reasoning as well? But keep it on the quiet side. I'm still figuring out the best way to bring everyone around."

"I'll do that, sir. I'd be happy to." She'd hoped to make her way to Nassau soon after joining the pirates, but it sounded like it might happen more easily than she'd thought.

"Knew I did the right thing, taking you on." Jack handed her the wine. "The rest of that is for you, son. Drink your fill!" He reached into the boat and pulled out the other bottle. He opened it and held it out. "To freedom!" he shouted, loud enough that his voice echoed down the beach.

Others joined in as Mary responded—"To freedom!" Her bottle clinked against his, splashing wine onto the sand. Voices roared in unison as she tipped the bottle back.

CHAPTER EIGHT

Isla de Cotorras—1719

The wine left grit on her tongue as Mary drained the last of it. She discarded the bottle and rocked forward on her knees, wobbling there as she considered Anne over the sheep carcass hanging between them. Anne's voice had just risen and she'd said something about Nassau, which had caught Mary's attention. The smoke distorted her vision, the red of Anne's dress bleeding into the night around her. Beyond her other fires flared, each pit with its own spit and a ring of raucous men around it. There must have been close to a hundred men, all told, now that they'd met up with the rest of the crew. Parrots and monkeys and God knows what else screamed from the dark wall of jungle beyond the beach, so loud it was hard to hear.

"What was that you said?" Mary called to Anne.

Paddy's soft eyes flicked from Anne to Mary. "Are you cracked?" He shook his head, stringy hair sticking to his neck where it had come loose from its pigtail.

Mary made a face at Paddy as she stood up. "What's this you're on about?" she asked, scuffing through the sand and plopping down next to Anne. Jack had said Anne needed some sort of *convincing* about returning to Nassau, but Mary was still unclear about what he'd meant. "You mentioned this morning that we're only staying on this island till we decide what's next."

Anne gestured at Mary with the bottle. "Aye, that's just what we was"—she gave Jack a sideways glance—"*discussing*."

"So where is it *you* want to go?" asked Mary. She was in love with Anne's boldness.

"Jaysus, Mark," Paddy said. "Come back here, I'll tell you where to go to keep your arse in one piece."

A couple of men laughed. Jack said, "No, no, my lady is in need of an audience. Go on, my dove. Tell the boy your damned plan."

The fire popped loudly as Anne wiped her lips. "I'll start by asking you this. Why are we here? Why do we have to hide out on some deserted island, when most of us call New Providence home?"

"That's easy," said a man on the far side of Paddy. He popped up to his knees, sliding hands over his mouth. What Mary had thought was a sneer earlier was actually a slight harelip that gave him the appearance of a perpetually curling lip. "Since the new governor came with all his plans for a god-fearing colony, we can no longer expect a proper homecoming." A smattering of laughter broke out around the circle, and a couple of hisses as well.

"A proper hanging's more like it," another man called.

Anne bared her teeth. "Exactly! But if we hadn't spent our time dithering and arguing among ourselves, we could have sank Rogers's fleet and kept Nassau for ourselves. Am I wrong?"

There were a couple of ayes, but a couple of nos as well.

"We did what coves like us do." A big chap in gold earrings leaned toward the fire. "People like us find a place to moor our brigs without fear during war, while kings are too busy drubbing each other to notice—but we have to scupper our hides out of there quick once all settles down and the attention turns to us."

"That, or take the pardon," Jack remarked.

Anne pounded a fist in the sand. "We don't need to take the bloody pardon to go home! A new governor with a scrap of paper in his hand ran us out—I still don't quite understand how he managed it. But look at us! A hundred men, almost, and that count rising! What's to stop us from taking Nassau back?" Anne cast her eyes to the men circled around her. Shadowy bodies ringed the fire like a rock wall. Here and there an eyeball or wet lip glistened in sharp relief from the blaze. Some men were nodding, some were shaking their heads.

"We're freebooters, not a rebel army," Jack said. "And we'll lose any chance of pardon if we try and fail."

"I think someone's got a bit of a chip on her shoulder about a certain husband of hers turning coat and following Rogers," remarked the man with the harelip. "Anne's intent on sailing back to Nassau just to see *him* swing."

He had to duck when Anne flung her bottle at him in response. "This is about *justice*, not about some stupid sailor who wasn't man enough to fight back." Her eyes fixed on Jack, the light from the fire arching her brows maniacally. "But I'll *never* go back to New Providence seeking pardon from the governor, when I know I'll have to beg it from that bastard as well."

"Jack's plan is sensible," said Mary. "Why not take the pardon, if they'll let us keep our plunder?"

"I didn't say that was my plan," said Jack, putting a hand on her arm. "It's just one of the options." Mary met his eyes, and his gaze was a warning before her released her. Too late, she remembered—*keep it quiet.* Christ. She was drunk, but the disagreement Anne had joked about aboard the *Vissen* seemed less trivial now, as Jack's lips pressed into a firm, disapproving line.

"Pardon might still be an option for you, Jack," a voice growled out of the dark beyond the ring of firelight. Bill, the quartermaster, was standing beyond Paddy's silhouette, hands clasped behind his back. Who knew how long he'd been listening. "But there's some of us who will lose every freedom we have if we return to Nassau, not just the little you would give up."

"That's it exactly!" Words began rushing from Anne as she stood, and Mary's pulse quickened. "We've two brigs now, with almost twenty guns between them. Wait till the word gets back to New Providence and Jamaica. Our brothers will be joining us here any day now. Another ship or two, and we'll have a fleet that will rival Blackbeard's. Get the element of surprise on our side and it'll be Rogers who swings, not us!"

"Apologies, captain." The gritty voice came out of the darkness again, and Bill stepped into the firelight, his illuminated face impassive as rock. Beside his muscled bulk Anne looked like a spark, burning hot but so small. "It might've sounded like I agree with Anne on this, but I don't. All she's doing is filling your men's heads with fairy stories. We need to make a real plan. One all your men can stand behind."

Anne stiffened, and Jack jumped to his feet.

"I know, Bill." Jack placed a hand on Anne's shoulder, to comfort her or hold her back, Mary couldn't tell. His tone was mild. "Sure, we're all just speculating here."

"No, Jack. You keep dropping hints about the pardon, that maybe we should take it. Just one more plunder. Maybe two. Just enough to waltz away rich after we turn ourselves in." Bill looked away and spat into the sand. "In the meantime, you're ignoring the real threat. We drew ire when we took the *Kingston*, and I'm sure there are plenty searching for us as we speak. We need to find a better place to hide out, somewhere we can defend ourselves proper if we're discovered."

"You're just afraid, old man," Anne hissed at Bill, pulling against Jack's grip as he tried to still her. "And there's no room for cowards here."

"Anne, that's enough." Jack tried to tug her back but lost his grip when she resisted.

"That might be up for debate," said Bill. "But what's never been is whether there's room for a woman." He looked pointedly at Jack. Voices began to swell around the fire.

"—don't have the right to be on that throne, let alone making proclamations—"

"—here till the wine runs out—"

"—what you get for bringing a woman on board—"

"—will do him in, if anything will. Never should've gone back for her."

Anne's eyes flicked to the men ringed around her, to the jungle and ocean beyond, to the lone pistol at her hip, and Mary's stomach soured in fear. This crew had already mutinied against one captain. What would happen if they mutinied against Jack?

When Anne lifted her face to the light again the rage was gone, replaced by something softer. She took a step back, closer to Jack. Her lashes fluttered as she turned her head away. "You know it could be more than just fancy, men like yourselves standing up to the law." As she turned her head her throat caught the light. "I just know what kind of men you are. I've talked with all of you, and I know you want more than to run your whole life."

Mary's fingers contracted into the sand, stomach sinking at the change in Anne's tone.

"Bill, this is exactly why I made you quartermaster." Jack's hands came to rest on Anne's shoulders, the fabric dimpling under his fingers as he squeezed. He stepped lightly around her. "The voice of caution, reason, and all that."

The arguing subsided. Bill inclined his head and spoke quickly. "Sir, there's no harm in resting here for a few days, but we mustn't stay. There are places we could go, in the northern colonies—"

"Our last captain listened too much to those who were fearful of capture." Jack paused to crush an ember out with the toe of his boot. "And because of that, we languished under his command. Since I've been captain, haven't we seen a drastic turn of fortune? We've taken risks that have made us all rich men, but that doesn't mean anything in the jungle. Might it not be time for a different kind of risk, one that allows us to enjoy the wealth we've gained?"

The other men were silent.

"We didn't mutiny because of Charlie Vane's cowardice." Bill's tone was slow and even, each word a stone dropped into still water. "We mutinied because he went against the will of his crew. Sir."

Jack pressed earnest hands to his chest. "And I have done everything you ask of me! Have I not? I led you to treasure and then to safety, have I not? We *both* want Avery's Madagascar, don't we? We just have different ideas about how to get it." He shook his head. "I've every intention of taking your concerns into consideration. I want what *you* want, mate, don't forget that."

Mary found she could breathe easier. So *this* was why Jack was captain, despite his silly britches—the way this man talked, all gold and honey, made her want to trust him.

Anne leaned into Jack, but he moved away as the conversation around the fire rose again, and she stumbled as he left her side. She looked around as if searching for something to hold onto that might bear her up again, and her eyes landed on Mary.

Anne came over, but when she squatted down her gaze was full of contempt. "Maybe you should keep your mouth shut about things you don't understand." She stood, sand flinging from her skirts into Mary's eyes. When Mary finished rubbing sand from her lashes Anne was gone, disappeared into the darkness.

Paddy was shaking his head. "Come back over here, lad," he said, patting the spot beside him. "I think it's time you kept your head down for a bit."

Mary crawled over and sloshed to sitting beside him. "Aye, I'll listen to you next time you tell me to mind meself."

"I doubt that," Paddy said fondly, scruffing her hair. "But I'll be sure to tell ye, all the same."

CHAPTER NINE

Wapping, London—1717

Mary stood on the landing for a long moment, staring at the tenement door. It was a stained, splintered piece of wood, nothing like the door in Granny's garret, with its brass fixtures and fresh varnish. She liked her little space at Granny's house in Westminster so much better than this. But she'd felt like she was going mad with her the only one in the world knowing she was a girl.

When Mary pushed the door open she found Mum sagging in her usual chair by the fire. The hearth was cold, a candle sputtering on the table. Mum's hair was still beautiful, golden and in soft disarray around her face. "Mum?" Mary whispered.

Mum's head whipped up and she put a hand to her forehead, squinting at the doorway. Her face looked gaunt and shadowed. Mary frowned at the empty bottle on the table, and the glass of tipple in Mum's hand.

"Mark!" Mum's hand went to her chest. Even her smile was thin. "You gave me a fright."

Mary shut the door behind her. "It's *Mary*, Mum," she said. "Please."

Mum leaned forward, gesturing for Mary to come close. "What news have you for your mum? Granny's just loving having you, is she?" Mum struggled to sit up in her chair and Mary approached to help her. Mum grabbed Mary's hand and pulled her close. "You know I've had nothing to get by on since you left. Tell me you've brought a bit of shine. You did, didn't you, Mark?"

"Me name is Mary, Mum." Maybe she really was mad. Maybe she was the one under some strange delusion, and she really was a boy.

"Come on, child. Show me what you've got."

Mary detangled her shirt from Mum's grip with clenched teeth. The thought of giving Mum the fine silverware she'd pinched from Granny's had pleased her—but now she felt angry, picturing Mum pawning it for gin. "I came by to—check on you. To see you." Mary closed her eyes. "And to bring you something."

Mum crowed. "I knew it! And only tonight I was thinking I might not make it, what with the parish being so bloody stingy with me. You're a godsend, child. I once cursed being left with a son like you, but the Lord had a plan all along."

"Bloody hell, Mum!" Mary struggled to pull her shirt over her head. "This isn't some divine plan! This is your daughter, parading about as something she's not." She picked furiously at the knot in her binding and managed to loosen the knot far enough so that she could push the binding down around her waist, almost expecting to prove herself wrong. If it were something that you could will into being, she'd have been a boy a long time ago.

But no, she wasn't a boy, and she wasn't mad.

She held Mum's gaze defiantly. "Look at me and tell me I won't go straight to Hell for this."

Mum turned her face away, setting her cup down on the table with shaking hands. "Cover yourself, Mark. You look obscene."

"It's you that made me *obscene*, Mum. This was all your scheme!" Mary grabbed Mum's face and made her look, trembling with anger. "Meanwhile *I'm* the one risking me life, not to mention eternal damnation!"

"You make it sound like some crooked plot." Mum pushed her hands away and looked at Mary for a moment, her lip curling. "I prayed and prayed for God to take the girl and leave me the son. What use to me is a bastard girl, I asked Him. We would have slaved to death in the workhouse long ago." Mum stood up, her eyes igniting with a familiar fire. "But God sent me a vision. A way to fulfill the promise of Mark's life. He blessed *you* with his life, so much better than you would have had otherwise."

Mary's hands curled to fists. "I want to believe you," she said quietly. "I'm trying to have faith."

Mum shuffled behind Mary and pulled a blanket around her shoulders. "Come, now. You've enjoyed what his life has allowed you. Living in that beautiful house with Granny! Having run of the city like a proper boy! You should be grateful to have had the chance."

Mary bent her head and clutched the cloth of her binding around her, suddenly cold and embarrassed. Mum was right. "I'm sorry," Mary whispered. "It's just so hard. I want to—there's things I want." She wanted Mum's certainty. She wanted to be worthy of a divine plan. But if there was a God, she knew He didn't have love for someone like her.

Mum snorted. "Good thing you didn't grow up a girl, then. That's nothing but wanting things you can't have." She came around and plopped back down in her chair. "Don't let any foolishness get in the way of what we've worked so hard for. Don't let Mark's death be for nothing. Soon enough the old broad will die, God willing, and me prayers will be answered at last." She rubbed her hands together. "Now. Let's see what you've brought me, eh?"

CHAPTER TEN

ISLA DE COTORRAS—1719

JACK WAS SINGING.

Mary cracked an eye and went to sit up. Someone needed to tell him to keep it down; honest tars were trying to sleep—

She moaned and lay back, her head throbbing as sensation flooded in. She was sweating, sand sticking to every pore of her body. The sun beat down without a whisper of a breeze. She managed to prop herself up on an elbow, slowly this time. Most of the crew lay sprawled around the blackened remains of bonfires, but a few were up and about, squinting into the sun and muttering at each other. Near the water, Captain Jack was singing an overly enthusiastic rendition of "The Handsome Cabin Boy" and rousing sleepers with the toe of his boot.

"Attired in sailor's clothing she boldly did appear
And engaged with the captain for to serve him for a year—"

Jack singing that song gave Mary pause—but she could barely feel her fear over the pounding in her head. She groped around until her fingers closed on the neck of a half-drunk bottle of wine. She took a few pulls, and the pounding in her head seemed to lessen.

Near the water Anne sat up, a splendid mess. Her red dress was ripped rather spectacularly, all the way up to her waist, revealing most of the glossy petticoats she'd foraged from the *Zilveren Vissen*. Mary remembered snatches of the night before: Anne, a tiny red volcano with sparks and smoke swirling around her; Jack, a patterned parrot with a pretty song; Bill, an unmovable mountain.

Mary stumbled down to the shore, her eyes closed as much as possible against the glaring light. "High tide, gentlemen, in just a few hours," Jack called. "And we've a few things to take care of before then, if we're planning on ever leaving this island for whatever reason. Let's get a move on!"

After almost everyone had gathered, it was agreed that hauling water from the headwaters up the beach was first on the list. After a quick, pained discussion, a couple of men set off in a jolly boat with empty water barrels. A few boats headed out toward the two brigs standing in the harbor. The crew needed to take advantage of the deep harbor and careen the ships for cleaning before they could set off.

Mary excused herself on account of her bladder, and ran up to the tree line to make water. As she hurried back, glancing at the jolly boats nosing into the surf, Anne caught her eye. She was hunched on a charred log by the water, frowning at the huge rip in her skirts.

Mary's steps slowed as the boats left shore, and by the time she reached Anne they were a good way out. The air was strangely hot and still. Flies and insects whined and swarmed around them. "I could fix that for you, if you like," Mary offered, pointing at Anne's skirts.

Anne shaded her eyes and squinted up at her. She looked like she felt about as awful as Mary. "What, this?" She fingered the tear in her skirts. "Right, you mentioned you're handy with this sort of thing."

"And look what I've got here." Mary produced the needle and thread she'd tucked into her binding before they'd left the *Ranger*, not wanting it to get lost and hoping to impress Jack with her forethought. "It's only heavy cotton thread, and a sailcloth needle, but it'll hold together until you find another dress."

"Well, aren't you thoughtful," Anne said begrudgingly. She stood and held out the cloth on either side of the tear. Black smudges darkened the corners of Anne's eyes, where ash from the fire pit had gotten caked. "You'll have to mend it while I'm wearing it," she said. "It wouldn't do for Jack to find me sitting with you in me shimmy."

Mary squinted toward the glittering water. The ships were still a way out. "All right then," Mary said. She took Anne's place on the log. "Lean your hip in so I can reach."

Mary threaded the needle, bit the thread off, and knotted the end as Anne moved closer. She smelled good, like wood smoke and salt. Mary tugged at the top of the rip, by her waist, and pressed the frayed edges together. Anne's hip shifted toward her, and Mary's cheeks flushed. She pushed the needle through the cloth, keenly aware of the girl watching her hands. "I—I wanted to apologize if I offended you last night," Mary said.

Anne huffed. "If you're going to pick sides without considering how things might work for anyone but you, you can keep your bloody apology."

Mary's nerves were on edge from the night before, her hands shaking so that she could hardly sew. She watched her fingers tremble as she slowly worked her way down the rip. She had never worked on such rich fabric. The velvet was too giving, too soft, and it troubled her to press the needle through it. This was a poor idea, but it was too late to stop now. "Tell me then," said Mary. "Tell me why you can't take the pardon."

"It's a matter of principle," Anne said indignantly. "What right does the king have to impose his rules on us, thousands of miles away? Thaddeus—he came down with a couple others from

Virginia—he says there's talk of revolt in the colonies. Fighting back against England—I'm not the only one with that idea. Quite a few men agree with what I had to say last night, you know." She looked away, glaring toward the ships in the harbor. "I haven't the faintest idea why none of them thought to back me up."

"So it's not about your husband, then."

"You know *nothing* about me husband," Anne said through her teeth.

The row of silver buttons up the front of Anne's dress flashed in the sunlight, making Mary's head ache harder. "Tell me about him, then," Mary said. Anne's anger made Mary think he had *something* to do with it. "I'd like to know."

Anne stared at her for a long moment, and Mary held her gaze. "James Bonny's his name. He got me out of Charleston," Anne said finally, looking away. "Bloody stinking swamp that is, and with me da watching me every move—I had to get out, and marrying Jimmy seemed a decent way to do it."

Mary fumbled with the skirt as she tried to pull it straight. Anne sighed and brushed Mary off to hold it in place for her. Mary hesitated, then put her hands beside Anne's and placed another stitch. Her fingers bumped against Anne's, though she tried to avoid it. Anne's were smaller and surer but they were as cracked and rough as Mary's. If Anne ever washed her hands before you couldn't tell now, black as her fingernails were. "How old were you then?" Mary asked.

"Fourteen. Jimmy was only twenty—me da thought he wasn't enough of a man for me, and after a couple years I figured he'd been right."

Mary imagined herself at fourteen. Living in the tenement with Mum, still marauding the docks with Nat and the other boys. Still thinking of Nat as her mate and nothing more. She couldn't imagine marriage, or anything that came after, at that age. "What happened?"

"When I first met Jimmy I loved how tough he was." Anne's voice was calm. "And he loved how bold I was, if you can believe it. I'd give him cheek and he'd wrestle me down." She sighed. "Me da was as hard as they come, but he always took fierce care of me; I thought Jimmy would be the same way."

"He wasn't, though," Mary guessed.

"It was different, once we got to Nassau. Once we was married. We wasn't making a fortune, not in the least. We was drinking away any money he made, and he made little enough. He was cross all the time, thinking everyone was out to cheat him and keep him jobless." Anne took a shuddering breath, and when she spoke again her voice was strained. "Then he started thinking I was out to get him, too, that everything I did was meant to hurt him. Now when he pushed me down, he wasn't waiting for me to squeal or giggle. He'd twist an arm or grip me hair until he saw me frightened."

"Christ. That sounds—really dreadful." It sounded worse than *Kapitein* Baas. Sadistic as he was, he hadn't been someone she'd trusted to take care of her.

"I can't remember why he hit me, the first time." Anne's voice was flat. "But he did it all the time after that." Her voice broke. "I kept thinking he'd go back to how he'd been at first, that if I could just make him happy . . . but he never did."

Mary wanted to kill him, just imagining it.

"Jack was so different. Bloody fool that he is—Jack's a decent man."

"Is that why you ran off with him?"

"Oh, he was after me from the start. Kept going on about how in love with me he was, and he gave me all sorts of lovely things. Why wouldn't I run off with him? He kept me safe from Jimmy." Anne gave a bitter laugh. "But then the new governor came, with all those bloody religious fanatics. And suddenly I was a whore for being with Jack, and I'd be put in the pillory if I didn't go back to me husband. People hissed at me in the streets, started throwing things and threatening me. It was only a matter of time before I was made an example of and returned to Jimmy."

"That's horrible," Mary said, aghast.

"I can't believe Jack thinks I'll go back to Nassau with him, when he knows what I'll face," Anne spat, fingers clenched her skirts so Mary had to stop sewing. "I'll kill Jack and Jimmy *both* before I'll ever let a man beat me again."

"I swear, if I had known all that—I would have been on your side last night."

Anne smiled down at Mary, her eyes going soft. "Well, I suppose I accept your apology then."

Their gazes locked. Mary couldn't believe how white Anne's skin was, with the sun beating down as it did. It looked so smooth and cool, the air and everything else so infernally hot. After a moment that stretched too long, she looked back down at her stitches.

"Thank you so much for doing this," Anne said, putting her hand on Mary's. "It looks so much better."

Mary cleared her throat and tried to speak normally. "I don't know about that, but at least it'll keep you decent."

"The brigs are coming in," said Anne quietly, releasing Mary's hand. "I think you'd better tie it off."

The way she said it, so soft and intimate—Mary dropped the needle and had to fumble in Anne's skirts until she found it again. She bit it off and tied the thread as Anne watched, amused. She'd only sewn about halfway down the rip, but the ships loomed close to the beach, and it was better that she got some distance from Anne before Jack caught her with her hands in his woman's skirts. "There you are," she said gruffly. "Should hold up well enough."

Anne grabbed her hand, and the touch sent a hot bolt of energy through her. "I know your sweetheart is in Nassau," she said earnestly. "We'll find a way to get you there."

Anne let go and ran down the beach as the *Kingston* ground onto the sand in shallow water and listed heavily to one side. Bill heaved himself over the side and slid down a rope and into the water, followed by a score more. The men hauled at the ropes, yelling and motioning for help pulling the ship forward.

Mary followed, and ahead of her, Anne lifted her skirts to step into the swash, briefly leaning into Jack before lending a hand. Her skirt had been sewn far enough down that Mary couldn't see the rip, but Mary knew what it looked like up close. Strong thread stood out from the velvet in bold dashes that didn't blend like they should.

CHAPTER ELEVEN

WAPPING, LONDON—1717

MARY WANTED TO FLEE THE TENEMENT AS QUICKLY AS POSSIBLE, BUT SHE couldn't help knocking on the door to Nat's kip before she left. She was still shaking. She'd been ridiculous to think she could go to Mum for comfort. Mum's callous scheming made her feel just as lonely as living at Granny's.

When Nat opened the door, pale light through the open casement illuminated his face, gleaming off his pale skin in the dim hallway, his eyes dark in shadow. "It's you!" he said around a mouthful of something. "I thought I heard something. I'm waiting on someone, you know—but you'll do for now!" He swung the door wider and gestured her inside. "Hungry?"

"It's you?" She crossed her arms, hoping the warmth flushing her cheeks wasn't visible. "What, no tearful reunion? It's been weeks since you saw me last!"

He gave her shoulder a thump. "Oh, come off it. You do realize what you're smelling is me mum's famous meat pudding, don't you?" He grabbed her elbow and pulled her into the tiny room he'd grown up in. A dying fire; a broad, rough table; two filthy pallets on the floor. Nat kicked at the hearth coals to stir them up, took a knife to the pudding, and flopped on his pallet to devour it, licking gravy from his fingers. Mary set her coat and waistcoat on one chair and sat on the other to eat.

"This is as good as anything they've served me at Granny's," she said.

"I've no doubt," he said. "Now you tell your old granny me days as a poor pickpocket are over, so there's no shame in associating with me. I went and got me a shift down at the yard. Bloody backbreaking work, that is—but I keep a weather eye out, looking for a good venture to join. It's only a matter of time before I get out of this bilgewater city, mark me words."

She felt a pang but shook it off. "Finally got an honest job, did you? Still, I'm sure Granny would hate to think of me consortin' with a laborer."

"Granny's got her claws in that deep?" He shook his head. "Too bad, I think a bit of honest work might be good for you, too. What do you say? I could put in a good word for you down at the docks."

Imagine working with him every day! But she couldn't just waltz away from her position at Granny's. "Oh, I don't know about that. Me muscles might scare them off."

He rolled his eyes. "I suppose why bother yourself, when all you've got to do is dance a jig when dear old Granny says to?"

"Here now, enough of that," she said crossly, pushing her pudding around her plate. "I am working, you know. And it's a sight better than any other job I'd be halfway decent at."

"Aye, I know. I don't blame you. You got yourself out of old Wapping on the Ooze, and that's nothing to sniff at. That's all I'm aiming to do meself."

She watched him scrape the last of the pudding from his plate and flop back on the mattress. He ran the spoon back and forth over his lip as he stared at the ceiling, lost in his thoughts. She recognized that sappy look—it was the one he got when he was sweet on a girl.

"I met a girl, Mark," Nat said, as if he'd heard her thoughts. "Susan. Down in Billingsgate Market selling mackerel a few weeks back, and I ran into her again not two days later! Fate's what that is, I say."

Mary's stomach twisted. *Fate*. That sounded serious—but it wasn't the first time he'd said something like that about a girl, and she'd never felt jealous before. She'd never minded being Mark to him. And suddenly all she wanted to do was get close enough to examine all the lines and freckles on his face.

She choked down the last of her food, stood up, and walked over to the pallet. Flopped down beside him, the picture of indifference. "So, er, this girl. She fancies you, does she?" Mary shifted her leg so that it brushed his as if by accident. Far from easing the urge to touch him, it only made her want more.

"It appears she does." He seemed lost in his thoughts, leaving his leg touching hers.

The straw beneath them was old, she could tell, and hard under her elbows when she propped herself up on them. She checked the pallet's holes for rodents or bugs. She studied the stains on the fabric. Anything but him lying so near to her, staring at the ceiling, crumbs on his face. His shoulders and arms had filled out from his work on the docks. Even his hands looked stronger.

She'd made a mistake getting this close to him. "How do you know she fancies you so much?" she managed.

"I kissed her behind the tobacco shop yesterday," he said softly, and Mary's heart lurched. "And she kissed me right back. For hours, it felt like, yet not nearly long enough."

Mary sank back against the pallet. "Doesn't that sound lovely," she said wretchedly. Nat knew she'd never kissed anyone, and he'd teased her endlessly about it, ever since his first kiss when he was eleven. It had only gotten worse with the second girl he'd kissed, and the third. Until lately she'd only been envious of being able to kiss someone without worrying she might end up imprisoned for it.

He turned toward Mary, head on his elbow, and she felt him watching her. Their faces were so close that if she turned she thought their lips would touch. The room was awfully dark.

"Aw, don't worry. You're filling out—soon the girls won't be able to keep their hands off you." He tapped her cheek with the spoon. "You'll get your first kiss soon enough, I'll reckon."

She couldn't help turning to look at him. He was so close she could see that damned freckle out of the corner of her eye, though the light was dim.

He gazed back, a troubled look settling on his face. Slowly, he touched the spoon to her lips. Her breath hitched. The moment stretched interminably, Nat's hand suspended, the spoon barely brushing her lip. Mary couldn't breathe, afraid the moment would end.

Someone tapped on the door, and Nat let the spoon drop, breath rushing out of his mouth. Mary fell back and kept her eyes fixed on the ceiling as Nat got up to open it.

It was the girl he'd been waiting for. Susan. Green eyes and bright yellow hair that burst free at the edges from a roll upon her head. She seemed to bring in the last rays of sunlight with her, all color and energy. "Christ, it's dark in here! Too much bother to light a bleedin' candle, is it?"

Nat scrambled to stir the embers until they flared. Mary sat up shakily as he added wood to the fireplace, and Susan leaned into Nat with all of her lovely curves. "Fancy a walk down by the wharves to watch the sunset?" she asked.

Nat wiped the crumbs from his face. "Aye. Me and Mark was just finishing up supper. You done, mate?" He avoided looking at her.

"Aye." Mary slowly pushed herself to her feet.

"Well then. Glad to see you're faring well. Don't fret, it'll happen for you soon enough." He put his arm around Susan and finally let his gaze meet Mary's, winking as his hand slipped down to Susan's rear. She squealed and whacked at him, but he ducked out the door before she could land a blow. Mary could hear them whooping down the stairs and out onto the street. She went to the window and watched them race toward the wharves, hand in hand. Nat let go and grabbed for Susan's waist, but she wiggled out of reach. Then they were gone, out of sight, and Mary was left behind.

CHAPTER TWELVE

Isla de Cotorras—1719

The two careened ships settled in the shallow water like beached animals, hulls groaning under unfamiliar weight. The plundered *Kingston* pitched all the way to one side, almost completely out of the water, with the *Ranger* nestled up to it so the pirate's flagship stood almost upright on its keel, both sides of the hull accessible. It had taken hours and a high tide to wrench them up on the sand, and Mary's fingers burned from hauling on the ropes. In the London harbor the ships would have been strung up on the dry docks for cleaning, their massive weights suspended by rope and chain, but here they'd had to improvise.

As Mary toiled she kept looking over at Anne. She wanted Anne to look over and meet her gaze, but since Jack had gotten back to shore Anne had eyes only for him.

The jolly boat finally returned with barrels full of fresh water. Mary drank her fill and then a bit more, sucking down a last mouthful as Jack and Bill organized men into groups and argued about the best manner to boil pitch to tar the hull. Anne was nowhere to be seen. Mary circled the *Ranger* until she was knee-deep in water and peered into the shadowy tunnel created where the two hulls came together, but Anne wasn't there either.

The hollow sound of restless water echoed around her. She breathed in, the briny stench strong enough to make her head spin. It smelled like the hallway of her old tenement in Wapping, where the sun never shone, where air never stirred. Cool, decaying, damp, wooden, salty, familiar.

The cool slip of slime soothed her chafed fingertips, and it was a relief to get out of the sun. She wandered down the hull, the gentle slap of waves against the curving wood lulling her. The shouts of the others sounded as if they were coming from a great distance. She pressed her forehead into the slime and inhaled the marine stink, working her fingers into the ooze.

"You're not going to get much filth off with your bare hands, boy."

Mary's head jerked up. Bill loomed between her and the nearest opening, his face difficult to read in the uneven light reflecting off water. He jammed the tip of a machete beneath a barnacle, snapping it off the hull in a quick motion. *Plop*. "You know the first thing about careening a ship?" He looked at her sideways, and she shook her head. "Maybe you should be listening a bit closer to those who know better than you."

"Sorry, sir," Mary said hastily. "Just needed to get out of the heat for a moment."

"Here, I'll go over the rudiments." He moved closer, popping a few more shells off with neat flicks of his wrist as a couple of men ducked into the tunnel behind him, carrying flaming sticks. They whistled at the state of the hull. "And I'll keep an eye on you while you're working," Bill said, "so you don't get any wrong ideas about the way things should be done." Flickering light caught the lines furrowing his dark skin, brows and lashes graying with his hair.

"I'm a quick learner, sir," Mary said uneasily, wishing she'd stayed with the group.

He stabbed his blade at the hull, nodding absently when the wood refused to give. "So, as to the proper methods of cleaning this here muck." He tested the wood with another sharp stab. This time wood blistered around the blade. He frowned and was silent for a moment, touching the damage with his fingers. "Bloody shipworm."

Mary wasn't sure if he was talking about her or the ship. "Sorry?"

Bill grimaced, a row of white and broken teeth. "They don't have 'em in the cold water where you're from, but down here they'll take a ship down every time. You wouldn't think it—a tiny worm? But they do more damage than a cannonball ever could." He went back to fingering the splintered muck as the men behind him went to work scraping the algae off. "No matter what you try, the worm always takes them down in the end." He glanced at her. "Same thing can happen with a ship's crew. All it takes is one person who doesn't belong, worming their way in and riling people up. Spreading ideas that don't need to be spread."

Mary's skin prickled. "Sir?" Did he think Jack had made a mistake, taking her on?

He ran his hand over a couple of shells adhered to the hull. "Barnacles, now—there's a way to rid yourself of them parasites, so the ship goes more efficient-like. You just have to clean everything out at regular intervals, so they don't slow you down. That can bring a crew down as surely as the shipworm, but with barnacles, there's something you can do." Bill waved to one of the men carrying the smoldering branches, who started slogging through the thigh-deep water toward them. "You heard we had another captain a while back?"

"Aye."

"Ol' Charlie was more of a barnacle. We got rid of his drag, and that of his supporters, and we've been moving at a steady clip since then." The man with the flaming sticks passed one to Bill. "As of late we've found it harder to catch a fair wind once again."

Bill held the smoldering end of the branch to a shell, and it darkened beneath the flame. Then—*plop*—off it came. He smiled at her. "See? Easy enough. Now, let's find you a stick and light it on fire." His smile darkened. "Burn the buggers off—that's the best way to do it."

Mary followed Bill out into the sun, feeling unsettled. Anne was standing next to a bonfire, its flames licking sideways in a sudden breeze as black smoke billowed. She grinned in satisfaction as the end of her stick began to flame, and when her gaze landed on Mary she smiled wider and motioned her over. As if they were friends; as if whatever Anne was doing, she wanted nothing more than to do it with her.

Bill gave her a warning look, and Mary turned away from Anne, heart pounding. *A tiny worm . . . they do more damage than a cannonball ever could.* She'd heard the way he talked about her last night.

Bill nodded and offered Mary a stick. She took it and lit it on the far side of the fire from Anne, looking anywhere but at her. She hurried back between the ships and began burning barnacles off. But Anne's laugh echoing down the tunnel made it impossible to focus.

All it takes is one person who doesn't belong . . .

And then Anne was right beside her, nudging her with her hip. "This is some proper excitement, ain't it?"

Mary looked up and down the tunnel, but Bill was nowhere to be seen. She gave Anne a quick smile. "Seems like you're having a grand time."

"Who would have thought that burning barnacles off a ship was about as thrilling as life could get?"

Mary's eyes fell on a spark smoldering into Anne's skirt. She wet her fingers quickly and pinched the spot, putting it out easily. "So long as you don't burn yourself up in the process. I'm not sure me sewing skills would be enough to fix that."

"I'll be careful," Anne said with a wink.

"Listen," Mary said in a whispered rush. "Bill just talked to me. He said some things—" She paused. What *had* he told her, really? Observations about shipworm and barnacles? "He was telling me about how they mutinied against Charles Vane—"

"Ugh, Bill," Anne huffed dismissively. "He's always grumbling about something. Don't worry about anything he says, all right? Jack knows how to handle him."

"If you say so," said Mary uneasily, looking around. There was Bill, talking with Jack out in the sunshine. Bill laughed at something Jack said, and the tension in her stomach eased.

"Your technique is terrible, by the way," teased Anne. "Slow as anything I've seen. Watch me for a look at a real master."

Mary watched Anne flit down the tunnel, going from shell to shell, gleefully sending mollusks to their death. She couldn't help looking at her again and again, hard as she tried to focus.

To Bill, freedom meant being a true equal to your fellows and never having your life subject to another's will. To Jack it meant getting away with a fortune in the end, slipping back to normal life once the money was made, with a willing woman and an untapped cask. And to Anne, it was something you had to fight for; it meant taking a stand and not settling for less.

Mary wondered what freedom meant to a mollusk—if they loved the shell that kept them fixed tight in one place—or if they longed for a fire that might ignite them, force the husk from their backs and reveal their soft insides to the world.

If Anne carried the flame, she thought with a heady rush—perhaps they wouldn't mind the brand so much.

CHAPTER THIRTEEN

Westminster, London—1717

Mary blazed down the hall between the servants' quarters and the dining room, then spun and paced back again. She couldn't eat dinner right now, with her insides such a roiling brine. All she could think about was that moment with Nat on his pallet, that rush of *something* that had surged between them. She couldn't stop herself from imagining that something more could have happened—and then she'd thank God Susan interrupted before it had—and then she was in agony, thinking of how *something more* would never come to pass. And in the meantime Susan and Nat were holding hands, Susan was leaning her curves into Nat and he was pulling her close—

"Hallo, Mr. Reade." Someone was right next to her, and there was a note of amusement in her voice.

Mary whirled. "Beth—Miss Hartley!" she gasped. It was one of the servant girls, smiling as she stood against the drapes. "I didn't see you there." Who knew how long Beth had been watching her pace.

"Clearly." Beth laughed. "I stepped aside to let you pass, and before I could go on you cut me off . . . I wasn't sure I'd ever make it down the hallway if I didn't make meself known."

Mary grinned sheepishly. "Sorry about that. I was, ah—you headed to supper, then?" Another supper with the servants all looking askance at her, wondering what the lady's grandson was doing eating dinner with the help. Though now that she thought about it, Beth always had a smile for her.

"Aye, just after I finish up clearing the missus's plates."

Mary liked the way Beth held her gaze. "I suppose I'll see you downstairs then." Mary inclined her head before she turned to go.

"Here now," said Beth, stepping forward to touch Mary's arm. "Are you *really* the grandson of the missus?"

Had Beth's touch lingered just a moment longer than necessary? "I am. What of it?"

"I heard you was recently of Wapping," Beth said, twisting a chestnut lock of hair around a finger. "But I thought to meself, the missus surely wouldn't have relations in Wapping! And what of you eating and sleeping with the servants? Seems a bit queer to me."

Mary was almost certain Beth was making eyes at her. "Aye, well. Granny's not overly fond of me mum, but she was terrible fond of me da. So I suppose I'm under suspicion till I prove meself clear of Mum's influences." Beth's eyes widened delightedly. Was this what it was like for Nat, to be a boy alone with a pretty girl? Mary leaned closer and whispered. "But the stories are true, I'm from Wapping sure enough! I saw pirates hung on Execution Dock from me own window, that's how close to the docks me kip was."

"You didn't, surely!" Beth crowed. "And you the grandson of the missus. Me mum would have a fit!"

"Where you from, then?"

"Grew up in Saint Martin in the Fields. Me sister Sarah's got a position as a nanny in Clerkenwell now, and I'm here. Quite an equally respectable position, me mum says, on account of the missus being such a lady. Tell you the truth though, it's dreadful boring work." She dropped her gaze, rubbing a smudge on her arm. "Must say, havin' you around makes things a bit more interesting." She looked up again, her gaze a challenge.

Beth fancied her. Mary had studied Nat long enough to see the way a girl looks at a boy when she thinks he's handsome. They would stand very close, their mouths turned up prettily. Mary could see where the dark of Beth's lashes faded to blond at the tips and felt a thrill at the girl's unfamiliar nearness. "I can't say I'm put out that you're here, either," she said with a smile. Beth looked away but a giggle escaped her. Mary ran her hand across the drapes as she leaned closer. "It's strange, ain't it? Granny having me eat supper with servants, hoping to make a proper gentleman of me?" Her hand brushed the curve of Beth's waist.

"Oh!" Beth jumped and started down the hall. "*Damn*, the dishes—"

"Oh, that's right," said Mary, voice trailing off. Maybe she'd been too bold.

"See you downstairs, then!" Beth turned with a wave, candlelight glinting off the hair escaping her cap as Mary watched her go. This was something Nat would do—stay where he was and watch a girl leave. Beth looked back once more, a faint smile on her lips, then bent her head to tuck a strand of hair behind her ear before she turned the corner.

Mary walked down the hall and turned off toward the kitchen. Her appetite had finally returned. She was looking forward to dinner.

Mary would keep the seat next to hers empty, in case Beth wanted to come sit next to her.

CHAPTER FOURTEEN

Isla de Cotorras—1719

Mary awoke in her sailcloth tent with a start, nerves singing. All she could hear was the drone of the jungle behind her, as usual, a rush of wind, and the slight patter of oncoming rain—but something else had woken her.

She reached for the bayonet she kept tucked beneath a corner of the sailcloth and listened with all her might, straining past the buzzing of the insects, the screech of parrots, and the shush of the surf. It had taken her forever to fall asleep. That morning, after two days of careening the ships, the crew had righted them and maneuvered the vessels out into deeper water—and the *Ranger* had gone right on sailing, straight out of the harbor. A couple of Bill's supporters had informed the remaining men that Bill and Jack had arranged to take a quick trip to Hispaniola with a skeleton crew, to scout potential hideouts and prizes before they decided where to head next. Anne's face had gone blank when she heard the news. She'd disappeared into her tent, and Mary hadn't seen her since. The mood around the evening fires had been sour. There were rumors that Jack hadn't been entirely willing to go.

She wished Paddy were there to reassure her, but Paddy had been on the *Ranger.*

She stiffened further when she made out the sound of footsteps coming in her direction. Mary crouched on her haunches. It was just beginning to rain—she could see fat drops landing on the sand beneath the edge of the tent and hear them tap-tapping above her.

She faintly heard a wet hiccup of sadness before the edge of her tent was thrown up to reveal the gleam of damp, sandy, red skirts—Mary barely withheld her strike as Anne flung herself into the dark tent. She knocked Mary back against the sand as she clutched her.

"That's the second time he's left me," Anne whispered. Her shoulders felt thin, shaking under Mary's palms.

Anne was in her tent.

"Shhh," Mary said. Her hands patted nervously, trying to quiet the girl. The crew might accept their strange connection by the light of day, but Mary doubted they'd be understanding if someone caught Anne and Mary together in a tent at night.

"I've been everything to him, done everything he's wanted—how could he leave me like this?" Her voice was a raspy wail. Mary smelled wine on her breath.

"There, there," Mary murmured. "He'll be back soon."

"When he took me away from James before, I thought—I thought that was it, he'd keep me and the baby safe. And then he *left* me, and nothing kept me safe when the baby came too soon—and he *promised* he wouldn't leave me like that again! He promised—" Her voice broke. Her face glittered in the darkness, wet with tears.

Through the buzz of nerves Mary took in Anne's words—the *baby?*—at the same moment that she became aware of girl parts against her, curves and dampness easing her back against the sand. Mary shifted so that they didn't touch so closely, wedging her arm between them. "There now," Mary said, as she struggled to sit upright. "There's naught that'll hurt you till he gets back. The men know you're his girl." Her heart pounded as she moved away. "He's mad about you, he is."

The rain was coming down hard now, nothing audible above its steady thrum against the sailcloth. The other men would be in their tents, and Anne's voice coming from her tent would be drowned out. Hopefully no one had seen her enter.

Anne leaned back in the sand, her hand on Mary's thigh, eyes glistening as she stared up into the dark.

When she spoke again her voice was calmer. "All I want is to be one of them. But no matter what, they always make it known that I'm only suffered because of Jack, and against his better judgment. And now it seems even Jack is sick of suffering me." Her voice went soft as her hand trailed up and traced the line of Mary's chin. "Not you, though. You make me feel welcome." Her fingers rested on Mary's jaw, soft as raindrops.

"You, Anne—you're the equal of any of us, and it's a shame they don't see that." Mary sat up and leaned over her. Anne should know—how extraordinary she was. "You shouldn't have to cater to Jack and the rest, just so they'll let you stay."

"Aren't you something," Anne murmured. Mary could hear her smile in the dark. "The boy who shot the captain, gone all soft and sweet on me." Her hands came up again, brushing against Mary's arm.

Mary pushed her away. "I'm not just saying—"

In a rush Anne sat up and pressed her lips to Mary's, quick as anything.

It took a moment before Mary got over the shock of it, and then she found she wasn't pulling away as she knew she should—but pushing forward instead, as Anne's hands came up to her neck and wound through her hair. The grit of sand on Anne's lips, the taste of salt and wine, the crinkle of velvet under Mary's hands felt so warm and right—

Mary ran her hands down to Anne's waist and pulled her in. Mary's head bumped against the sand. She must have leaned back, and Anne followed in a tangle of breath and texture. They puddled on the ground together as rainwater ran under the sailcloth.

"So timid!" Anne said softly, right against her lips. Mary could feel her smiling. "Haven't kissed such a boy as you in a while."

Such a boy *as you . . .*

Mary suddenly remembered how things like this ended—how another kiss like this had ended.

"We can't—" Mary pushed her away and struggled to sit up. "Jack—"

Anne pulled her back down. "Jack won't know," she said, and straddled her. Mary could just make out Anne's head thrown back, a waterfall of curls spilling down, her dress slipping off a shoulder. Her hips moved in a slow, delicious way as she pressed her hands into Mary's waist.

Desire pooled deep inside her.

"We can't." It came out in a gasp this time, and Anne laughed. But her movements stilled, and she leaned in, her hair falling forward to tickle Mary's face.

"You're going to have to give me a better reason than that bloody *man* of mine."

If Mary were a boy, she'd press up against Anne. She would pull her down and feel all that softness and forget about thinking, give in like she'd never had the chance to before—but she always wanted impossible things, and this was surely one of them. She wasn't the boy Anne thought she was. And as much as she wanted to kiss Anne as if she was a boy, she also longed for Anne to *know that she wasn't*. She'd wanted that, she realized, from the moment she'd first seen Anne on the deck of the *Vissen*, brandishing her pistol and cutlass.

Heart pounding, mouth dry, she arched up off the sand and tugged her shirt above her head. Anne gave a satisfied *huh* when she realized what Mary was doing and leaned back to give her room. "Here," Mary said. She fumbled for Anne's hand, then guided it to the knot in her binding. "Here's your reason, then." Her voice sounded different in her ears—lungs emptied of air beneath Anne's curious fingers. She felt Anne shift, smelled her wine-sour breath move closer; she could almost see the puzzled look on Anne's face as her hands began to move, trying to piece together what Mary was showing her.

All those times she'd imagined Nat's hands on her, her body unbound—Mary felt dizzy, the shock of skin on skin as Anne touched her, the tightening deep in her belly that made her gasp—

Just as Anne sucked in a breath as well. Mary didn't have time to be embarrassed at the sound she'd made, or the muddle of feelings that left her tingling. "You—" Anne sounded tongue-tied. She was tugging on the knot.

This was wrong.

Dread surged through Mary. She was a girl like Anne—yet she knew without a doubt that she was also *not a girl at all*. And now Anne knew what she was. Mary groaned, pushed Anne's hands away and crossed her arms over her chest.

And then—"*You*." Anne said it clearly this time, with what could only be called delight. She shoved Mary's arms away and began picking furiously at the knot. "I *knew* there was something about you from the start!" Mary hadn't undone the binding in months, and it was cinched tight and was stiff with salt and dirt, but somehow, Anne made short work of it. There, the knot came loose, Mary's ribs expanded as the fabric fell away—and then the shock of Anne's cold hands on skin that was never touched, not even by air.

It made Mary want to cry out and curl into a ball. "Miss, please." Mary could hear the meekness in her voice as she wormed away, and it maddened her.

"Oh, you have got a bit of something, don't you? Now that it's unwrapped." Anne sounded satisfied. She seemed to have forgotten that they'd been kissing. "I *knew* it could be done—didn't I tell Jack? But he would never let me try it."

This certainly wasn't the reaction Mary had feared, but still she felt sick.

"You have to tell me," Anne said, grabbing her hands. She was still straddling Mary's hips. "You have to show me how. I've always dreamed of doing this, just like you—I knew it was possible!"

"Like *me*?" That gave Mary pause. "But I'm—" Not a girl, not a boy. "I'm nothing."

Anne snorted. "The way I see it, Mark—" She giggled. "It ain't Mark, is it?"

"No, miss." She hadn't heard her name in so long. "It's—it's Mary." She whispered it, shivering as a gust of rain-cooled air came under the tent.

"The way I see it, *Mary*—" Her name said aloud brought another surge of aching as Anne took Mary's hand and pressed it to her chest. "This way, you get to be *everything*."

The binding coming off, her name being said—it was all happening the way Mary had envisioned it, only there was this girl instead of Nat. And they were not kissing, now that Anne knew what she was. Somehow, that was the thing that Mary wished was different. She wished there was a world where Anne knew who she was—and kissed her anyway.

Anne sighed contentedly. "You'll show me how to do it." Her words came out heavy, syrupy, as she rolled over and lay beside Mary like they were nothing but friends. "I'll get along famously then. I won't need Jack or anyone—just like you."

They were quiet for a moment. The sickness in Mary's stomach was subsiding, now that Anne relaxed against her. Maybe—if she had something Anne wanted—she could ask her—

Mary sat up, reached for her shirt and pulled it over her head, but she left her binding off. "And—you might show me how . . . to be . . . a bit more like you?"

Anne snorted as Mary lay back down again, her face flaming. "Oh, that's the easy part." Anne curled in beside her. "You're a girl, ain't you?"

She sounded so sure.

She put a hand on Mary's ribs, just below the place where her hammering heart was beginning to steady, and sighed sleepily.

Mary could feel each finger against her unbound skin.

CHAPTER FIFTEEN

WESTMINSTER, LONDON—1717

MARY SPLASHED HER FACE WITH WATER AND RUBBED THE DUST FROM her shoes. She couldn't help but grin, though her nerves were ablaze. Granny had invited her to sup with her at last, at the grand table! Supper with Granny, instead of the servants. Like a proper grandson.

She clattered down two flights of stairs and composed herself before walking into the dining room, slicking the hair back from her forehead. Granny loomed already at her place behind a battery of candles, a glass of claret at her elbow, a set place just across from her. Mary cleared her throat and sat down as Jenny filled her cup with small beer. The food was much the same as what she ate with the servants, the glorious difference being that it was all steaming hot instead of middling warm. There were five or six vegetables, all in lumpy heaps of slightly differing colors swimming in butter, the usual pudding, some boiled beef and gravy, and Mary's favorite, oyster pie.

Without a word, Granny clasped her hands and bowed her head, and Mary scrambled to imitate her.

"Dear Lord, we thank thee for this food . . ."

Mary's attention wandered as Granny droned on. She wondered what the gossip around the servants' table would be, since Granny had suddenly invited her to dinner. Would Beth miss seeing her tonight?

Mary had been flirting shamelessly with the servant girl. She knew she should be careful, but she couldn't help it. She loved making Beth laugh, and the more outrageous Mary was, the brighter Beth's laughter. She'd give her a wink across the dinner table when no one was looking, and whistle the refrain of some cheeky song whenever she passed a room where Beth was cleaning. Whenever Mary could get back to the tenement she told Nat about her, almost keeping pace with him when he told her about the girls he met. Sometimes her cheeks warmed when Beth's fingers grazed her hand—sometimes, lying awake in bed, it was Beth's soft lips she pictured kissing, instead of Nat's.

Mary's attention snapped back to Granny as her voice grew more forceful. "The temptation to sin is great, but we strive with all our power to be righteous. Help us to avoid sinful pursuits, those of the flesh, in pursuit of righteousness."

Mary's stomach twisted suddenly. No matter whose lips she was picturing, she thought, God wouldn't approve.

Abruptly Granny stopped. "Amen," she finally finished, looking up to stare directly at Mary. Mary echoed her uneasily.

Granny began piling beef on her plate. Mary sat for a moment, unsure of her manners, then reached for the oyster pie.

"Something came to my attention that gave me cause to rise early this afternoon," Granny said finally. "Beth, do you know her?"

Mary's heart jumped. "Which Beth do you mean?" she asked, though of course she knew who Granny meant.

Granny looked sharply at her. "The maid, Beth Hartley. She came to get the keys from me for a bit of cleaning today."

Mary's throat closed up as she continued ladling cabbage onto her plate. "Aye, I know her. From eating dinner with her. With the servants, I mean."

"She mentioned she'd been getting some help cleaning the second-floor library as of late," Granny continued. Mary choked down a bite of pie and kept her eyes on her plate. "She said you've been quite friendly with her. What a gentleman she thinks you are!" She took another sip. "But following girls into empty rooms doesn't sound like the behavior of a gentleman to me."

Mary set down her fork and put on an innocent face. "Oh, I honestly was only trying to be helpful—"

"You may be my footboy," Granny interrupted, her sharp eyes unimpressed, "but you are also my grandson. Has it occurred to you that I have no other family, no heirs but you?"

Mary wrinkled her brow and tried to look thoughtful and surprised, as if this idea was new to her. "I suppose I am, Granny. It is just me, ain't it?"

"*Isn't* it, Mark. Please try to speak properly. And I'm sure you've imagined it could all be yours." Granny ran a slice of beef through the gravy on her plate. Mary gave up on eating, her stomach now too knotted to try, and sucked down the rest of her beer.

Granny poked her fork in Mary's direction. "A girl like Beth could get you in trouble. Do you hear me? My son was ruined by a pretty-faced harlot who knew how to get what she wanted, and I've no intention of letting the same thing happen to you."

Mary clenched her jaw and looked down. "It wasn't like that," she mumbled, but she felt a flash of fear. If Granny wasn't satisfied with her excuses, everything she'd worked for could be lost so easily—and if disguising herself as Mark didn't ruin her in God's eyes, being tempted by another girl certainly would.

"Now I find you're carrying on with a girl that could very well do the same to you." Granny began to wheeze. "I may be sick, but I'm not blind. Take care and stay away from her." Mary nodded chastely as Granny took a sip of claret to clear her throat, relieved that she'd be escaping with a warning. "Or I'll discharge her and send you back to the bilgewater you came from. Do I make myself clear?"

"Yes, ma'am." Mary kept her fists hidden under the table. She would *never* go back to that tenement room in Wapping. She'd do whatever it took.

Granny eyed her. "It's partly my fault. From now on you'll eat with me, and I'm having one of the rooms on the second floor made up for you. A real room, one suitable for my grandson. Take care you don't give me cause to regret the expense. Do you understand?" Granny drained her glass and set it on the table with an authoritative smack.

Just when Mary was starting to enjoy eating dinner with the servants, joining in on the conversation and cracking jokes. And *Beth*. Spending time with her had been the best part of being at Granny's. But going back to Wapping and living with Mum was impossible, and she had her soul to think of. Whatever raged inside her, she knew what she had to do. She looked across the table and nodded somberly. "Aye, Granny. I'm sorry. I won't disappoint you again."

CHAPTER SIXTEEN

Isla de Cotorras—1719

"Why don't those who want to go to Nassau just head there, while Bill and his supporters continue on the account?" Mary asked Anne. They had rowed a jolly boat up the shore to the nearest river's headwaters, promising to haul back some fresh water—but really hoping to steal a few moments away from the crew. Mary hopped out of the boat into ankle-deep water, silty mud mushrooming up around her feet.

"Well, pretending for a moment that those who want to head for Nassau are in agreement about the manner in which we'll be arriving," said Anne, climbing out of the boat as well, "who gets the *Ranger*? The one left with the *Kingston* is just asking to be captured—she's so slow, and every British ship in the sea is looking for her since she was taken." They began pulling the jolly boat toward the shore, water soaking up Anne's skirts. "But the biggest sticking points are money and pride. Bill doesn't think a captain who begs pardon deserves to take a double share with him, and Jack won't give that up."

"Jack only gets a double share of the spoils?" asked Mary, sidetracked. "Is that really true?"

"Aye," said Anne.

"If only everything worked that way." If only Granny had just double what Mum did. If only Baas had double what his sailors did. "Imagine if the king himself could only have twice as much as the poorest beggar. The world would be a different place."

"A *better* place," agreed Anne. "There wouldn't be a need for piracy at all." She gave a short laugh. "But I'm sure, even if the world worked the way a pirate crew does, they'd still find a way to keep women from getting any share at all."

Mary paused as the jolly boat nudged the shore just past the tree line. "Wait a minute. Don't tell me you don't get a share?"

Anne looked at her pointedly. "I'm telling you, Mary, you should stick with the britches. Speaking of which—hand them over."

"What's that?" Mary scooped a palmful of water up to her mouth. It was brackish from being so close to the sea, and warm. She spit it out and made a face.

"Your britches, and that bit of linen you keep wound 'round your chest. Hand it over." Anne attacked the buttons running down the front of her own dress one by one, the neckline sagging open to reveal a dingy chemise.

Mary fretted with the knot in her binding through her shirt, staring back the way they'd come. "Perhaps we should row a bit farther in?"

"I'd like to see you try and haul water in me skirts, while I try on your togs!" The dress was open to her waist.

Mary tied the jolly boat to an exposed root. The headwaters were only a mile or two easy walking from the main camp. She squinted into the undergrowth, but of course no one had followed them.

Anne dropped her dress on the bank and waited expectantly. Her chemise was thin, almost threadbare; Mary could see the swell of curves, the darkness of a nipple beneath. Mary dropped her eyes quickly, but her mind continued to trace the soft lines of Anne's silhouette.

"I don't think me binding will do you much good. You're too, ah—womanly."

The corner of Anne's mouth crooked up. "You can keep your shirt on 'neath the dress. I'll use me shimmy as me shirt, so I just need the britches and the binding if you please."

A mess of green parrots swarmed above them, screeching and shaking the palm fronds until the whole canopy danced. Anne had told her that *cotorras* meant parrots, and that the whole island was swarming with them. Mary looked up. The birds twisted their heads around and fixed their little black eyes on her, calling and preening, taking off and landing here and there.

Mary climbed onto the bank, untucked her shirt, and reached beneath it for the knot. After Anne had untied it the night before last, Mary had cinched it extra tight, and she couldn't find a way into it again.

Anne laughed. "Maybe you'd do better if you took your shirt off so you could see?"

Mary turned away, blushing furiously, and lifted her shirt, tucking the hem beneath her chin. She finally managed to loosen the knot. Once the binding was gone she dropped the hem of her shirt, made sure it fell straight to her knees, and then eased out of her britches.

Suddenly the red dress was in her hands, and Anne was giggling as she wrapped the binding around herself. Mary pulled the dress over her head gracelessly, floundered her arms into the holes, and did the buttons up with shaking hands.

When she turned, Anne was swaggering along the riverbank in Mary's britches. "Oooh, just look at me!" she squealed. "Don't I look like a proper cove now!"

Mary watched her, annoyance rising in her chest as she buttoned up Anne's red dress. "You look as much like a boy as I do a girl."

"What's that, my dove?" Anne swaggered over, her version of a manly stride just serving to enunciate the sway of her hips. Likewise, it seemed even a dress couldn't make Mary look like a girl. The sleeves cut into her armpits, the soft velvet contrasted with her cracked, broad hands, and the neckline drooped away from her negligent bosom. She remembered the men she'd seen dressed up in women's clothes, and she knew just how she appeared.

"I look like a molly." She swallowed a wave of nausea that rose up at the memory of the cart going by—and then of Nat's arms around her. Somehow she'd thought becoming someone he might desire would be as easy as putting on a dress, but this didn't feel right at all.

Anne wiggled up close. The britches clung to her thighs, and the binding slimmed down her bosom. She looked leaner, certainly, without her skirts billowing around her—some new sort of *virility* hung about her. She looked as if she could scale a mast or helm a ship much more easily than she could have before.

Anne cocked her head. "Here now, let's see what we can do." She pulled Mary's hair out of its pigtail and down around her face. Anne took a look, then shook her head and braided it over one shoulder. "There now. Tilt your chin down."

Mary obliged, and Anne studied her again as Mary snuck a peek through her lashes—girlishly, perhaps—but that felt wrong, more an act than wearing a dress. She wasn't the kind of person that looked at anyone like that. Perhaps she'd spent so much time being a boy that it was impossible for her to be anything else.

"Aye," Anne said finally. "Britches is the better look for you." Anne bit her lip in an arresting manner, like Nat used to do with that freckle of his. "Too bad I've taken yours."

She shrieked as Mary lunged for her. Mary stopped, changing tactics, fumbled the buttons open, and pulled the dress over her head, throwing it with great show in the river. Anne stopped with a gasp and ran toward it, and Mary dove at her. She wrestled Anne down, yanking the britches from her waist as Anne shrieked and hung on to them—

Mary realized she was only wearing a shirt, and though it came to her knees she still felt awfully exposed. She froze and for a moment they were nose to nose in the dappled sunlight, parrots screeching as they stared breathlessly at each other with wide eyes. Mary's gaze dropped to the full curve of Anne's bottom lip—

Mary let go and jumped to her feet. She crossed her arms over her chest and glared, breathing hard. "Give them back," she said gruffly.

"Well aren't you cross all of a sudden!" Anne rolled her eyes as she wiggled out of the britches and unwound the binding from her chest. She jumped in the river to fish her skirts from the water.

Mary set her appearance right again with trembling fingers.

Anne had been staring at her for a while now, abandoning all pretense of hunting for mussels.

"What are you doing?" Mary hissed, dropping a mussel into the makeshift shoulder bag she'd sewn from sailcloth. "You're making everyone uncomfortable. Especially me." The tide was out and they stood in the swash, looking for shellfish among the exposed rocks. Others were building a fire to cook over, fishing, or hunting for mussels. Everyone was on edge, but they had settled into a resentful routine, still hunting and fishing and hauling water, still keeping watch from the crow's nest on the *Kingston*. Waiting for Bill and Jack to return.

Anne cocked her head. "I'm watching the way you walk. I've realized I'm never going to pull it off just by putting on a pair of britches—there's a whole act you've got going on."

Anne didn't realize that it wasn't an act. "How do I walk?" Mary asked.

"It's the way you carry yourself. No extra flourishes. A sureness. Something like that." Anne lowered her voice. "It's rather thrilling, when it's a girl pulling it off."

That made Mary painfully aware of her own strangeness—but she had never considered that someone might like the looks of her act. "Let's see you try it, then, and I'll tell you if I find it as thrilling as you do."

Anne handed her sack of mussels to Mary and smoothed her skirts. "Well. It'll be hard without the britches." Then she took a deep breath, closed her eyes—her lips twisted up very seriously—and she walked across the sand like a mummer acting the constable, all stiff-limbed and waddling.

Mary's hoot of laughter caught the attention of the men. They were all looking, or trying not to look.

"Don't feel bad," Mary said, when Anne mock-scowled at her. "It's not as if your life depends on it."

"It will if I ever need to make it on me own," Anne said determinedly. "Jack's proved that he can leave me to fend for meself more than once, so I'll not trust him to protect me once we get back to Nassau, whether we storm the fort or go back with our tails between our legs."

Mary frowned. "If it's any comfort," she said, changing the subject, "it'd be just as ludicrous if I tried to walk like you."

Anne crossed her arms, but there was a glint of daring in her eyes. "Let's see it then."

Imitating a girl in front of the whole crew seemed like an awful risk. But after their clothing experiment a few days before, Mary expected she was so thoroughly *boy* that she could try it and no one would be the wiser.

She passed the mussels to Anne, copying her skirt smoothing and deep breath in preparation—the other pirates watched askance—and then Mary sashayed down the beach, hips swinging wide as she tossed her head back. She must have done a good imitation, for the pirates watching her began to guffaw and cracked a joke or two at Anne's expense.

Mary's heart sank. She didn't have to worry that acting like a girl would give her away. Her disguise was so complete, playing a boy was no act for her—it was who she was.

She didn't know whether to feel proud, or to despair.

CHAPTER SEVENTEEN

Isla de Cotorras—1719

"I'm glad we butchered the last of the sheep, even if Jack and Bill should be back soon," Cager said as the men that had been seated around the fire stood. "It's lovely when there's more than enough to go around!"

The other men laughed and nodded, but they looked pensive as they rose to make water and find another bottle. Mary glanced up as she hacked a second helping of meat from the ribs of a sheep carcass, trying to gauge Anne's reaction to the mention of Jack's return.

"It's odd," said Anne, looking sideways at Mary as she licked the grease from her fingers. "I'm almost sad Jack is coming back. I thought I'd be so lonely and scared while he was gone, like I always am—but it's been fine. I haven't been lonely at all."

Mary managed to tug a meaty rib from the spit and sat back down. "I know what you mean," said Mary, with a flash of nerves. "It's been—nice. I've never been able to be free with someone before."

"So you've never been honest, even with a boy?" asked Anne, raising her brows. Light from the fire flicked across her face, lips glistening.

"No." Mary spat a bit of gristle into the fire.

"Have you ever wanted to?"

Mary thought of Nat, tapping that spoon against her lip on a dusk-darkened pallet. "Aye."

"Oh," Anne sighed. "How terribly *star-crossed*. I can just *imagine* it!"

All the little bits of Nat she'd memorized—Mary had never talked about them with anyone. She tried to picture him, all of him, but found she had trouble recalling his hands, his eyes, his shoulders, his smell. He was starting to grow dim in her mind, even his freckled lip not as real to her anymore as the one Anne rubbed a stained sleeve against to wipe off a smear of grease. "I was speaking the truth that first morning we met," she said. "Chasing him is what brought me here to the islands." She needed to remember all his sweet details, the passion that had driven her across the ocean. She needed the last time she'd seen him to not be the end of their story.

"Well. When we return to Nassau, guns blazing, we'll be sure to demand your sweetheart is delivered straight to you."

Anne was still going on about rebellion and seeing the governor swing. The fire snapped and flared, and Mary remembered Bill's mussel-burning brand. When he and Jack got back, the winds would shift one way or the other. "I've been meaning to ask you," she said casually. "Why don't you side with Bill? Why don't you stay as far away from New Providence as possible, if you're so afraid of your husband?"

Anne's jaw set. "It's me home. Before Governor Rogers came I felt safe enough there, protected by Jack and others. I'm livid every time I think about what Jimmy did to me, but you know what enrages me even more? How people started to think that he had a *right* to do what he did, and that I was the one who should be put in the pillory. That whole town needs to be burned to the ground and started over."

"There must be some way to get justice besides that," Mary mused. "There must be some way for you to go home without destroying it."

"Have you ever been made to feel completely powerless?" Anne challenged her. "Have *you* ever been dismissed, just because you're not a man? Why no, I don't believe you have. You have no idea what it's like."

That made her teeth clench, and Mary chose her words carefully. "That *has* happened to me, actually. But it's not as simple to fight back as you make it sound. Some things are the way they are, and all there is for us to do is to find a way to live with them."

"You sound just like Jack, you know that?" Anne snapped. "I shouldn't have to be content to accept things as they are. I deserve better."

"What if you could go home to Nassau and find a way to keep you safe from James?" Mary asked, an idea dawning on her. You could end a marriage if you had a man and enough money. "Jack gets that double share. So long as the crew is behind Jack, a couple more prizes like the *Vissen*, and Jack could pay James off for you, whenever you end up returning to Nassau."

"Ugh, like I'm a bloody cow. He could *pay* for me, and then he could leave me or do whatever he wanted because I belonged to him? I'd only marry Jack if I had no other choice."

"It wouldn't be so different from what's happening now, would it?"

"How's that, Mary?" Anne's eyes narrowed. "Please, I'd love to know."

"I'm just saying that Jack's not the worst person to serve. I'm rather enjoying the freedom I enjoy under Jack's command, and it seems like you enjoy quite a bit of it yourself."

Anne's mouth twisted in disgust. "You're *never* free, so long as you're subject to someone—to a captain, or the crown, or whatever good-for-nothing man decides to lord over you."

"You'd rather burn New Providence to the ground than compromise?"

"Not if I'm the only one who has to compromise!" Anne's voice rose. "If we went back to Nassau and Jack paid James off, I'd have to see Jimmy's smirking face every day and know he got away with being such a devil. No—he got *paid* for it. He got *rewarded*. Can you even imagine?"

"You're being ridiculous," Mary said exasperatedly. "Storming Nassau is *never* going to happen, no matter that there's a handful of rebels egging you on. In the meantime, what happens if the crew decides Jack shouldn't be captain? What if the crew mutinies, and you're caught in the middle of it? Or what if he goes back for pardon and leaves you here to rot?"

Anne stared at her for moment, lips parted. "I can't believe this," she said finally, outrage building in her voice. "You act *so* sympathetic, so *sorry* for what happened, but then you refuse to do anything about it, just like every other bloody man. You've spent so much time living as Mark that you haven't had to think about how it might be for someone like me!"

"You have no idea how hard it's been for *me*!" Mary said, voice rising to match.

"It's been just as easy for you as for every other arsehole parading around this beach!" Anne shouted. Men sitting at other fires quieted their conversations, turned to look. "Otherwise you'd understand!"

Mary stood, tossing her bone into the flames. "If that's what you think, you can go to hell," she said and stalked off.

CHAPTER EIGHTEEN

Westminster, London—1717

Mary plucked a few sprigs of catmint out of the front garden and caught up with Beth as she hauled a bucket of filthy water down the steps from the kitchen, her hair steamed into frizzy ringlets around her face. The leaves of the trees above their heads exploded in yellows and reds and oranges, and Beth's smile when she saw Mary approach matched their exuberance.

As Mary held out the flowers, she realized what a bad idea they were. She'd wanted to soften the blow, but Beth's expression when she saw them made Mary think they'd only make it worse.

"I think they're the last thing left blooming," Mary said. Beth set down her bucket, setting the violet blossoms to nodding as she took the flowers from Mary's hand. She looked pleased but tired, and Mary felt an unexpected rush of concern. Beth was hard at work every time Mary saw her, always in motion. "I hope your day's been easy enough?"

"Seeing you eases it considerably," said Beth warmly. The maid looked expectantly at Mary.

"Ah, good. That's good." She didn't know how to begin. Disguising herself as Mark was bad enough, but that was a matter of survival. God would never forgive her if she didn't end this—and neither would Granny.

"Tomorrow's me half-day," Beth said after a moment.

"Is it," Mary said. Should she be firm? Should she make a joke out of it? Should she blame Granny, or make it sound like it was her own idea?

"You're done after supper, ain't you?" Beth asked. "Tomorrow?"

"Aye."

The corners of Beth's mouth turned up.

She was waiting, Mary realized. For her to say she'd like to steal a few moments with Beth tomorrow evening, if she guessed it right.

The silence stretched too long, and Beth sighed. "Would you like to meet up with me then, for a walk about the garden?" she asked.

No. Mary couldn't let herself. "Listen, Beth. Granny—You see, I—"

Beth leaned in and kissed her.

At first, Mary was too surprised to pull away—and by the time she remembered that she should, it was very hard to follow through. Not at all as slight as she appeared, with their lips touching suddenly Beth was all curves, out at the hip and in at the waist, a slight roundness to her belly beneath Mary's thumbs. She parted her lips, and Beth did too, and then they were really kissing, still soft and warm but now something secret as well. Beth made a *hmm* noise against her lips as Mary leaned into the kiss—and at that sound a wild feeling rose up in her, longing and sick-to-her-stomach and queasiness and elation. She never wanted it to stop.

All of a sudden Beth's fingers caught on the binding of Mary's chest, paused there, then seemed to study the contours of the hidden wrapping with her hands, fingertips bumping over the subtle, uneven layers. Beth's body stilled and Mary froze, her stomach dropping.

Tracing a strip of binding to the worn knot, Beth tapped it a few times and then pushed away so she could look at Mary. She ran firm hands over Mary's chest and drew in her breath. Mary stood there, unable to move, too shocked to speak, still trembling from the heat she'd felt.

"Is there something you've been meaning to tell me, Mark?" Beth asked. Mary, prepared for anger, heard only bemusement in her voice.

They stood still as pond water, Beth's hands still on her chest, staring at each other. Beth remembered herself before Mary did and pulled away abruptly. She looked at her splayed fingers, as if they were what had shocked her. Her lips had a shine to them, but her eyes grew shadowed as her brows drew down.

"You let me think . . ." Beth put her hands to her mouth, looking at the leaves along the walk as they turned belly-up in the breeze. She'd dropped the catmint on the cobblestone, and the blossoms were strewn around their feet. When she looked at Mary, her mouth twisted in disgust. Suddenly she bent, grabbed the handle of her bucket, and heaved. Cold, stinking water struck Mary like a blow that left her gasping and drenched.

"Don't come near me ever again," Beth said evenly. "Don't talk to me. Don't even *look* at me."

Mary nodded, shaking and sputtering.

Then something dawned in Beth's eyes, and she took a step back. "Grandson of the missus, are we?" she said slowly, and in her tone Mary heard the beginnings of the shocking, gossipy tale Beth would put forth to everyone around the servant's table that night.

Mary turned and ran.

CHAPTER NINETEEN

Isla de Cotorras–1719

Mary lay on her back in her tent, hot with anger—and shame, too, because Anne was right. Mary didn't know what it was like to live as a girl, to have your safety and freedom tied to a man and his whims. But Anne didn't know what life had been like for Mary, either! Still, her stomach lurched at the thought that she might lose her only friend.

Mary flung the sailcloth aside and stalked toward Anne and Jack's tent, a dark shadow by the tree line. By the time she stood beside it she was trembling.

"Who's there?" Inside the tent, Anne sounded scared.

"It's okay," Mary said gruffly, squatting. "It's me."

"Mary," said Anne, with relief in her voice. "I'm so glad it's you. I—well, I might have been a bit hard on you, even if you were being an arse."

"It's all right," Mary whispered, relieved, reaching toward Anne until her fingers brushed the canvas of the tent.

"I just thought—I felt that *finally*, here's someone who understands me. And then to hear you dismiss me like everyone else."

"You're right, I don't know what it's been like for you," Mary said softly. "But every little bit you tell me about how you see the world—I want to know more. I want to understand."

Anne was quiet for a moment. "You are so sweet," she said ruefully. "Not sure why I took a fancy to you. Sweet isn't exactly me type." Her laugh was sad. "Too bad you're not a boy."

Aching suffused Anne's words, and Mary was filled with a familiar longing. If only she were a boy, if only wishing hard enough would make it so—but she wasn't. She was just confused, messed up, not girl and not boy. Nothing about her made sense—especially the yearning that had been growing stronger since Anne kissed her.

Anne lifted the sailcloth and peered out from beneath it. Her eyes were dark shadows. "You might as well come in," she whispered. "Before someone sees you sitting outside me tent and starts to wonder."

Mary sank to her knees, crawled inside, and sat facing Anne in the dark.

"I know you want to get to Nassau," Anne said. Her skirts brushed Mary's knees as she shifted. "So you can see your sweetheart again. I know how much you must want that."

Nat. "Yes. But I also—I don't want you to think I don't care about what happens to you."

Anne fumbled for Mary's hand and squeezed it. "We'll get you to Nassau, one way or another."

They were both silent, fingers entwined. Mary was afraid to move.

"I've been thinking about what we was talking about before I got so angry," Anne said, her voice a little unsteady.

"What's that?" Mary asked hoarsely.

"About what you're going to do once you find your Nat, and how you've never kissed a boy before." Anne cleared her throat.

"I think you've got to put a bit of thought into how you're going to show him how you feel."

Mary knew what Anne *showing* someone her feelings was like, but couldn't picture herself being that forward. "I was thinking I'd just tell him," she mumbled.

"Well I think—a girl in your position, looking so, well, so much like a boy, I suppose—"

"All right, now. Let's talk about this some other time." It made her instantly cross, how Anne summed up all her awkwardness so carelessly.

"Remember how I kissed you?" Anne pressed, her voice sounding surer.

Mary had been trying to forget it—every heated, confusing moment. She shook her fingers from Anne's grip.

"I think you ought to show Nat like *that*, next time you see him." Mary sensed Anne leaning forward. "But you have to do better than how you kissed me."

"What's that supposed to mean?" Mary felt a dart of irritation. "You didn't seem to mind it."

"It was lovely," Anne said. "But the way you went about it, I didn't think you was a girl for one moment."

Mary tried to remember the way she'd kissed Anne. She hadn't been thinking. She'd just reacted—a visceral, instinctive response. Mary leaned forward on her knees, until she could feel Anne's breath, so close, against her lips. "I don't know how to kiss like a girl, any more than I know how to look like one."

Anne was unreadable, a dim silhouette against the moonlit sailcloth behind her, but Mary thought she saw her smile. "Why don't you try it, and I'll tell you what I think."

Mary tried to stifle her breath so it didn't sound so loud. How in the hell did someone kiss like a girl?

Anne tugged her in confidently. "Pretend I'm Nat," Anne said. "You be the girl, now."

Mary's hand clunked against Anne's side as she tried in vain to touch her softly. The more she thought about softness, the stiffer she became. She leaned in anyway, pressing her mouth gently against Anne's.

Anne giggled breathlessly when Mary pulled away. "Here now, you're thinking too much."

"I can't—"

"Maybe you're right, and you're incapable of it," Anne teased.

"*Maybe* I just need a proper demonstration." Mary pushed Anne back and leaned over her, the heels of her hands grinding into the sand on either side of Anne's shoulders. Her heart was racing. "Show me again how you do it, since you're such a master."

"All right," Anne said. It sounded like she was trying to catch her breath. Her hands came up to Mary's hips, rested there like butterflies, then tugged her gently down. "Come here, then."

Mary slid down until she rested against Anne, and Anne's hands slipped up to her hair, and Mary leaned in and kissed her, hard. Anne pressed up against her and Mary's mind went blank, forgot that she was supposed to be—that this was pretend. Their bodies softened like wax against each other's heat, melting into each other.

"I was wrong," Anne murmured against her lips. "Forget everything I told you. You kiss him just like that, he'll fall for you."

The sudden quiet between them was deafening as they stared at each other in the dark, mouths close, Anne's hands still softly pulling Mary into her.

It's you *I want to fall for me.*

It echoed again and again in her mind. She wanted this girl. What was *wrong* with her? She was mad to want this—but she couldn't pull away, not while they were hidden from the world, Anne's hands twitching against her skin as if she wanted to pull her closer still.

Mary leaned down gently and kissed Anne again, and Anne arched up against her. Mary kissed her lips, her eyelids, her smooth forehead and cheek and throat. She grazed the neckline of Anne's dress, longing for the skin beneath it. She only had to shift a bit to gather the shoulder of the dress and tug gently, exposing just a sliver more of Anne's skin to her lips. Then another.

"Mmm," Anne sighed, fingers tightening on Mary's waist. "Just—like that—"

There was nothing Mary needed outside of Anne's breath catching and turning to soft, liquid sound. She would do anything to make this last forever. She would do anything Anne wanted, storm bloody Nassau if she had to, Nat be damned.

Suddenly a roar cut through the night noises outside, and the sailcloth above them ripped away with a shout. Anne shrieked and flung herself forward, balling herself up beneath Mary.

When Mary turned, a pistol pointed at her face, Jack behind it, snarling like a devil. "What the bloody *hell* is going on?"

CHAPTER TWENTY

ISLA DE COTORRAS—1719

ANNE WAS UP IN A FLASH, SCREAMING IN JACK'S FACE. "WHAT IN *GOD'S* name makes you think you've got the right to ask me that, Jack? What?"

She shoved the pistol away from Mary's face, but then came the crack of Jack's palm against Anne's cheek. She screamed again, turning away and cradling her face. Jack closed in above Mary, pistol retrained. "You're a dead man, Mark."

Mary could feel every grain of sand, rough against her palms, and the breeze off the ocean whipping away the little warmth lingering where Anne's body had pressed into hers. She could smell the tang of smoke off the bonfires along the water's edge. The *Ranger* had to be standing beside the *Kingston*—there, she could see its lights glowing over the ocean. The pirates must have come in only minutes before, dropping anchor and rowing to shore. She should have noticed them arriving as she'd walked to Anne's tent, heard them hail the men on the beach to let them know that their crew had returned. If only she hadn't been so distracted. She tried to remember, but all she could hear was

Anne's voice, whispering against her neck—*You kiss him just like that, he'll fall for you—*

"D'you hear me, boy?" The metal barrel made a cold imprint on her forehead, snapping her sharply back to the moment, and she jerked away. "You might have been the boy who shot the captain," Jack growled, "but you're about to be the boy the captain shot—and there's none here who'll blame me."

Suddenly the cold pressure on her forehead disappeared, and she flinched as red skirts sprayed sand in her eyes. "You think you can leave me without a word, and come back thinking you have some right to me?" Anne was sobbing, pounding on Jack's chest so that he took a step back. "You *knew* how much it would hurt me!"

Jack refocused on Anne, and Mary took a gasping breath and scrambled backward. Jack grabbed Anne's wrists and shook her. "I didn't *leave* you! I had to go without you, the way you was going on about Nassau, how dead against Hispaniola you were!" He pulled her toward him and whispered fiercely, "You *know* I had to do it. And you knew I'd be back for you! This—what you've done—"

Behind them a smoldering bonfire on the beach flared to life, the flames splintering, then coming closer—Mary saw they were brands held aloft by a few men as they ran up the beach to see what the shouting was about. The flickering light caught the glisten of tear tracks across Jack's cheeks, the queer twist of his mouth. "What the devil have you done, Anne?" he asked. Men slowed their approach, lowering their flames uncertainly.

Somehow the tears in Jack's eyes filled Mary with more dread than a pistol to her forehead. Mary slowly stood and began inching toward the tree line, as if the jungle might save her.

"What did you expect?" Anne hissed, struggling weakly against his grip. "What did you think would happen, when you act as if I'm nothing to you?"

Jack pushed Anne's hands away. "You made a fool and a cuckold out of me, in front of my crew." His voice was rising. Mary struggled to her feet.

Anne didn't even look in Mary's direction, just bowed her head and leaned against Jack's shoulder. "What did you expect, when you knew how much you'd hurt me?" she repeated softly, but a pleading note had entered her voice.

Mary's eyes met Paddy's, his face illuminated starkly against the darkness, familiar and strange all at once in the orange light. His mouth opened as he took in Mary's cowering form, Anne's fury, Jack's tears. Mary grinned at him nervously, baring all her teeth like a cornered cat. He'd be sad, but he'd still believe she brought death on herself.

Jack's mouth curled up, his voice cracking. "I should shoot you as well, and be done with it." He stepped away and held the pistol up again, this time pointed at Anne's breast.

An arm caught Mary, stopping her from stepping between Jack and Anne. When she looked up Bill stood above her, an iron grip on her shoulder.

"You don't mean it, Jack," Anne whispered, the pitch of her voice rising as she backed away. "You love me."

Everyone stared with wide eyes.

Jack's eyes closed. "Of course I love you, Annie." The pistol was shaking—or perhaps that was a trick of the uneven light. "But all you do is prove, over and over, that you're unbiddable. You do as you like, and damn the rest of us." He cocked the pistol's hammer.

Mary's eyes flicked between them, a sour taste rising her in her throat. But she made her voice strong and confident as she spoke. "What if I said that you was mistaken?"

"There's naught you could say that would convince me that she don't deserve this," Jack said, but his tone was unconvincing.

Almost as if he was begging her to prove him wrong. "That you *both* don't deserve this," he added sharply.

"What if I told you it wasn't young Mark she was in that tent with?"

Anne's mouth opened—and then realization sparked in her eyes and filled her whole face with hope. "Aye, that's right!"

"You know you can't let them get away with this," Bill said, releasing Mary and stepping forward. Murmurs rose up from the men surrounding them, all in agreement. "In front of all your men? You know it would mean your crew's loyalty. It would certainly mean mine."

Mary looked at Anne, the flames surrounding her licking closer. She remembered how Anne had squealed when she'd found out what she was, her delight at hearing how Mary had dodged her own fires.

"Jack," Mary said loudly. Jack turned to her and Bill folded his arms. Mary lifted her chin. When the men shifted their brands toward her she imagined it was lights coming up on her like at the theater: Mary Reade making her debut.

"What I say is true."

The men began to laugh.

"Tell them," Anne said. She was standing strong again, though Jack still held the pistol to her heart. Mary searched her face for some sign that might mean—she didn't know what. All she saw was Anne's manic intensity, her chest inflated with the breath she held.

"My name," she said, "is Mary Reade."

CHAPTER TWENTY-ONE

Wapping, London—1717

Mary buzzed around the tenement room like a fly trapped in a bottle, throwing herself down on the pallet, then bouncing up to the chair, then bolting to her feet and pacing. Beth would tell Granny—she probably already had. Would Granny call the constable and send him after Mary? It wouldn't be too hard for him to find her—Granny knew she'd be in Wapping, and the constable wouldn't have to ask around long before being pointed to the right kip. Maybe there was a chance that Granny wouldn't come after her, but she couldn't bet on that, and then there was *Mum*, Lord knows where she was right now but she'd be back soon, and when Mary told her what had happened—she *couldn't* tell her what had happened. Mary flung herself onto the pallet and pressed her fists into her eyes. She'd ruined the one thing that made her worth anything in Mum's eyes—and whether it had been God's plan for her to masquerade as Mark or not, Mary was just a girl who had lied her whole life. She couldn't go back to living with Mum in this filthy room as the nothing she would be to her now, she *couldn't*.

A thump from the landing pulled her from her thoughts in a panic. But it was Nat's door across the hall slamming open and something heavy crashing down, followed by a smattering of footsteps and a curse—"Christ almighty!"

Nat's voice.

Whether she ended up in gaol or fleeing the city, the thought of never seeing his face again was suddenly unbearable. Mary jumped from the pallet and crept to his door.

Nat crouched over a lockbox on top of the table, fumbling with a key. A floorboard creaked under Mary's foot and his head snapped up, the key clattering to the floor.

His face was a mess. "Would you look at this?" He sounded oddly triumphant as he gestured to his eye. "When I got home last night he was back." His left eye was swollen shut, his cheek puffed out, crusted and purple. His other eye had a mad look in it, his breath coming short and fast. He bent and picked up the key. "Me da's back, been laid off from his ship same as everyone, and it's no use I got a job now. He'll do nothing but drink me money away, as he's got none of his own." His hands jumped about, key rattling against the lock as the metal touched. "But no matter. This is the last of it."

"What's that supposed to mean? You finally going to make good on your threat and finish him off?" She wouldn't put it past him, in this state. Nat didn't seem himself at all.

"I'd kill him soon as look at him again." His gaze landed on her and he stilled. "What are you doing home, mate?" he asked. He dropped the key, grabbed her arms and gave her a shake. "You finished with that bloody boring life you have with Granny? You ready for an adventure?"

"Bloody hell," she said, her voice catching a little. "I think I am."

He was leaving. They could leave *together*.

"That's brilliant, mate—listen to this!" Nat began pacing back and forth. "I was up early for me shift at the yard, and the cove I work for there, Johnny Thresham, told me about the reward the king's just posted for pirates—twenty pounds for regular pirates, up to one hundred for the ringleaders! There's a fortune to be made hunting down men like me da that take what's not theirs!"

He was leaving to go hunting *pirates*? "Aye. That's a fortune sure enough, but—"

"The West Indies, mate! There's money, endless sunshine, and plenty of land to be had. Johnny's got a plan to chase down pirates, a ship, and a scheme to get the shine to back it! We've got to be on that boat tonight if we're to leave in the morning—we're sailing straight for Flanders first thing. There's a rich man there he's worked for that owes him a favor, and hates pirates besides—Johnny's sure he'll want to buy shares in the venture. How's that for you?"

Mary sank down on a chair. "Chasing pirates, then." It wasn't what she dreamed of, when she imagined the New World. She'd been more inclined to envy the pirates than the men hunting them. For all their treasure. For starting a new life, out of reach of London law . . .

And then—she couldn't possibly survive a journey on a ship full of men. Where would she relieve herself? Where would she sleep? Could she really fight pirates, if she had to? And there'd be nowhere to run, should she be discovered.

Nat squatted in front of her. "You've got to come! Johnny's still looking for able men that can leave in the morn, and I know you're as wild to get out of here as I am. I'll vouch for you—he's sure to take you on!"

Nat wanted her to come. Even if it was just as his mate.

"Mark," Nat said. "You living in Westminster—it got you out of Wapping, but you're still Mark Reade. Your Granny's still breathing down your neck, and your mum's still a drunk, and that'll never change."

"Aye, that's bloody well true," Mary said bitterly.

"You sail to the other side of the world—you could be anyone you want!"

Mary's heart started to beat faster.

"We could find our fortune." He nudged her. "Buy our island."

She nudged him back. "Find you a parrot to sit on your shoulder."

He laughed. "Aye! Exactly."

The New World—and Nat would be with her. Mary would get out before Granny or the constable came after her.

She looked at Nat. The eye that wasn't swollen shut was so hopeful, so black and deep and promising. She let herself imagine running her hand along his jaw, across his bottom lip. Pushing the hair from his forehead.

She rose to her feet and banged the table. "I'm in, mate. Let's get the bloody hell out of this city!"

He cheered. "That's it! That's the spirit!"

When she laughed it sounded almost like crying, coming from somewhere breathless and deep inside her chest.

CHAPTER TWENTY-TWO

Isla de Cotorras—1719

"My name is Mary Reade," she said. "I've lived as a boy all me life, but it don't change what I was born. What I am, still."

She couldn't look at anyone. Not Anne, not Jack or Bill, and certainly not Paddy. "I joined your crew under false pretenses, sir, and for that I'm sorry. But what Anne said was true; I am no man. She knew this when I came to her tent." Mary's face went hot as she remembered Anne sighing against her lips—but that didn't matter.

Silence descended, broken by a few uncertain birdcalls from the jungle behind them. The brands popped and hissed around her as the men drew closer.

"What is this?" Jack said finally, to Anne. "Some scheme of yours?"

"It's no scheme, but the truth," said Anne. "She revealed her sex to me when you left, so as to better comfort me in your absence."

"I don't believe it," he said, but the pistol wavered, dropped a bit.

"Believe it or not," said Mary. "I am no boy."

"Didn't I tell you it could be done?" Anne gestured grandly, her voice growing stronger. "It's something I should've done meself, then I wouldn't have been so dependent on you bloody lot living up to me expectations—sure, *I* could've been captain!"

They both might survive the night. "Oh, you wouldn't have fooled a soul," Mary said, exasperated. "Haven't I told you? Jack was right about that." She stared pointedly at Jack, willing him to go along with this. All he needed was an excuse to forgive Anne.

There was shuffling and murmuring from the men.

"Aye," said Jack. He sounded bewildered by the turn of events. "Sure you're too much woman to wear britches and pass for a lad . . ." Then it seemed to hit him, how this might change things. He lowered the pistol. "Annie! Sure, leave it to you to spring a surprise such as this!" He laughed with relief and pulled her in for a kiss.

"Girl or not," said Bill, "there's nothing natural about—that—" He pointed to Mary, as if struggling to name something he'd never seen before. The circle fell silent again. "What I mean is—how could someone like *that* offer comfort, except in some unnatural way? I saw how they lay together, when they was discovered."

"Aye," said someone, with a note of titillation. "It didn't look innocent to me, neither." The circle of men shifted and a lewd comment or two escaped. Someone laughed.

Mary's stomach curdled. Bill knew what he'd seen and it was wrong, whether she was a boy or not. Even *more* wrong, since she wasn't.

"I don't like what you're getting at, Billy boy," Anne growled.

"You can't wiggle your pretty arse out of this one," Bill said. "She was straddling you, and kissing—they was kissing, I saw it!" He pointed a finger at Jack. "You saw it, too."

"I—" Mary started, but she couldn't think of an argument. Bile rose in her throat.

"I was giving her love advice," said Anne. The words sounded smaller than the ones before. The popping of the brands almost drowned her out.

"Were you now." Bill folded his arms.

"Oh-ho, is Mark-the-girl sweet on someone?" asked Jack, ignoring Bill. Anyone could see he was desperate to have the men buy into Anne's version of the story. "The unfortunate tosser, a dog like that on his heels!"

"She's not a dog, no matter that she don't look a proper girl," snapped Anne. "I know for a fact half the crew was sweet on her, even when they thought she was a boy." There was a bit of laughter at that, and then a wolfish whistle that made Mary start nervously.

"I saw them when we came up, captain," said Bill. "That weren't no friendly advice she was giving. I knows an act of passion when I sees one."

"Aye," said Tommy Snipes. "I saw it, too."

Jack looked at Anne.

She smiled up through her lashes as she took his hand. "Sure, what do you think a girl could do for me, after having a man like you?"

Mary's chest tightened, but she held still. Mind blank. Face pleasant.

Jack puffed up. "Well now that I know Mark's a girl, I don't mind the looks of this situation so much as I did." He twirled his pistol jauntily and slid it into his waistband. He looked at Mary and rubbed his chin. "In fact, I might not mind the looks of it if I saw it again."

"Well I mind it more so," said Bill, as a few of the men chuckled.

"Listen, I'm willing to get rid of Mark-the-girl, if it'll calm you down a bit," Jack cracked.

"You won't, either." Paddy's voice startled everyone, it came out so strong. "She's done nothing here but try to get along. Just as we're all trying to do." The last bit came out as more of a mutter, but there were men that nodded their agreement. His words made Mary's heart leap—he was still on her side, despite her betrayal. But Anne remained silent, curled safely under Jack's arm, content just to watch now that she wasn't in danger.

Jack nodded. "All right then, I'll forgive the chap—er, *lass*, what comforted my lady in my absence. So long as the story is true." He strode and held out his hand, and Mary took it.

Jack pulled her in and lifted her shirt.

There were whistles all around. Mary swallowed a gasp, but didn't look down as Jack studied her. She made her face as impassive as Bill's. She was stone, a statue, though her eyes flicked to Paddy's as the men crowded close.

"What do you think, boys?" Jack asked, stepping back so that everyone could see her bound chest. "Does it look to you devils as if there's a lass under there?"

"I think ye need to check and make sure," someone called.

"Come off it," Paddy said. "You know she is, else why would she be bound like that?" Mary's throat tightened. She would smile at him, she would thank him for that, if it wasn't so important that she stayed completely still.

Jack pulled a knife from his waist and laid it flat against Mary's stomach. The cold metal burned as he slowly moved it up, catching the edge of the linen, tugging upward against the blade until it split. One strip—then the next, and the next, until the whole binding unspooled and dropped to the ground.

Jack stepped back, clearing his throat as he gestured to her body with a flourish. "Seems she's a lady after all, gentlemen."

Men's voices raised around her in hollers and shouts, whistles and laughter.

"That ain't so convincing!" someone called. "Ye need to check better than that!"

Mary's eyes met Anne's—and Anne *smiled*. Slowly, she clapped her hands together. Once, twice. Applauding Mary's performance. Then Anne grabbed Jack's hand and leaned against him.

"There you go, now that that's over with. I missed you so much." She tipped her chin up, her mouth tempting and sweet. "But don't think I'm going to forgive you, just like that."

Mary's mouth fell open.

"Aye?" said Jack. He dropped Mary's shirt, put away his knife, and pulled Anne close. "I've got a few ideas for how I could convince you."

Anger flared in Mary's stomach as Anne nuzzled into Jack's shoulder, pressing her whole body to his as he kissed the top of her head. It wasn't just about the kiss they'd shared, although the sensation of it still burned in Mary's skin—as did the memory of the gun Jack had held to her head.

"Isn't it mad that she's a girl, and you never would have guessed it?" Anne laughed. "Come here, you—" She pulled Jack's face in and kissed him deeply. "You know there's no one else for me but you," she said, hanging around his neck.

"It's still not right," said Bill, raising his voice. "I know what I saw."

Mary looked at Bill, lip curling, then back at Anne. They could both go to hell. "Jack," Mary said, squaring her shoulders. "Are we going to Nassau for that pardon or not? You should know you have me vote."

The shock that wiped the sugar-sweet softness from Anne's eyes warmed Mary's heart. The men fell quiet, their eyes landing on her. Then flicking to Bill. Then Jack.

"Aye, you have mine as well!" someone said. "We've had a good run, but it's only a matter of time before our luck turns." There were a few more ayes, and Jack started to nod slowly.

"The votes don't matter," said Bill loudly. "I made my case to Jack, and he's come around."

A few voices rose to agree with Bill as well.

Anne pushed Jack away. "Is that right? You want to go to Hispaniola and live with the *pigs*?"

"You know what?" Jack sounded exasperated. "You and Bill have both pressed me enough. I'm still captain of this crew. What use are our riches if the only people who'll risk trading with us are peasants with cassava and a couple of chickens? Still sleeping under sailcloth on the ground—no matter if it's this island, Hispaniola, or some godforsaken atoll, it hasn't been the same since we lost New Providence." Everyone was silent, light flickering on the whites of their eyes.

"What are you saying, Jack?" Bill said warily.

"Yes, Jack," said Anne, a tremble in her voice. "What are you saying?"

Jack put a hand on his pistol. "We're going to Nassau to beg pardon—and before *anyone* challenges me, you'd best be sure you have the votes. Or you're a dead man, mark my words."

Mary smiled. Bill and Anne could rot in hell. She'd be in Nassau soon enough.

Bill sighed. "I was elected to represent our crew's interests, just like you." He drew his flintlock as other men did the same, and he said, "Jack Rackham, I challenge you."

CHAPTER TWENTY-THREE

Isla de Cotorras—1719

"I don't believe it," said Jack through his teeth. "You heard the men. They want the pardon."

"Those of us not interested in begging pardon won't let you sail off with our shares, our ships, and our crew," said Bill. "What, did you think I was of a mind to start over in a jolly boat and work my way up again? Did you think I'd risk joining another crew, only to have them sell me with their merchandise when the money got tight?"

"That's too bad, Bill." Jack slid his pistol from his belt. "I like you. I would have vouched for your freedom when we got to Nassau."

"I've relied on promises like that before from men like you," said Bill. "And ended up in chains."

"*I'm* not going back to Nassau, either," Anne said. "You make the same empty promises to me. I'd rather vote for Bill."

"You'll go wherever I go," Jack spat. "My promises are the only thing you've got."

"The lady doesn't have a vote, anyway," someone said.

"Nor does that one," said Bill, pointing at Mary, "now that we know what she is. So there goes one of your backers, Jack."

Mary's jaw dropped. "I'm a member of this crew, just like anybody else!"

"I can't believe you!" Anne whirled on her. "After everything I told you, you still think we should beg pardon? You don't deserve a vote."

Mary felt her cheeks flame hot. "I'm not like her," she said loudly. "I'm not just the captain's plaything. I'm the boy who shot his captain, and I deserve a vote."

Anne's body went rigid, hands clenching to fists.

"It's a curious situation," Jack mused. "Given the circumstances, I think Mary should get a vote."

"That's because she's on your side," Bill said. "And you need all the votes you can get."

"I have *plenty* of support," snarled Jack. "I don't need her on my side. We can leave her out of it if you want."

Mary couldn't believe this was happening.

"You're getting a sense of what it's like for me now, aren't you?" Anne asked, a note of satisfaction in her voice.

"Come on, then," said Bill. "Make sure everyone is gathered. We'll meet down by the water once everyone's accounted for and settle this."

Everyone started trailing off toward the shore. "Even if the vote doesn't go your way, lovey" —Tommy Snipes leered at Mary as he passed—"I'm sure we could find you *some* sort of position on the crew."

Mary felt lightheaded. She crouched down, put her head on her knees and her hands in the sand, and waited for the world to stop spinning. She was someone else so suddenly. She couldn't even begin to get her footing.

A hand landed on her shoulder, light but solid. "You all right there, child?" Paddy's voice was hoarse with concern.

Mary hauled her head up. The lines of his forehead were worried, and his mouth was drawn down. He didn't mind if she was Mark or Mary. He just wanted to know she was all right.

"It's not fair," she said weakly. "I should have a say."

"Aye," he said, squeezing her shoulder. "You splice a line and mend a sail as well as any of them. You drink and eat and joke and fight and work as well as the rest of us. It ain't right."

Her jaw began to tremble, her eyes starting to burn. She could hear in the way he cleared his throat that his was tight as well. "All the days I was away with Jack," he said. "I worried about Mark. I worried about what that damned girl might have fooled him into thinking by the time we got back." He chuckled lightly. "But looks as though 'twas a different girl taking us for fools all along."

She deserved to have him hate her. "I'm sorry," she managed.

"For what? Surviving? For being me mate all the way across the ocean? The fact you was such a light to me, that you was a friend *despite* your predicament, just makes me think more of you. I came to think of you as a son—but it's just as easy to think of you as a daughter."

She inhaled slowly, her heart and lungs and stomach settling back into their proper places. "That brings me comfort," she said. "Thank you."

He leaned close. "I'll cast your vote for Jack, since you can't. It doesn't make it better, but I can do that much."

Mary's pulse quickened at the thought of how quickly the crew had discounted her, but she forced herself to nod.

He stood and offered his hand. "Give 'em a strong show tonight," he advised, pulling her to her feet. "Make them believe you're still the same person, all right? They'll come around." Paddy walked off to join the other men.

Anne was rummaging beneath the ruined sailcloth tent, coming up with a bottle of wine. She watched Mary as she uncorked it, her cheek starting to swell where Jack had struck her. "I know you're not used to it," Anne said, "but this is what you do when you're a girl. See what the men decide and then find a way to manage." She put the bottle to her lips—the lips Mary had just kissed. Then she held it out. "Here, have a drink. I find it makes it a little easier."

Mary took the bottle, her hands trembling with anger. Then she turned it upside down and let it drain into the sand. "You'll manage," she said, looking Anne straight in the eye, "so long as you've got your man." She dropped the bottle into the sand. "But I need my wits about me."

Anne stared at her for a moment, mouth open, then smirked as she slowly shook her head. "You're scared now that everyone knows your secret?" she taunted.

"I'm not scared," said Mary evenly. "I'm just nothing like you."

She spun on her heel and walked away.

CHAPTER TWENTY-FOUR

Isla de Cotorras—1719

Mary watched the vote from just inside the tree line. All the men were gathered; even those who had been keeping watch from the brigs in the harbor had been notified and rowed ashore. The wind whipping off the water was growing cool, stars slowly being blacked out by gathering clouds. The fires burned brightly and the wine flowed. Mary clutched the bayonet she'd grabbed from her tent. Whether Jack won or not, she'd be ready to protect herself.

Tommy and Cager went around to the fires one at a time. The men had divided themselves; at one fire, almost all the hands would raise in unison. Then, after they'd been counted, one or two men would lift a sheepish hand while the others looked on. But at the next fire, only a few would raise their hands at first, then the rest second. Mary counted feverishly along with Tommy and Cager, but she was too far away to know which vote was for whom. Sometimes, she'd think she did. At the fire closest to her she saw a vocal supporter of Bill raising his hand, and knew that everyone else raising their hand at the same time was for Bill.

But most of the fires were too far away for her to make faces out. She'd just have to wait until the votes were in.

Voices screeched and sang in the night. Anne held court at her fire as if she were still queen of the crew. But Jack sat slumped, staring broodingly into the flames, pushing Anne away when she leaned in close. Bill sat by the edge of the water, keeping watch on the horizon. Mary watched men stroll up to him, pause, squat down to talk.

Mary pulled what was left of her torn sailcloth tent tight around her. She had her bayonet in one hand, a broken wine bottle in the other, hunched just inside the tree line so that she was hidden in shadow.

She'd gone down to the fires at first, to prove she wasn't frightened. Paddy had sat beside her, fiddling with his pistol. "I won't let anyone mess with family," he'd said quietly. "I won't let no one touch you." She knew he'd be on her side if it came to it, but she couldn't rely on a man like Anne did. One man was no guarantee.

She'd felt a hundred eyes on her every time she stood, every time she moved. They'd stared outright, searching her face and body for a hint of softness, a whisper of curve, swearing now that they'd seen them all along. As they grew drunker they'd hollered at her, asking lewd questions as they leered.

Didn't Anne say she was sweet on one of us? Come on, Mark, give us a hint!

A girl that joins up on a ship, mates—what do you suppose she's after?

I'm still not so sure there's woman's bits under there at all. Come here, sweet Mark—

Come prove it to us—

Give us another glimpse, will ye? Just a wee little peek?

That strip of linen around her chest had been a safeguard, not a binding. As much as it had chafed Mary, now she wished her whole body was bound in linen, thick enough that no penetrating gaze, no curious hands could reach any part of her, no matter how hard they tried.

The men had burned what was left of her binding, tossing the scraps into the fire. The fabric wouldn't have been any use to her anyway, cut to pieces as it was. Even with all of that, she'd been determined to prove that she was still one of the boys. But when Anne had laughed and laughed—*Let 'em breathe, Mary, you've kept 'em tied up tight too long! That's no way to get your man*—Mary couldn't bear it any more. She'd given up her secret for Anne, and Anne only cared for Jack.

They'd go to *his* tent together tonight. Mary knew what they'd do: Anne would lie back in the sand. She would reach for him and draw him down to her—he would sink into her, put his lips to hers—Mary shuddered as she pictured it.

What do you think a girl could do for me, after having a man like you?

Was it the same between them as it was for Anne and Mary? Did it feel different, a kiss between a chap and a lass? Could anything feel and taste as good and right as Anne pressed up against *her*?

This was insane, this was nonsense. Mary had been enchanted, all her longing for Nat taken hostage by a girl. Mary had felt seen and desired and admired—everything she'd wanted from Nat. *He* was the one she longed for. She couldn't remember a time when she didn't study his body, memorize his movements, long for him to see her as she always saw him. Her longing for him had drawn her across a whole ocean. It had drawn her here, to the Caribbean, onto a pirate crew, onto this outlaw island. Into this trap.

Tommy and Cager walked up to Jack, and Mary sat up straight, straining to make out what was happening. Jack stood, his fists clenching as they spoke. Bill's head turned toward the gathered men, and he got up and strode over, hands clasped behind his back as he listened. He nodded and held his hand out to Jack, who was rigid as he shook it. Bill turned to Anne, and they faced each other for a moment. Finally he offered his hand to Anne. She stood up sharply, spat in the sand at his feet, and stormed away.

Mary's heart sank.

Men began to gather around the fire to shake Bill's hand. His supporters raised their bottles, shouting and laughing as Jack slumped back down, head in his hands.

He had lost.

A few men's voices began to rise in an argument. Bill intoned a warning as a couple of pirates stood and shoved each other, and a man punched the fellow next to Jack and knocked him to the ground. A man at another fire shot a pistol into the air and those surrounding him jumped up and wrestled him to the ground as Mary watched with a pounding heart. The pistol was wrenched from his grip, and the man sitting on his back tied his fists behind his back and left him to cool off. The shouting and laughter now had an edge to it, but a brawl had been averted. For now. Most of them were drunk, so anything could happen.

Paddy stood up, scanning the beach. Looking for her.

Mary swallowed the lump that rose in her throat, trembling as she tightened her grip on her weapon. She wanted to talk to him, but she was terrified to let the others know where she was.

Mark had earned his place on the crew, but Mary was someone else. And Nat might as well be in England again, for all that she'd find him now.

The future was dark, utterly unknown. Nothing was certain anymore. Mary stared at the fires. They burned black spots in her vision that grew until nothing was illuminated.

CHAPTER TWENTY-FIVE

Wapping, London—1717

Ships crowded the water as thick as tars swarmed the docks, three and four deep, men and boats all knocking into each other in a din of curses, shouts, groans, creaks, thumps, and booms that rang out over the roar of the river. A forest of masts with pennants snapping in a stiff wind blocked out the afternoon sun. Mary pushed against the throng, following Nat as he strode toward the *Queen Catherine,* his mate Johnny's ship. He kept looking over his shoulder, squinting past Mary as if afraid his da was after him—Mary was doing the same, she realized, trying to pick a Westminster constable out of the crowd. But Granny wouldn't know where she'd fled. She tried to keep her eyes on Nat, to keep looking forward.

Nat pointed ahead. "It's that brig, there—not a fighting vessel as it's rigged up now, but just you wait!"

The ship was middling size compared to those around it, with a couple of gun ports and two masts besides the bowsprit. It wasn't the prettiest ship in the river but it was clean, its paint fairly fresh, with a magnificent bust carved into prow.

Mary lost her footing and almost pitched into the river as soon as she stepped onto the plank connecting the *Queen Catherine* to the dock. "Careful," said Nat, catching her hand and pulling her upright. "You haven't been on a boat since we played around as kids, have you?"

She adjusted her standing and loosened her knees, Nat's firm grip steadying her. She took a breath, the scent of sun-warmed canvas and rope stronger than the stink of the river. Nat gave her an approving nod and let go of her hand as a man came down the plank.

"Took ye long enough, boy—we'll be run ragged before we weigh anchor yet, no thanks to ye." The man wiped his lips and pulled out a ledger. He must have been close to seven feet tall, bare-chested, gray hairs sprouting from every inch of him. He looked like an old wolf, silver and sinewy. His eyes flicked to Mary, and she had to keep herself from taking an involuntary step back. "This one a bit young, is he?"

"Same age as me, sir. Hasn't been sick a day in his life. Still has all his teeth. Can shoot a gun and obey an order, sir."

Mary had never shot a gun, but thought it sensible to keep that to herself.

The man looked her up and down. "And this one has Johnny vouching for him as well?"

"Aye," said Nat without hesitating.

"Indeed. Well, let me see here . . ." The man's gaze ran over the papers in his hand, and he flipped a page. "Suppose we've need of a nimble bugger to reach the topsails proper—what's your name, son?"

"Mark Reade." Mary could scarcely believe it was happening. "Sir."

The man shook his head, scribbled something, and turned up the plank, muttering under his breath. He had a silver pigtail that hung halfway down his back. "Come on, ye lazy bastards," the wolf-man growled. "It's down in the hold with ye. You've got till dark to prove you're worth the grub it'll take to keep ye."

Nat nudged her as they followed the wolf-man. "Don't let old Abe put you off none. Johnny's brother, he is, and a devil of a sailor. If he's signed you up, that means you're in—he knows we've need of you."

Johnny, another gray giant, was down in the hold. He was too worked up over the state of the sails to mind the second boy who willingly went to work threading needles and mending holes. Mary and Nat dragged a pile of canvas up to the deck and spent the rest of the afternoon bent over in the sun. Mary slowly worked her thread through sailcloth while Nat sat on the crate next to her and rattled on about which sail was which, how to splice a line, and which shroud did what. At some point Mary cocked her head. "Where's all this coming from, then?" she asked. "Here you are speaking like a regular tar, and all this time I thought you was a landlubber like me."

"I've sailed a few times since you left Wapping. Short trips—a few quick hauls to Flanders—this feller Johnny knows trades in that Flemish lace everyone's raring for lately. Johnny's been hauling it over as fast as he can."

Mary knew that lace—Granny had it tacked onto the cuffs and neckline of every dress she'd bought the past few months. "This feller," Mary said. "This is the one we're going to see before we set off hunting pirates?"

"Aye. The Dutch hate pirates more than the English, even. Seeing as it's English pirates always stealing off them." Nat tugged on a corner of his sail to smooth it, frowning thoughtfully at his work. "Anyway, Johnny says that if this feller's willing, he's got more than enough money to send us off with everything we need to round the scoundrels up."

They stitched on. Mary eventually put down her sail, rubbing the needle-sore pads of her fingertips as she stared up the masts. The topgallants flicked lazily now, the wind settling into a warm late-afternoon breeze. Ropes knotted in many different ways draped down from all sorts of bits and pieces above them. "You'll have to teach me all this cleverness you've picked up, else Abe will throw me overboard when he realizes how useless I am."

"I picked it up quick enough. A smart, book-reading feller like yourself should have no trouble."

She gave him a wry look. "You shouldn't be so cocksure—he might send you over too if I make a mess of it, seeing as you're the one who brought me."

He gave her a brilliant smile, his sweat-slicked skin shining in the sunlight. "We'll go down together, then, if we have to go down."

"Not so sure that's a comforting thought," she retorted, but his words warmed her. Here they were, the two of them. Together, whether they found their fortune or not.

He shook his head, still grinning as he bit through his thread. "Of all the coves in London, you're the one I'd have been saddest to see the last of," he said, knotting off his last row of stitches. "Thank God I found you before we shipped out, eh?"

She looked down at her work quickly, in case the pleasure she felt shone too bright on her face. He was just scared to go off on his own, desperate for a friend to commiserate with. But she couldn't help savoring those words. "What of Susan?" Mary asked. "Does she know you're leaving?"

"Things between the two of us have cooled," Nat said, shrugging. "It wasn't anything worth sticking around for."

"Would you have stuck around," Mary asked, "for the right girl?" She didn't need to pretend to be Mark for Granny anymore. The thought of being able to tell Nat—someday—made her dizzy.

"I don't think there's anything that could have made me stay," Nat said. "Mum gave me her blessing, told me she wanted me to go. If she didn't make me stay, there's no other woman who could."

Mary hardly slept that night, crammed between a damp wall and Nat's bony back. Belowdeck smelled like she imagined a coffin would after months underground: rotting wood, fusty cloth, and fermenting bodies. But she was beside Nat at last, the musky salt smell of him keeping her warm. She could feel his shape against her, a bit of his hair tickling her neck when he shifted. She hugged her arms around herself. Against all reason, she was exhilarated. This moment . . . what they were doing . . . it felt momentous. This could be something they wrote plays and told stories about.

She would find a way to tell him. What she felt was too big not to spill out into the open.

CHAPTER TWENTY-SIX

Isla de Cotorras—1719

A distant shout woke her. The air was gray, the sun a pale pink promise on the horizon. At some point she must have dozed off, once the fighting and revelry had quieted. She was stiff, disoriented, her tailbone aching from sitting up all night. She stretched her neck one way and the other to work the tightness out. Her mouth tasted awful. The bayonet was still in her fist.

It seemed she had survived the night.

She heard another shout, more like a hoarse scream echoing from far away, then the distant crack of a gun. She squinted down the beach. A few gently smoking fire pits, men and their makeshift tents pitched everywhere. No one moved. The *Kingston* and the *Ranger* stood silent in the bay beyond.

Still, someone shouted.

She squinted at those distant ships. Something looked amiss. Another distant gun fired, and the screaming stopped. She thought she saw movement in the *Ranger*'s crow's nest, a shape falling to the deck below. She didn't hear it hit; the ships were anchored too far off. The light was strange this time of day, all the shadows blurring together. Mary looked back at the water line, and a nervous feeling tightened her gut.

A third ship stood beside the *Kingston*.

She could see how she'd missed it at first glance. The strange brig was nestled right alongside the *Kingston*, almost hidden from view, a few fragile grappling lines connecting the two vessels. It almost looked like the ship's shadow, its bristle of masts blending into the *Kingston*'s rigging.

Was this some plot readied in the night by a man disgruntled over the vote? But what was that third ship, then? Mary sat up and strained to see.

There was movement beneath the *Kingston*'s prow. Shadows bulged, then detached from the ship. They bobbed closer, materializing into jolly boats being rowed ashore. More details became clear as they approached: men inside hunkered down beneath broad-brimmed hats, bayoneted weapons rising from their backs like sharp fins as oars sliced through the water.

Mary's whole body went cold. That wasn't her crew. What else could it mean but that they had been discovered by pirate hunters? It had taken her stupid, sleep-fogged mind too long to understand, and now these strange men were within gunshot range, and she had warned no one. All her crew could be picked off by gunfire if she screamed and they jumped too soon. If it was even enough to wake them, dead drunk as they all were.

She frantically scanned the bodies down by the water for Anne's familiar shape, the color of her dress, but she couldn't pick her out, thank God. Even now some of the men in the boats were taking guns from their backs and training them on the men that lay sprawled in the sand.

It would be a rout.

Jack's tent was near the tree line. She could wake him without alerting the enemy, and make sure Anne was safe. The thought of seeing them together was unbearable, but she had no other option. Jack would know what to do.

She stood, hunching down so that she was sure the bushes hid her, and scrambled for Jack's tent. She was trembling so hard she could hardly walk straight. Straggling grass tangled up her feet and tripped her. She pushed it aside with the tip of her bayonet and crouched as low as she could, praying that the shadows were thick enough to hide her.

The boom of a single cannon firing shocked her into stillness. She looked out to the water, past the men in jolly boats rising to their feet. Smoke wisped from a cannon on the *Ranger*'s starboard side. It wasn't quite oriented so that the cannon could shoot anything useful—the ball splashed into the water a ways beyond the *Kingston*'s prow—but some pirate on board the *Ranger* still lived, and he had fired a shot in warning. Someone had hoped to wake the men on the shore.

And there, on the beach—a man or two raised their heads, looking about groggily—

Mary bolted from the cover of trees. "Ambush!" she screamed, pointing toward the water as men rolled over dazedly to look at her, wiping the sleep from their eyes. "Ambush! We are attacked!"

She saw Paddy's sandy head lift by the water and turn to her. Her eyes met his, squinting and bleary as he pulled a sailcloth blanket from his chest. He sat up, frowning at her as she waved and screeched, then turned to look back at the water.

"Run, Paddy!" she screamed.

A volley of gunfire shattered the stillness.

Men rising from the sand staggered backward, bloodstains blooming on their chests and shoulders. A few grabbed pistols and fumbled with them, training them on the boats. A bullet pocked the sand beside Mary's foot as she took off along the tree line, still screaming at Paddy. "For God's sake, *run*!"

Paddy started to his feet, agonizingly slow. She watched in horror as the men in the jolly boats reloaded beneath a thin cloud of gun smoke, then aimed their weapons again. Paddy was up, lurching toward her, his whole body exposed. The pirate hunters had plenty of targets to choose from as everyone swarmed to standing. Another bullet kicked up dust in front of Mary as the second wave of gunfire echoed over the beach. She darted behind a palm and bolted for Jack's tent, frantically scanning the beach from between the trees.

Their attackers jumped into the shallows, aiming, firing, and shouting. Several dropped under the waves as the pirates discharged their guns, but most of her crew was stumbling for the jungle, weaponless and wine-stupid. Bill towered over everyone, pistol in his hand, shouting orders.

He hadn't drunk so much, she remembered. He never did. He swiveled, locked hair flicking like snakes around his shoulders as he picked off attackers, standing guard as a few pirates secured one of the stranded jolly boats. He dove into the boat with a handful of men, hunched down, and began rowing hard, as another pirate stood and picked off assailants with his pistol.

At last she was at Jack's tent. She whipped back the sailcloth. A warm, sour odor rose off the two tangled bodies beneath. "Up!" she yelled, yanking at Anne's limp arm. "Up! We're attacked!"

Jack put a hand to his forehead and swore. He fumbled his britches closed and flipped to his hands and knees, fingers scrabbling against the sand. He began digging without a look at the beach, though the staccato of gunfire echoed closer and closer.

Anne pulled her arm from Mary's grip and curled into the empty space he'd left, moaning as she covered her eyes with her chemise.

Mary put her arms around Anne's ribs and pulled her to sitting as the gunfire approached. A few pirates had reached the tree line, their pursuers not far behind. "Come on, Annie," she urged, whispering in her ear, fighting against her dead weight. "I'll not leave you behind."

Anne's eyelids fluttered, gaze fixing for a moment on Mary's face. But she was limp, eyes welling with tears as they closed again.

"Damn you!" Mary strained but couldn't lift Anne to standing.

Thaddeus crashed by, roaring and slashing his cutlass through the brush as he fled. Jack looked over his shoulder at the beach, cursed again, and abandoned whatever he had been digging for. He grabbed Anne's shoulder and helped Mary pull her up. "Wake up, Annie," he said. "Up we go now."

"Leave me here," she mumbled. "I want to die."

"You're daft." Mary pushed her into Jack's arms. She couldn't force Anne to safety, but Jack could strong-arm her. "*Go* with him, now."

"I'm dead no matter what I do." Anne's head lolled, a tear leaking out from beneath her lashes as she put her arms around his neck. "Best leave me here and save yourselves."

"For Christ's sake." Jack picked Anne up and hoisted her over one shoulder, then crashed into the jungle as Anne's flaming hair whipped behind them.

Mary looked back and saw Paddy hoofing toward the trees. "Paddy, thank God!" She held her hand out for him.

He was almost within her reach when the musket ball exploded through his shoulder, metal and blood and bone blossoming as he fell, screaming, to the ground.

CHAPTER TWENTY-SEVEN

Isla de Cotorras—1719

Mary screamed and ran for Paddy. "No, no, no, no—"

He moaned hoarsely as he tried to stand, terror in his eyes. "No, get out of here, get out before they get you, too—"

She grabbed his good arm and tried to heave him to his feet, but he was off balance and too heavy. His legs scrabbled to find purchase, his face contorted in pain. "Leave me, dammit—" Tears streaked the dirt on his face.

Mary dropped her bayonet and grabbed him with both hands. She gulped air—tried not to look at his right arm dangling—and finally got enough leverage to help lift him up. "Come on, Paddy. Come on, I'm not leaving you—"

I won't let anyone mess with family, I won't let no one touch you—

"I won't let them touch you, Paddy. You just have to stand—"

He coughed hoarsely, his legs fumbling weakly, grinding blood into the dust beneath his feet.

Suddenly Mary felt hot, sharp pressure between her shoulder blades. "Drop him," said a voice, the breath that carried it hot on her neck. The pressure at her back formed a picture in her mind—the powder-warmed muzzle of a musket.

Her eyes went to the ground, her bayonet half-upright in a nest of weeds, just out of reach. Slowly, she lowered Paddy. He clutched his useless arm and rocked forward, curling over it. She crouched and pushed sweat-soaked hair from his forehead. "Be ready," she murmured. He looked up at her, his face contorted, sucking air through his teeth. She wasn't sure if he registered her words.

Then the pressure between her shoulders pulled away, and the air that replaced it felt strangely cold. "Is that—"

Through the disbelief in her attacker's voice Mary heard some quality she thought she recognized—

"Is that you, Mark?" the man asked.

A straw-pallet beneath her elbows, the glint of a spoon in a dim room, fading light and the smell of salt through an open window—

Her head went light.

The bayonet lay just below her hand, Paddy's blood leaking into the dirt beneath it.

Paddy stared into her face, so desperate. Willing her to act. To run.

Anne hadn't cared when Jack and the other pirates threatened her. Mum, Granny, and the whole bloody world had done the same, even *Nat*, no one had stood up for her—

No one but Paddy.

She lunged for the bayonet on the ground, pivoted sharply to face her attacker, and threw her weight forward.

The first thing she saw was his hands, blackened from gunpowder, flying up as he lost his balance—and then his shoulders hitting the dirt, a bit broader than she remembered. His full lips with that freckle on it were open in surprise, and her breath left her as her gaze fell upon his black, black eyes, wide with shock—

She crouched on his chest, all her weight on her knees, flattening his shoulders to the ground, bayonet held to his neck.

Nat's throat worked beneath the blade, his clear astonishment quickly turning to anger.

"Take the musket and go," she growled to Paddy, her eyes never leaving Nat's face. "I'll catch up once I settle this."

CHAPTER TWENTY-EIGHT

Isla de Cotorras—1719

"I'll not leave you with him," said Paddy.

"You're no use to me—just go!" Mary's eyes never left Nat's.

Paddy was silent. Then a groan, a shuffling. The scrape of a musket being lifted.

Nat's nostrils flared, his lips tightening. But he lay still beneath her. She wasn't sure how long she could hold him if he did try to throw her off.

"Go, Paddy—now!"

She heard him stumble off, crashing into the brush.

The sound faded. She and Nat were alone—the pirates all fled to the woods, their attackers looting the beach camp. A bird called overhead, tentatively, but otherwise the air was so still around them. The shouts of the raiders seemed very far off.

He looked different than the Nat in her mind, though his lashes were as thick as ever. His hair curled long over his collar, and he had a bit of stubble on his cheeks and chin. His skin had tanned quite dark. She was keenly aware of his gaze; of the empty space between her shirt and her chest, where her binding had always been; of her hair sticking to her forehead with sweat; of the soot streaking her skin, and the soil of her britches and shirt. Did she still look like the scrawny mate he'd left behind, or had she changed as well?

This was the first time they'd seen each other since he'd found out she was a girl, and it didn't appear that this exchange would go any better than the first. She was so angry that they'd met like this. She had so much to tell him, so much she wanted to say. She wanted to throw her arms around him—she wanted to smack him in the face—she wanted to cry—

"Tell me you was pressed into this," Nat growled.

Anger took over. "I wasn't," she said. "Joined of me own free will, I did." She took the bayonet from his throat and set it aside. "Not every pirate's like your da, Nat," she said, stabbing his shoulder with a finger. "There's *plenty* of good reasons men find honest life impossible. I'd think you'd know that, growing up how you did."

His clenched jaw softened. "A dishonest life ain't easier, is it?"

Her eyes narrowed. "Aye, no thanks to the likes of you," she snapped. But her anger was subsiding. His eyes looked more concerned than angry.

Paddy needed her, and if Nat's crew caught up to them her life would be over, but she felt sick at the thought of fleeing. Her eyes flicked to the beach, where their attackers were piling booty into jolly boats and burning the rest. A handful of pirates had been rounded up and sat, shackled, in one of the boats. From this distance, Mary couldn't tell who they were. The *Ranger* was slipping out of sight around the curve of the island, surely under Bill's direction.

When she turned back Nat was frowning at her, as if searching for some missing detail. "I can't believe I thought you was a lad, all those years." He shook his head, voice hoarse. She felt tingly at that, and awkwardly shifted off him to sit in the dirt. "When we was young, I understand that. But looking at you now—" He looked pained as he sat up. "It was *you* the whole time, wasn't it?"

She nodded, unable to speak. How different would things have been, if she had had time to explain when her disguise had been ripped away from her that first time, on the *Queen Catherine*? And now, once again, there was no chance to tell him the whole story.

He struggled to his knees and caught her hand, his fingers rough and dry against hers. "We sail for Jamaica to return the *Kingston*, stolen by your crew a few months back. Then we're bound for Nassau to seek recompense from Governor Rogers for pirates killed or captured."

She squeezed his hand. "Go then, you bastard. I need to find me mate." Her voice sounded odd in her ears, choked off. She tried to pull away, but he held her fast. She heard voices traveling up the beach. They were coming.

She had to go.

"I thought I'd never see you again." His eyes burned as they searched her face. "I've never stopped thinking about you."

"What—what do you mean by that?" she stammered.

"Nothing," he said, his voice hard again. "You need to come to New Providence seeking pardon."

She looked over her shoulder, to where Nat's mates were securing the *Kingston* and her crew. "It isn't going to be easy for me to get there," she whispered.

"Look at me," he said urgently. "I'd take you back with me right now, but you would have to stand trial."

"Of course," she said, holding his dark-eyed gaze again.

"Come to New Providence. Turn yourself in and get the pardon. And—come find me. Me kip's just north of the main market. I can't stand the thought of not seeing you again."

Was he offering a pardon of his own, for deceiving him all those years? The heat of his hand in hers seemed a promise.

"I will if I can," she managed. Then she pulled from his grip and ran without looking back.

CHAPTER TWENTY-NINE

Isla de Cotorras—1719

Mary found Paddy's body beneath a flowering tree, broad red blooms marking the end of his blood trail. She sank to his side and checked for breath and pulse, tears streaming down her face, but he was gone. What she could have offered him had he been alive? She had no knowledge of medicine, no idea what to do to save a man from blood loss or pain. But she should have been there to offer comfort as he died.

Men crept out of the jungle all afternoon, looking haunted and sick. They were too subdued for Mary to feel threatened by any of them now, but she took a loaded flintlock from one of the dead and tucked it at her waist as a precaution anyway. Jack strode onto the beach angrily, Anne trailing him, and set about counting and identifying the dead. Anne looked like a phantom, pale and shaking, before she disappeared into a tent. Jack didn't seem to care that she left; his face was set into a hard, unreadable expression. They were all numb, a bitter taste in their throats from the gun smoke that hung in the air.

They counted almost forty of their men dead. There were another forty or so unaccounted for, either captured or escaped with Bill. Jack hadn't seen Bill take the *Ranger*, but when she told him what had happened he seemed cheered. Bill would be back for them, wouldn't he then?

That night they burned what they could of the remains of the dead. The next morning Thaddeus helped Mary carry Paddy's body from the jungle. She put Paddy out to sea on a raft she fashioned out of driftwood lashed together with rope, a bit of sailcloth laid over him. As she pushed it off the shore she imagined it headed for England, toward his beloved Katie.

She clenched her fists and walked into the water behind the raft. She sank beneath the waves so that no one could hear her scream or cry.

When she surfaced she was calm again.

Bill did not come back for them, the eighteen pirates left alive on the island.

"Nassau it is, then?" Mary asked. It was evening. They sat around a fire, picking meat off a few roasted parrots they'd shot out of the trees.

Jack rubbed his forehead tiredly. At his feet lay twenty silver pocket watches that he'd stashed in a hole in the sand beneath his tent. They'd taken account of everything they had left—two jolly boats and a sailing piragua, a couple of pistols, a compass, a bale of bedraggled silk stockings and lace hats. Their attackers and the deserters had taken everything else, even the wine. "Nassau, is it," he repeated, looking around as if for another alternative. He did not sound thrilled.

"Or ye could come with us to Hispaniola!" said Thaddeus, ever the optimist. "I know ye were keen to get to Nassau, but that's when you had something to show for yourself. Hispaniola is as good a place as any to start up again. Fresh water, meat aplenty, and a couple of jolly boats—we'll have a bigger ship at our command in no time."

Jack snorted. "I've no mind to raid sloops or merchant ships from a *rowboat*," he said. "Least, any longer than we have to. We should've gone for the pardon when it was worth our while, but our best chance is still in New Providence. I can figure out what to do from there."

"I'm only coming if you marry me," said Anne. "I need you to get me an annulment, Jack."

Mary opened her mouth—and then shut it again. Why should Mary care what Anne did once they got to Nassau? Nat would be there, waiting for her.

"We both know you're coming with me no matter what," said Jack, not meeting Anne's eyes. "What do you think you'd do otherwise, stay on this island forever?"

"I'll not go back without that promise, Jack. You know I can't, otherwise." Her voice broke a little.

Jack looked up. The hard look he'd had since the raid still hadn't left his eyes, but he nodded. "You'll get your annulment, Anne. I promise."

She leaned into him, but he turned away to throw his bones into the darkness.

"You must be just delighted, Mary," said Anne, shifting her attention, "about how all this turned out."

Mary fixed her with an icy stare. "Aye, I'm delighted Paddy's dead, that our treasure is gone, that half our crew will hang on the gibbet in New Providence. Just thrilled."

Anne rolled her eyes. "I didn't mean—"

"But yes, I'm eager to get to Nassau as soon as we can."

Anne leaned in and put her mouth to Mary's ear. "It gives me comfort to know you'll be there with me." Mary flushed despite herself, though she knew Anne's words were empty. "It gives me hope that maybe things won't be so bad."

Anne scooted away to pull another blackened bird off the fire, laughing at something Thaddeus said. Mary closed her eyes and pictured Nat in her mind, imagining it was his words that made her tingle so.

The next morning, nine of them were Nassau bound.

CHAPTER THIRTY

River Thames—1717

Mary awoke to muffled shouting in the pitching hold of the *Queen Catherine*, her stomach sour and unsteady, muscles cramped from the hard, cold floor. She stumbled onto the deck to see the Wapping docks disappearing into dense morning fog. She ran to the railing, gripping the wood as thick mist swallowed her home.

She'd been so close. Why hadn't she pulled back when Beth kissed her? Why hadn't she stayed far away from her from the start? It would have been so easy to avoid being found out. Everything she'd worked for, all her life, was all for nothing now.

"Come here, you," Nat called from above. Mary turned and looked up, squinting against the spray as her heart lifted. He swung down from a ratline—was that what he'd told her the rope ladders were called?—a few yards away, his black hair whipping about his face in the gray wet wind, and waved her over. "You best stick close with me, until you know your way around the rigging. Up you go!"

She had to make water, but she was more anxious about *that* than climbing a bit of rope. She walked over and put her hands on the lowest rung. Bristly, unweathered hemp cut into her palms as she heaved herself up, toes slipping off the wet railing. The ratline bellied out from the *Queen Catherine* as the ship listed, the ocean churning straight below her. She clung desperately to the rope, her feet scrambling for purchase. Then the ship rocked back in and her whole body planted against the ratline, rope scraping her face.

"By all means, take your bleeding time!" Nat called up. "At this rate we'll be in Rotterdam before you make it to the topsail!"

Mary gritted her teeth and looked up. The first beam that crossed the mast seemed impossibly high, so she focused instead on the rung just above her. She could make that at least.

She clawed her way up one rope at a time, trying to anticipate the rocking of the ship with each fumbling lunge. Finally she settled shakily onto the beam and tried to catch her breath. The wood beneath her was slick, and she kept a nervous grip on the ratline as the ship swayed sickeningly below. Nat pulled himself up beside her. "Now then, time for your lessons," he said, patting the beam beneath them. "This here's a yard, and that's the mainsail below us. Above us, we've got the main topsail—and a couple of bloody monkeys, from the looks of it."

Mary looked up. Two fellows straddled a platform just above their heads, scattering crumbs as they smirked down at them with their mouths full. They were broad boys with big hands and jaws. One was dark, the other fair.

"Oy, Nat!" said the fair one, yelling over the wind. "We heard you was aboard, but I didn't believe it. A skinny cove like you's no use against pirates, I said, but apparently Johnny didn't mind me none."

"He knows you've got to be smart to catch pirates, see," said Nat. "Which is why I told him not to take the either of you."

"And who's this?" said the dark one. He peered down at Mary. "He better be smart, from the looks of him—don't seem as if he could put up much of a fight."

"Hey, now." Nat slapped Mary on the back. "This is me mate, Mark, and though he's small he's sharp as a pin. He can *read*, even."

The fair one snorted and took another bite of his hardtack, showering them with more crumbs. "Oh, that's how you catch a pirate, is it? By reading him a bloody book?"

Mary smiled uneasily as Nat laughed and countered him. She was thrown by the boys' easy banter, not quite sure how to slide into the rhythms of it. She *knew* how to be a boy, didn't she? But around the three of them, she suddenly felt unpracticed and awkward.

The first one who'd spoken turned out to be Robbie, and the other Kit. They were a couple of Clerkenwell boys, a few years older than she, who'd worked for Johnny on some of the trips that Nat had sailed. Mary followed the three of them around, pretending as if she knew what sheets and clewlines were as Nat tossed clues to her. Her hands chapped raw on the ropes. She soon felt dizzy and exhausted, holding her water until she wanted to scream—all while Nat joked back and forth with the boys, as if this was the easiest work he'd ever done.

But she clenched her jaw and did it right along with him. Abe had been right—she was a nimble bugger, able to reach the topmost sails as the water swooned far below, and this at least made her feel like she might be able to hold her own. After a few hours she found she liked being high up—the farther away from the dark, stinking hold of the ship, the better.

"There you go, Mark!" Nat called up as she managed her first buntline hitch on a corner of the topgallant. "We'll make a proper tar of you yet!"

She patted the sail, content despite her aching hands and shoulders and bladder. She could do this.

The sun was finally breaking through the fog, the river giving way to sparkling sea ahead. Vast swathes of white canvas billowed below her, rippling as gulls soared, screeching, between them.

This must be what it would be like to sail on a cloud through the sky. Far away from London and the consequences of her lies. She closed her eyes and felt the sway of everything around her, her body swooping through the air like a bird.

Nat grabbed her ankle and she looked down. He said something, but up this high the wind whipped words away faster than he could shout them.

"*What?*"

"I said," he yelled, "you fancy a *leak?*"

Her nerves jolted. She needed him to show her where to relieve herself. She needed to get this test out of the way, to prove to herself that she could survive the long trip to the West Indies. But most of all, she needed to make water. She climbed down after him, Kit and Robbie following. Mary began to sweat. She didn't think she could pull it off for the first time in front of all of them.

But Kit and Robbie stopped above deck, arguing over something, and only Nat took the ladder below the main deck with her. They headed toward the front of the ship.

Could she really pull this off? There was more to worry about than just making water. Mum had taught her to keep extra linen bound around her waist, in case she bled—it was rare enough, but if her flow did make an appearance, she could rip a length off and tuck it into the belt in front and back to catch the blood. The fabric she had now was torn from the end of one of Granny's bedsheets, and if that ran out, she could always use a strip ripped from the bottom of her shirt. That would get her across the ocean at least. Still, she would have to be *so* careful.

The light filtering through the gun ports flickered against Nat's silhouette as he walked ahead of her, ducking under crossbeams and stepping over coils of rope until he reached a narrow door in the front wall of the hold. "Phew, that stench will remind you of home quick enough, won't it?" Nat asked.

It did smell like the stoop of their tenement, where the drunks liked to do their business as they stumbled home. Mary ducked through the door after Nat into a triangular room. There was a hole on either side of the peak and a trough in between for doing both kinds of business. It all emptied into the sea below, where the prow of the ship curved inward. Mary could see seawater churning through the holes, occasionally splashing up through the wooden slats. At least the flushing motion kept the boards reasonably clean. The stench must be from where tars had missed their mark.

She didn't hear Kit and Robbie coming down to join them. Only one boy to fool, instead of three. Nat stepped in front of the trough and opened the front of his britches.

She stepped up to the trough too, as far a distance as she thought decent, and opened her own, careful to shield herself. She pretended to hold herself with one hand, as a boy would do. With the other she pulled *up*, like Mum had shown her as a child in the tenement, when she'd aimed for the chamber pot set on a chair.

Thank God, the trick still worked—her water streamed right into the trough. She groaned with relief, her bladder emptying. She wasn't a particularly clean shot, but when she snuck a peek at Nat she saw that he was worse than her for getting his water over everything. He didn't seem to be trying as hard to aim as she was.

He finished, then shook and waggled a bit. She was sure to do the same.

Just like that! A giggle escaped her.

"What's so funny?" Nat asked.

"Laughing at your tiny willy, is he?" Kit said, clattering through the doorway as Mary scrambled to close her buttons.

Robbie followed, sauntering up to the trough. "Can't say I blame him—laugh at it every time I catch sight of it, I do." They both dropped their britches.

"Hey now," said Nat. "It's not so wee as all that. But we can sort this matter out quick enough if you like."

Kit turned, his britches falling to his ankles. "Well then, let's see how you measure up!"

Mary was out the door in a heartbeat. She couldn't get pulled into a game like that.

She pulled herself back up the ladder, into the sunlight, and leaned over the railing—the gunwale, as it was properly called. She'd learned so much already, just in the time it took for London to become a gray smudge on the horizon behind them.

She turned her head the other way. Ahead was nothing but shining, limitless water and an open sky. Nothing but possibility. She was still determined to tell Nat—but with boys like Kit and Robbie hanging around, she'd have to be careful to find the right time to do it.

CHAPTER THIRTY-ONE

Caribbean Sea—1719

Jack spotted the perfect target, finally, after weeks of raiding fishing canoes and small bateaux along the coast of Cuba. "There," he said, pointing it out to Cager as Mary came to see what the fuss was about. "Two masts. Some sort of schooner. And that's the Spanish flag."

Mary's skin prickled as she made out the ship, just coming around the curve of the island. They weren't too far off.

"Aye," confirmed Cager, squinting as he leaned over the gunwale. "Think it's time to hoist the Spanish colors and close-haul the sails."

"Approach with caution," said Jack. "If she seems like a ship we can take, let's do it as bloodlessly as possible. All we're trying to do is convince them to trade our ship for theirs. We can't afford to lose anyone right now."

Mary nodded as Cager ran to tell the others, her heart starting to pound as she remembered the frightened Spanish fishermen they'd stolen their flag from. The sailors they'd been raiding as they rounded the western tip of the island and closed in on

Havana were as ground down as she had been in her tenement in Wapping.

But this conquest was different. A schooner like this one, the kind of ship that could get to Nassau fast, but was small enough to commandeer from a piragua, would belong to someone wealthy. "I'll run the flag up the mast," she said, and ran to grab it.

They sailed close to the wind to within shouting distance, then hailed the schooner innocently, Anne leaning over the gunwale and waving a friendly hand. *"Por favor!"* she called in the snatches of Spanish she'd learned from an old crew member. *"Estamos perdidos!"* The schooner obliged by turning toward them.

Anne smiled at Jack, eyes bright with anticipation. "Look at that," she said. "Whatever would you do without me, Jack?"

"Not now," Jack said shortly.

Anne's smile tightened, but she pushed her hair back and returned to waving at the ship. Without cannon they'd have to get close enough to board quickly, with surprise on their side. Mary clutched her grappling hook tight behind her back as they drew close.

"I count only seven on board," Anne said, all playfulness gone from her voice. The pistol and cutlass she gripped were mostly hidden by her skirts. "There may be a few more of them out of sight, but it's not a big ship. This should be easy enough."

"Aye," Jack said. "Prepare to board on my command."

Blood pounded in Mary's ears as they came up broadside. Two men peered over the gunwale of the schooner, calling to them in Spanish.

"Let's go, gentlemen!" Jack commanded.

Mary widened her stance and imitated Cager as he swung his grappling hook toward the target's gunwale. She flung her hook in an awkward arc, but it caught as the schooner's passengers disappeared behind their railing, shouting. She swore and held on tight, hauling against the motion between the ships. Once Mary's and Cager's lines were steady, Stephen and Davie stretched a ladder between the two ships and scrambled across, Jack and Anne following.

Mary lashed her line to the gunwale of the piragua as two musket shots blasted into the deck beside her. She swore and clambered onto the ladder, splinters biting into her palms as seawater roiled below. The ladder pitched up and down wildly as the ships shifted on the waves, spray making every rung slick. She kept her eyes on the dirty hem of Anne's skirt as it dragged in front of her, moving one hand at a time until Mary fell over the gunwale. She staggered to her feet, a thrill shooting through her as she readied her pistol and took in the scene.

Stephen ran toward the helmsman, brandishing his cutlass. One of the Spanish crewmen trembled as he trained a musket on Stephen's back—but Cager shot past Mary and knocked him to the ground. Jack and Anne had another two men up against a mast, both of them weaponless, hands up as they pleaded.

Davie was steadying himself against a barrel, blood soaking through the fingers he held pressed to his stomach. "Got me right as I jumped aboard," he gasped, pointing toward the captain's quarters, "then shut himself in there."

Will crouched beside Davie to look at his wound, while Tommy and Jeremiah swung themselves up on the ratlines toward a sailor on the mainyard, who was screaming down at them but didn't appear to have a weapon.

Mary cocked her pistol and approached the cabin warily. She made herself put her hand on the knob, her breath coming fast.

She threw open the cabin door with a strangled yell and aimed her pistol at one side of the small room, then the other—a child was against the wall, eyes wide. Mary gasped, eyes flicking between the corners as she lowered her pistol. Where was Davie's assailant? The child couldn't have been more than six, dressed in fine clothes, tears streaking his face.

Anne panted as she came up behind Mary and peered into the cabin. "Christ," said Anne, "you're scared of him? Come here, child." She reached out her hand. "It's all right. We won't hurt you." She strode into the chamber.

"Wait!" shouted Mary, grabbing for Anne as a man leapt from behind the door, roaring, and grabbed Anne, holding a knife to her throat—

Jack lunged through the door past Mary, firing his flintlock. He swore as the man released Anne and fell to the ground with a gargling cry. Anne stumbled upright and spun around, pressing her cutlass to the man's neck.

"*Papá!*" the boy screamed.

Mary clutched the doorframe as Jack and Anne froze. Blood bubbled between the man's lips as he rolled onto his back, struggling to breathe, and Anne slowly drew her weapon back, her eyes flicking to Jack. The man reached for the child with trembling fingers, chest spasming as he tried to speak.

When Jack turned, the anguish on his face made Mary's heart skip a beat. "Go!" she said, grabbing his arm and pulling him out the door. "I'll make sure the cabin's secure." Jack stumbled back toward the deck as she ducked into the cabin and peered around, breathing hard. No one else was there.

Anne started after Jack, cursing under her breath. Mary watched helplessly as the man's head fell back against the floor of the cabin, his eyes losing focus. Mary crouched down in front of the sobbing child and grabbed his shoulders. "Stay here," she ordered, but she was sure he didn't understand her. His mouth was open, eyes squeezed shut. "*Papá, no!*" he wailed. "*Papá!*"

Mary stood shakily and walked out of the cabin, shutting the child and his dead father in, away from the fighting. Then she ran to help the others. It would be over soon.

They won the schooner without any deaths on their side. It was well-made ship, the ropes and sails fresh and stiff, the deck newly whitewashed, with a good supply of sweet water and food, though they found only two bottles of rum on it. The Spanish crew had been convinced to board the piragua without further trouble. The child had been subdued as he climbed down the ladder, watching with bottomless eyes as the body of his father was passed down after him.

Will soaked Davie's knife wound with rum and bound it, and both of them seemed optimistic about of the chance of staving off an infection. But a pall hung over the crew as they trimmed the sails and headed for open water. The rush of the fight had worn off, leaving Mary shaky and sick. When she rubbed her forehead her hand came away with blood on it, and it wasn't hers.

Jack paced the deck. "I always swore I'd never be the pirate who killed some child's nurse in front of him." He flung himself down on a crate and dragged his fingers through his hair. "Instead, I killed his bloody *father* while he watched."

"You didn't have a choice," said Cager from behind the helm. "You did what you had to do."

"Aye," Anne said, sitting on the crate next to Jack. She looked exhausted. "It was that or he'd've slit me throat."

Jack jumped up and started pacing again. "If you hadn't let your guard down, no one would have had to die," Jack muttered. "Bill was right—we'd've been better off not letting a woman fight after all."

Anne looked at him incredulously. "You think that would have gone so much better without two of your crew?"

Jack leaned on the gunwale and stared at the horizon. "I didn't mean Mary."

"Oh yes, that's right," Anne said, her voice dripping sarcasm, "she's '*nothing like me*.'" Anne threw Mary a pointed look. "I thought we were both women at least, but I'm beginning to get the idea that I was wrong about that as well."

Mary bit back a retort. With a cold look, Jack stalked over to the cabin and shut himself inside. Anne looked small and alone, watching Jack disappear from her perch on the crate. But before she could turn back Mary took off, pulling herself up on the ratline, to see if she could get a little more wind in the sails. She couldn't get to Nassau fast enough.

CHAPTER THIRTY-TWO

NASSAU—1719

MARY JUMPED INTO THE WATER THE MOMENT THE JOLLY BOAT RAN aground on Nassau. "I need to find the main market," she said to Anne. "Can you show me where that is?" She was sunburned and filthy, her hair tangled and thick with salt, but she wanted to find Nat as soon as possible. It had taken them weeks to get to Nassau from the waters outside Havana. The sea had been swarming with Spanish and British ships engaged in yet another war.

Anne vaulted over the side of the boat. "I'm headed that way, and I can't stop you from following."

Mary ground her teeth as she pulled the boat up onto the shore by herself while Anne took off without looking back. They'd been cool with each other since Isla de Cotorras, and worse since the fumbled attack—and yet Anne still had the power to nettle her with one careless remark.

She and Anne had made landfall on a deserted strip of beach out of sight of Hog's Island, where Jack was docking the Spanish schooner and surrendering to the authorities. Mary planned to slip into New Providence quietly, and at the last minute, Anne had jumped into the jolly boat with her. If they pretended they'd come to Nassau on their own, no one would know that Mary had ever been a pirate, and Anne wouldn't be instantly jailed as an adulteress.

It was a hot day, but a stiff breeze kept it bearable. Anne led Mary along the beach until they were directly across from Hog's Island, where Mary could just make out the shape of the docked Spanish schooner. She recalled how the whole crew had grown quiet approaching Nassau, wondering if the pardon that had been offered would be honored, or if they were walking into the lion's mouth. She squinted across the water, but there was no way to tell what was happening on board.

She followed Anne away from the shore, down a short, sandy path. Anne groaned as they scuffed their dirty feet up the path and the first stalls of the market came into view. "You should have seen it before!" she said. "All set up along the ocean—full of amazing things from all the world over, oozing with excitement, nonstop drinking and dancing. Now look at it. Rogers brought a bunch of bloody Protestants with him and they ruined everything."

It didn't seem so terrible. The sandy soil glowed hot and white; the water behind them shone blue; the trees and scrub rising ahead were green, lush, and shady. There were no tall buildings; no foggy air, no gray, damp stone, no steel-blue water. The gloomy, stinking markets of London were far away. Still, something made Mary's heart clench as they approached what could almost be mistaken for Billingsgate Market. Silvery fish were laid out, freshly gutted, alongside piles of conch and crab. The squalor, the mewling of kittens and barking of dogs, the smells of broiling fat and the smoke of cook fires, the stench of piss pots emptied into the sand—this market was full of the people she had left behind, come here to find a new beginning. Just like her.

She heard a sharp inhalation behind her and turned to see that Anne had stopped. "There he is," she whispered, staring toward the market. "The bastard." Her knuckles whitened as she bunched her skirt between her fingers.

Mary turned, shading her eyes. "Who?"

"Jimmy."

There were plenty of men in the market. "Which one is he, now?"

She turned to find Anne backing away. "I've got to make sure Jack's got his pardon first, before Jimmy knows I'm here. I shouldn't be wandering about. I can't have someone see me and let James know before we have a plan—" Anne talked fast and almost to herself as she turned and hurried back down the path.

Mary began to follow her; then she remembered how Anne had taunted her for being scared back on Isla de Cotorras, and turned away. She needed to find Nat. She poked around the stalls, running her hands over swaths of fabric and baskets of fruit. The pocket watch Jack had given her swung against her hip—she'd need to turn it into money for food and clothing and a place to stay, but first things first.

Not seeing Nat at any of the stalls, Mary lifted her eyes to the scruffy buildings behind the market. A few yards down she spotted a tavern with a thatched roof, its walls wide open to the breeze. It was crowded with men seated around tables with tankards in their hands.

There! She sucked in a breath when she spotted him standing near the corner closest to her. He was in profile, handsome and tall as she remembered—and clean and well-dressed. She fingered the chain on her pocket watch, wondering how much a hot bath and new clothing would cost.

Then her eyes fell on the man next to him.

Robbie. His broad shoulders, his frame a few inches taller than Nat's. The thick wavy hair. That stance, feet spread wide, like he was straddling something.

Him standing over her, just like that—

His bulk pinning her to the floor, bones grinding against her. Running—him only arms-length behind, breathing hard—

She wanted to flee. She wanted to jump back in that jolly boat and paddle *away*, she didn't care where—back to Isla de Cotorras—she could eat parrots and fish and be alone for the rest of her life and forget Nat and this silly notion of a place where she'd fit.

But she *would not* run. Nat had hinted, at least, that there might be a place with him, if she came looking for it.

She forced herself to exhale, to unclench her fists. Of course Robbie was here. He'd come to the islands with Nat on their pirate-hunting venture. Why wouldn't he be here? She scanned the pub as she approached but didn't see Kit, thank God. They were in public, she reminded herself, and she had a pistol tucked into her belt.

"Nat," she said when she stood, only trembling a little, on the other side of the low wall across from him. Nat and Robbie wore similar outfits, something like a uniform: clean white shirts, tan britches, gleaming pistols at their side. Nat turned to her. Shock flashed across his face when he recognized her, and his eyes darted to Robbie. Bile rose in Mary's throat as Robbie looked at her, but his face was blank, and she had a moment to swallow and steel herself.

Then Robbie smiled broadly. "Well fancy that." He turned to a man who had just walked over and lifted a hand in greeting. "Here's that friend of Nat's I was telling you about the other night. The boy shaped like a girl—or was it the other way around?"

Nat gave a short laugh and patted the stranger on the back. "The other way around, Robbie. You know that." He turned to the stranger, who was looking Mary up in down in a way that made her skin crawl. "This is—well, I knew her as Mark, but I suppose that's not her real name. We'll have to ask her what she calls herself these days."

She hated how Nat kept looking at Robbie to gauge his reaction. "It's Mary," she said through clenched teeth.

"So you've come begging pardon," Nat said, nodding approval, and Mary felt a stab of nerves. Please, dear God, let him not have told Robbie about their meeting.

"Why would I beg pardon?" Mary asked, forcing innocence into her voice. "Why, I've just come in on a merchant ship these past few days. I've done nothing wrong."

Nat's eyes narrowed. "I'd say you've done nothing *but* wrong."

Mary's stomach twisted. Where was the softness she'd hoped to see in him again?

Robbie snorted. "Aw, he's still put out about what happened on the *Catherine*. You should've heard him moaning, all the way to the islands! About how his best mate had betrayed him."

Mary forced herself to exhale. It didn't seem like Nat had told Robbie about Isla de Cotorras after all. But if Robbie didn't know she'd been a pirate, why was Nat acting so cold?

The third man snorted. "*This* is that lass? The one Robbie told me you was always going on about?" His lip curled as he leered at Mary.

"I didn't *go on* about her," said Nat.

Mary flinched at the hardness in his tone. This was going nothing like she'd wanted it to. "So I've done nothing but wrong." She couldn't keep the hurt from her voice. The last time she'd seen him, he'd given her so much hope.

"You know what I mean. You need to beg pardon, Mark—Mary."

She looked from Nat to Robbie to their friend, then fixed her gaze firmly back on Nat, swallowing a meek reply. She wasn't the only one needing forgiveness, but she was the only one expected to ask for it.

Well, she wouldn't. Not like this. She set her jaw, turned on her heel, and strode away.

Mary stomped back down to the beach, breath hissing through her teeth, tears burning behind her eyelids.

"Mary, wait!" Nat called from behind her, and anger roared up inside her.

She spun around to face him. "You here to drag me off to the governor?" She stalked back and shoved him. "Fine. Take me then!"

"Hey, Mary." He flinched when she pushed him, but held his ground, and she couldn't help noticing the way her real name sounded in his voice. He caught her fisted hand and held it. "You took me by surprise—with Robbie, of all people, and bloody James, who he's told everything to. I—you threw me off a bit."

"James—*Bonny*?" Of course Robbie was best mates with Jimmy. Of *course.*

Confusion flickered across Nat's face. "Aye, you know of him?"

"Never mind." The warmth of his grip on her hand was distracting, but she kept her fingers clenched. "Me best mate died, you know that?" she said. "The one you shot right in front of me, remember?"

"Did you know Kit died on that beach as well?" Nat asked, and with a shock Mary realized he was as close to tears as she was. He dropped his head and took a deep breath. "Neither side is innocent," he said quietly.

They were both silent for a moment. She wanted to say *I'm sorry*, because she *was* sorry he'd lost his mate even though she'd hated him—but he hadn't apologized for Paddy, either. "I won't beg pardon, Nat. From you or the bloody governor."

He released her hand gently. "Of course. You're right. I'll just keep me mouth shut and no one'll know better. No one needs to know you was ever on the account. I should have thought of that."

Mary nodded tensely, lowering her hands.

"It's good to see you," he said quietly. "I've kept an eye out for you ever since I saw you, praying you'd show up."

A lump rose in her throat. Here was the softness she longed for. "I—it's good to see you, too."

Nat cocked his head, the corner of his mouth turning up. Shadows of palm fronds shifted across his face as the breeze picked up.

"Where are you planning on staying?" he asked.

Mary's chest tightened. "I thought I'd just stay on the beach tonight, until I get me bearings."

"No need for that!" he said, lighting up. "There's a place you can stay until you get settled. It's close to here. Follow me." Nat spun around and strode toward the water, gesturing for Mary to follow. They followed the shoreline around a curve, out of sight of the main beach, where the tree line dipped closer to the high tide mark.

Not long after, they stopped beneath the shade of a palmetto stand, in front of the oddest structure Mary had ever seen. It looked something like the disembodied captain's quarters of a ship, with a whole wall of old glass windows across the front, a few of them shattered. It was as if a ship had sunk into quicksand, leaving the stern end thrusting up toward the sun. A doorway on the side was hung with sailcloth. A phalanx of mastheads stood along the top—a fierce-looking gull; a bare-breasted maiden; a rearing dolphin. All listed to one side or the other, tied in place by knotted ropes, perched along the roof like drunken birds. "Here you go!" Nat said, holding open the sailcloth door. "This used to be a whorehouse, but Rogers had us clean it out not too long ago. No one's been staying here since."

Mary ducked under the sailcloth and found herself in a gloomy room, illuminated only by sun through the wall of windows. Hammocks, straight-backed chairs, a broad wooden table, a number of low cots along the back with moth-eaten curtains dividing them. Rats scurried from the pitch-dark corners, but it was dry and protected, and sleeping on a straw mattress would be a luxury.

Nat stepped in behind her, letting the sailcloth fall and dim the light. "There you go. You can stay here until you get settled."

Mary felt his fingers touch hers, then take her hand and clasp it. She turned—what did it mean that he'd taken her to a brothel, of all places? But when she looked at him, there was no lechery in his gaze. His grip was firm, his face unsure. "This is confusing for me," he said quietly. "You look like Mark, but I know you're someone else. I want to see one or the other—girl or boy—not both."

"I—I'm not sure that's possible." Her breath was loud between them. "I think I might be permanently mixed up."

He gave her a lopsided smile. "I've thought about you a lot," he said. "What it might have been like, if you'd always been Mary. I couldn't help wondering—" He paused.

Mary swallowed hard. "I'd like to see what it's like between us," he said finally. "Now that you're Mary. I'm excited to meet her. You."

Mary exhaled. "I'm excited for that, too." Even more than Nat meeting her—who would she be, when she wasn't Mark to everyone?

"I'm at Jacob's tavern most evenings," Nat said casually, giving her a sideways look as he gestured to her britches. "Maybe Mary could stop by sometime, when she comes to town?"

"You arse." Mary grinned. "Yes. She'll be sure to swing by."

The morning sun coming through the palmetto fronds outside the windows made the room glow green. They were alone, the sounds of the beach outside muffled by the walls. He was so close. He had a bit of stubble on his cheek—that was new. But he had the same freckle on his lip. The same dark eyes, long lashes, the same easy smile. He pulled a flask from his pocket and popped the stopper out with one hand. "A drink, Mary. To you. To getting to know the girl I grew up with. To forgetting about the boy." He took a swig and held it out.

In truth, she didn't know if it was possible. Even she didn't know where one ended and the other began. But if Nat was asking it of her, standing so close and looking at her so intently, she knew she could try. "All right then," she said. She took the bottle and tipped it back. "To Mary, whoever she is. To making a proper girl of her."

CHAPTER THIRTY-THREE

New Providence—1719

Mary steeled herself and went back to the market the next day, dragging her feet as she approached a stall where a sempstress was selling dresses and underthings. She made herself ignore the fine britches and shirts, clean and freshly pressed like Nat's, and instead picked a plain blue linen dress out of the gaudy, beribboned confections that surrounded it. She could see herself, she decided, in its simple, clean lines.

The sempstress came huffing around the side of the stall, leaning heavily on her cane. "Lord have mercy," she said, landing on a chair with a thump. Sweat stood out on her forehead. "Who would have thought I would be busier on a godforsaken island than the center of London. There's no competition, is what it is, and I can hardly keep up."

"Business is good, then?" Mary said conversationally, trying to keep the tremble from her voice.

"Aye, I should be thanking God, shouldn't I? It's a sin to complain." The sempstress's eyes landed on the dress in Mary's hands. "Have a sweetheart you're hoping to impress?" she asked, brows waggling.

"No," Mary said, heart racing. "It's for me."

The sempstress went silent, looking Mary over. Her eyes narrowed when they landed on Mary's unbound chest, her gaze sharp as it fixed on her face again. "Two shillings," the sempstress finally said. "I'll throw in a gown petticoat to match."

"Two shillings?" Mary asked incredulously.

"Came all the way from London, that did," she said. "And I've got enough work that I don't need to bargain, keep that in mind."

Mary exhaled. "If you help me figure out the underthings to go with it, I'll pay you that and more."

The sempstress pinched her lips together. "I suppose I could do that," she said finally. "God favors the charitable. Let's see. You need a shift, stays, dickey petticoat, all of that?"

"Everything," Mary said, swallowing.

"Well then. Let's see. Stays for someone about your size." She fumbled through a couple of baskets and stood up with something in her hands. She came around the table and held the stays up to Mary. "This looks like it should fit. I'll throw in a day cap and apron as well. Give me a moment and I'll get everything together."

"I'll take whatever this can buy," Mary said, setting her pocket watch down. "That's worth five shillings if it's worth a penny. And I'll take a few extra shifts if you have them."

The sempstress's eyes lit up. Then she looked around furtively. "Contraband ain't legal no more," she said slowly. "I'd be taking quite the risk in accepting this. We could both end up in gaol." But then she seemed to change her mind, palming the watch quickly. "All right, then. Dress, three shifts, stays, and the dickey and gown petticoats. That should be a start. I'll wrap them up for you."

The sempstress bustled around with crinkling tissue paper for a couple of moments, then piled a stack of soft packages in Mary's hands. The paper gave delicately beneath her grubby fingers.

"Come by if you need the gown tailored any, you hear?" the sempstress added generously. "I'll throw that in for you as well. If I'm not here, just ask around for Molly Hatch."

"I won't need any help with that," Mary said, then an idea dawned on her. "I'm very handy with a needle. Tell me, what would you pay for help with your orders?"

Molly gave her a skeptical look. "I pay a half-penny per piece. *If* the stitching is impeccable."

Piecework. Mary did the figures quickly in her head—she was going to have to sew *awfully* fast to make anything, and it would still be nothing like what she'd been promised as a sailor, or what she'd made for her three months as a pirate off just the one pocket watch. Still, it was better than nothing. "Would you be interested in my help?" Mary asked.

Molly narrowed her eyes again. "Tell you what. You come back in those togs tailored to fit, and I'll take a look at you and your stitches and tell you if I'm interested."

"Thank you," said Mary, a thrill running through her. "I'd be very grateful."

Nat was sitting at the bar, a half-full mug of ale before him, empty stools on either side. Mary ran an uneasy hand over her cornflower skirts and tugged nervously on the braid that she had plaited that morning. The braid was fine; she was used to a sailor's pigtail. And she was gloriously clean, head to foot. It was these damned skirts that made her feel so uncomfortable, like an actor on a stage. She definitely hadn't been Mark, that was true. But she wasn't so sure she was this *girl*, either.

This would surely be the test. She ducked under the palmetto awning. "Well, well. Just the cove I was looking for."

Nat's face split in a grin when he saw her. "If it ain't Mary in the flesh!" He pulled a stool out. "Let me buy you a drink?"

Did she imagine that he looked her up and down appreciatively as she approached? She smiled and tried not to walk too stiffly. "I'll have the same," she said to the barkeep as she took the stool, then wondered if that was the proper thing to do. She tried to remember: did girls drink ale? Mum had drunk gin; Granny, port. Anne liked wine, but she wasn't exactly a standard for proper girlishness.

"Prepare to be impressed!" Nat raised his mug. "This is no taplash, but a fine English ale—can't believe it made it all the way from London without the tars downing the whole keg!"

The barkeep set a mug down in front of her, and Mary took a sip. It was light and malty, with an aftertaste of honey. "It is good," she agreed.

Nat nodded.

She was at a loss. What would a proper girl say now? She knew what Mark would have said, but that was probably exactly the wrong thing. Her cheeks were heating up under the warmth of Nat's gaze.

Damn it.

"It's good to see you like this," he said, and touched her sleeve. Not quite her arm, but almost; she felt the fabric tug in his grip. "It's as good as I imagined it."

Way back when, she'd imitated Nat to learn how to flirt with girls. Perhaps she could try to flirt with him like Anne. God, Anne was good at it. The comments, touching her hair, raising a brow as she leaned in close. A light touch that went on a little longer than it should. Mary couldn't begin to imitate all of it—but she could raise an eyebrow, at least. She tried it. "You imagined me like this, did you?" Eyebrow up. There.

He leaned back on his stool. "Lord, I've said too much."

It seemed to be working. She took a long pull of her ale and kept going. "Robbie *did* say all you talked about was me, after I left."

He laughed, sounding pleased at her boldness. "That's a bit of an overstatement. It was just a shock to lose you like that. And after learning you was a girl—" He shook his head. "It was hard to get you out of me head, I'll admit."

She took another drink. A good start—but she wasn't sure where to go now. She had the feeling that from here it might get away from her.

"You were hard to get out of my head, too," she said.

"Was I, now." Nat bit his freckle in that way that used to drive her crazy. Mary shook the sudden image of Anne looking up through her lashes from her head. Had someone distracted Nat in the meantime as well? The thought of him with another girl had driven her crazy since Rotterdam—but she couldn't bring herself to ask.

"I got a job," she said instead. "I think. Working for the sempstress."

Nat frowned. "I hate to think of you having to work."

"How else do you think I'm going to survive?" Mary asked incredulously. "What do you think women do, when they don't have a man to support them?"

"I suppose . . . I don't know any women your age on the island who work," he mused. "They all came to the islands with a man, or because of one. At least, that's the case since we shut down the bawdy house. I suppose sewing is better than that."

"Christ, Nat," she choked. "Aye, it suits me a bit better."

"All I know is, my wife won't have to work," he said. "I'm about to ship out on another privateering mission. If it goes well, I'm going to have enough money to build a real house." He took a long drink. "I'll be looking to settle down. Live a Godly life."

Her heart skipped a beat. The last time she'd thought to yearn for God's love, she'd been someone who never could have earned it. But she was starting over, trying to do right this time. "You sound like you've got someone in mind," she said lightly.

He chuckled, but it sounded forced. "Well now." He looked deep into his beer. "If Robbie has his way, it'll be his sister Livie."

Her heart sank. "She the kind of girl you're looking for, then? Doesn't work, and goes to church on Sundays?"

"I suppose, something like that." He cleared his throat and leaned in with a smile. "But right now, what I'm thinking of is all the money I could make on this mission I'm heading out on."

Mary took another long swallow of ale, jealousy hot in her stomach. "Is that just because she hasn't lifted her skirts for you yet?"

He looked shocked. "Mary Reade!"

She shrugged irritably. "What? You would have told me straight off, back when we was mates."

"Back when—" He shut his mouth, throat working. "I would have, wouldn't I?"

"Aye," she said, and raised her mug to her lips, but it was empty.

She smacked it down on the bar and gestured for another.

He looked at her askance as he signaled the barkeep as well. "You know, sometimes it seems that Mark's the one that was real, and you're him pretending to be Mary."

"We're one and the same, you know—Mark and Mary. Both are me." What had she thought, that she'd put on skirts and transform into the kind of girl Nat liked to charm? The kind that lived a righteous life? A dress was just another binding, fooling people into thinking she fit the spaces she filled. She took her second mug of ale.

Nat nodded uncomfortably. They drank in heavy silence for a moment. "Why do I have to act differently, now that I'm a girl?" she asked. "I'm the same person I was then—just as much as you are." She didn't know why this aggravated her so much.

"It is different, though. You have to see that."

She shook her head.

"You're a *girl*, Mary. I think about you different than I did."

"And you're a bleeding tosser," she snapped. "Just like you always were."

He laughed. "Right enough." He put a hand on her thigh and rested it there, casual.

Oh.

He never would have touched Mark like that.

He gave her thigh a squeeze. "I suppose I could get used to it—you a girl, but maybe still be the cove I knew as well."

She didn't move away. Nat's hand on her was solid and assured. "Lucky me," she squeaked out.

He leaned in, eyes serious, his perfect lips inches from hers. "What I was trying to say about Livie is—she's lovely, but since I saw you on that beach, I . . . it's you I think about."

Her head was spinning from the ale. If she was a girl like any other, there was only one thing all of this could have meant—his hand on her thigh, leaning in to whisper about how he couldn't stop thinking about her. But was she a girl like any other, to him?

Only one way to find out.

She leaned forward. She curled her fingers into his hair and pulled him in and brushed her lips against his.

You kiss him just like that, he'll fall for you . . .

Nat's hand tightened on her thigh and she kissed him again, trying to wipe Anne from her mind. This kiss was different. This was *real*. This was soft and tasted like malt and honey and was just as good as how she'd imagined it.

She pulled away unsteadily, and Nat looked as disoriented as she felt. "I've been wanting to do that for a long time," she murmured. His lips were just as warm as Anne's, his response just as eager. Mary leaned in again, determined to kiss Nat until there was nothing left in her mind but him—but Nat glanced up and pulled back suddenly. "How's it going with Burgess, Robbie?" he said over her shoulder, letting his hand slip from her thigh.

Mary made her face pleasant before she turned.

Robbie was glowering at her. "Burgess himself sent me to find you," he said, taking in her new attire. Mary tried to hold his gaze defiantly but looked away after a moment, and he focused his glare on Nat. "They're struggling to ship out on schedule, no thanks to you getting into your cups."

"It was only a pint of ale," said Nat. "I just stopped for one last drink."

Robbie folded his arms. "Burgess says you're needed at the fort. Says you ship out *tomorrow*—or had you forgotten?"

"Fine, fine!" Nat laughed, pushing back his stool. "I'm coming."

"Hurry up then." Robbie turned and stalked out of the tavern.

Nat grabbed Mary's hand. "Can I see you again, when I return?" Nat asked. His smile was a brisk wind on a fair day.

Mary squeezed his fingers. After so much confusion and so many mistakes—maybe she could still right her course. "Go on then," she said, "I'll be waiting for you."

CHAPTER THIRTY-FOUR

ROTTERDAM—1717

ON FIRST GLANCE ROTTERDAM WAS JUST LIKE LONDON. TO GET THERE, the *Queen Catherine* tacked up a river like the one they'd left just days before. Wharves and shipyards lined the waterfront, just as they did in Wapping. The ship dropped anchor at a dock like the one they'd left, thronged with a similar bustle of goods going this way and that. But this river was not the Thames; it was blue and calm, smelling of salt instead of sewage. Mary overheard snatches of conversations she couldn't understand.

Lights winked on as the sun set, beckoning the crew in all directions at once as they finished docking the ship and headed into the city.

Mary grabbed Nat's elbow, her stomach humming with nerves. "You want to grab a pint of ale with me? It's been a while since it's been just the two of us, and it'll be months before we have the chance again, once we ship out!"

But Nat looked toward Kit and Robbie, who were shoving each other up ahead. "We're headed to a pub we found on our last trip here," he said. "But me and you will have a beer before we ship out, just the two of us. What do you think—want to come along?"

Mary nodded, the tension in her belly releasing. She wanted to tell him everything before they left, but another day or two to work up the courage couldn't hurt.

Every street they turned down was pretty and wide, and every person they passed was fatter than the last. The taverns had spotless front steps, glass in their windows, and bright tiles on their roofs. The horses were fat and freshly curried, the hackneys gilded and gleaming. The air smelled heavenly, like roasting meat and whitewash and the damp of rain. Even the cobblestones were clean. Where was the dirt and filth, the gray air, the stench, the gangs of starving brats and pockmarked beggars? Where were the rotting warehouses and crumbling tenements? Where did these people empty their chamber pots and throw their refuse, if not in the streets and the river?

The hot scent of roasting meat filled her nose as Mary followed Nat, Kit, and Robbie into the pub. She was ravenous. They found an empty table, Nat hailed a serving girl, and Kit whipped out a deck of cards and started dealing them all in. They'd been playing Ruff and Honours every time they had a free moment. Mary had just started getting the hang of it, and was eager to make up for all the points she'd lost over the past few days.

The air crackling from the fireplace blazing in the center of the room was hot, and Mary soon shrugged out of her tarred jacket. A girl bearing a tray of tankards dropped one off in front of each of them. She had yellow hair that wisped around her face and a wide gap between her front teeth when she smiled. She left a lovely, soapy trail of scent behind, and Nat turned and watched her glide back to the bar.

Mary nosed her own sleeve, smelling her own sour stink. She *never* smelled like that girl.

She bent as if to scratch her leg, and inhaled Nat's stench as she leaned over the bench. That same unwashed odor smelled so good on him.

When she looked back up, both Kit and Robbie were giving her narrow-eyed looks. They said nothing, and Mary grew uneasy. "What?"

Robbie's nostrils flared. "Your turn, mate."

"Oh. Aye." Perhaps they hadn't seen her smelling Nat.

She'd just *smelled* Nat. She needed to mind herself.

They were playing two against two. Kit and Robbie were up three points. The serving girl approached again as Mary threw down her card, carrying two plates full of meat and gravy that she set down before Kit and Robbie. "I'll be back with two more?" the girl said with a broad smile and a thick accent. Nat stared up at her, blinking, then nodded slowly. Robbie laughed as she left and gave Nat a shove. "In love, are you?" asked Kit.

Mary kept her eyes fixed on her cards as Nat grinned and shrugged.

"Looks like we picked the right alehouse," said Robbie. "Wonder if these girls work the rooms upstairs as well, eh?"

Kit glanced at his hand and pulled a card. "Oh, what I'd do for an extra shilling . . ."

Mary felt a bit sick, the strong ale turning her empty stomach. She put her cards down and looked to the bar, hoping to see the girl returning with their food, but the maid was chatting with someone instead. When Mary turned back, Nat was grinning. "Liked what you saw as well, did you?" he asked.

"I'd like her better if she brought me a plate."

"I'd like her better if she brought me upstairs," Robbie quipped, nudging Nat again.

Nat was distracted by his hand. "Damn," he said, and played an honour. Mary was never going to win if he kept playing like this.

"This place reminds me of the Red Ox back home." Robbie slopped gravy around his plate with a crust of bread. "They was a lot of common doxies, but they did know how to treat a feller right."

"Sure you know, the amount of time you spent hanging over the taps there." Kit took the trick.

"Only reason you saw me there is you were there all the bleeding time yourself!"

They fell silent for a moment, staring at their hands.

"Did you ever go?" Mary asked Nat suddenly. "To one of them bawdy houses?"

"Aye." Nat frowned, wiggled a card free of his hand, then changed his mind for a different one.

She hadn't known that.

"So our young Nat's fallen for a loose woman's charms before," Kit said.

The way the conversation was slowing the game's pace was beginning to get to Mary. "Your *turn*, Kit."

"You unrig the drab, then?" he asked Nat, ignoring her.

Nat sighed and nodded wistfully. "I was sure she'd taken a real fancy to me, but turned out the girl that took me innocence was only interested in me coin."

"That's all that ever interests them." Kit finally played a card, and Mary put down hers. Finally, she'd won a point.

"I don't know about that, now." Nat tilted his head at the leading card Mary played, but his eyes wandered toward the bar. "That yeller-haired angel might be different, and I've a mind to find out."

"Are we playing cards or not?" Mary threw down her hand. "If you lot aren't going to play, I'm out."

"Now Mark, no need to be jealous," Nat said, laughing. "I'll find out if she's got a sister when I'm getting to know her."

Robbie leaned back in his seat. "If that girl's got a sister, she's mine. Sorry, Mark." His smile grew nasty. "But it's her brother you'd fancy more, eh?"

Mary stared at him, mouth open, unsure if she'd heard him right. "What—what's that?" He couldn't have guessed. Could he? He had a sly look on his face.

Then suddenly, she understood.

He didn't think she was a girl—but he didn't think she was a proper chap, either.

She stood. She should make a crack, or ignore him and go back to the game. But she couldn't. She was shaking. "You—you're a bastard, Robbie, you know that?" Why did her voice have to sound so weak? She shoved the bench back.

"What the devil are you getting so worked up about?" Robbie asked, a smug expression on his face as she stumbled over the bench. He loved her reaction, and she hated herself for giving it to him. "Sure I was just poking a bit of fun."

Mark stalked toward the door.

"You've ruined the teams, Mark," Nat called over the crowd. "Get back here. Come on, Mark!"

She pushed through the tavern and out the door, breaking into a run as soon as cold air hit her face. She didn't get far—she stopped when she hit a railing at the water's edge of a little inlet, and then she crouched down on the dock, arms over her head, breathing hard. Why? Why couldn't she just play the game, keep her mouth shut, and eat her supper? Why couldn't she take a joke with the rest of the boys?

Nat caught up quickly. "Bloody hell, Mark! You're in rare form tonight, aren't you?" His boots stopped beside her. She kept her head bent so he couldn't see her face, but he squatted down next to her, grabbed her arm and gave her a gentle shake. "Come on, sure it was just a joke."

"I'm pretty sure it was more than that!" She twisted out of his grip and lost her balance, falling against the railing.

When he saw her face, his expression changed. "Crying over it, are you? God Almighty."

She pushed herself upright and wiped her cheeks furiously. Now. She should tell him now.

"Christ, Mark. Is it really—" Nat's throat worked. "Are you—?" He didn't finish.

"No, Nat, I'm not." *Say it. This is the moment.*

Nat put his hands up. "Mark, look, I've been trying to tell them. But I don't know, sometimes I wonder meself—"

Mary held her breath. "What?" she whispered. "What do you wonder, Nat?"

"I just—nothing." He looked away, sounding embarrassed. "I'm stupid to listen to them, ain't I?"

She wondered how he couldn't see the answer shining in her face through the darkness. "Nat, look, I—" she said, stammering. She'd worked so hard for so long not to let it slip.

"You know what? It's fine," he said, standing up. All questioning was gone from his voice. "You don't have to convince me. I know you, and I trust you. If you say you're not a molly, then you're not."

She stared across the water. Lights blazed up on the inlet's opposite shore, their reflections lapping out toward her. It was so hard to break his trust. And what for? Did she think he'd fall in *love* with her, with her face and body that passed for a boy's, when pretty Dutch serving girls smelled so good and curvy girls like Susan kissed him for hours?

"I'm not a molly," she said finally.

"I'm sorry I gave it any credence," he said. "I'm on your side, all right? I know it's true, you was always going on so about Beth."

"Aye. I was." She looked at Nat's earnest face, remembering how quickly Beth's eagerness had hardened to contempt.

"Come on, she's surely brought our plates by now. Our food's probably going cold." He offered his hand, but withdrew it before she could grasp it. He looked ashamed, but he turned away. "I'm starving," he said, walking off. "Let's go."

Mary used the railing to pull herself to her feet, then followed him to the tavern, wishing she could just return to the way it was before, back when they'd been children playing pirates down on the docks. If there was any way to go back to that easy fondness, she would have gladly done it. But as her gaze lingered on his broad shoulders, easy gait, and unkempt hair, she knew there was no hope of that.

CHAPTER THIRTY-FIVE

New Providence—1719

"Molly Hatch?" Mary asked, approaching the sempstress's stall.

Molly looked up from her stitches. "Well now!" she exclaimed. "Don't you look lovely in that color."

Mary came close, and Molly leaned in to see her work. "I'm still interested in doing piecework for you, if you're in need of the help," Mary said.

Molly set down her work. "Let me take a good look, now. Me fingers *have* been dreadful arthritic as of late." She came around the table and lifted the skirt, inspecting Mary's needlework. "The lines are unconventional," she said, raising her brows. "Still, the stitching is neat, and I'm desperate for some relief."

"You won't regret it," Mary said. "I can start as soon as you like."

The sempstress gave her a hard look. "I'd be grateful for the help, so long as you stay in your skirts. Won't sit right with me customers if I seem to have hired a godless wench."

Mary fought a flush of anger. "Of course not," she said agreeably.

"Come back at the end of the day then, and I'll give you work for the week," said Molly.

So long as you stay in your skirts? Mary laughed to herself as she walked away, imagining how Anne would have responded to that. At least Molly had given her work. Fine. She'd keep the skirts on to please Nat and Molly and everyone else if it meant things kept going her way.

The smell from the stalls selling pasties and puddings was making her hungry, but she hadn't any money. She was just deciding to retrieve the jolly boat from where she and Anne had stashed it and take it out to fish until it was time to come back for her piecework, when Anne's unmistakable auburn curls caught Mary's eye from across the market. Her heart lurched, but she quickly shifted direction and headed toward her.

Anne was sitting at the foot of a tree, head bowed. "What do you think of me new togs?" Mary asked with false bravado, crouching down and nudging Anne's arm with hers.

Anne raised her head, and Mary gasped. Anne's lip was swollen and crusted with dried blood, her cheekbone bruised, her eyes red-rimmed. "Oh God, Anne."

Anne's lip started to tremble. "I was hoping to find you here, but I'm trying to stay out of sight." Her voice was meek. "I—is there anywhere we can go?"

"Follow me," Mary said quickly, helping Anne to her feet. "Come on, I've got just the spot."

"Old Nan's place?" Anne asked with a sharp laugh when Mary pulled open the sailcloth at the door of her masthead hut. "Jimmy better not find me here, else all his vile ideas about me will be confirmed."

"He won't think to look for you here." Mary checked to make sure no one had followed them, then let the cloth drop. "Here, let me see your face." She took Anne's hand and led her to the wall of windows. She tilted Anne's chin up and studied the gash in her lip as a tear slipped down Anne's cheek.

"Nothing to do but clean it up," she said, gently wiping the tear away. "Jimmy did this?"

Anne squeezed her eyes shut and nodded. "I ran into him last night. I was fuming from what Jack had done, and I wasn't thinking—"

"Slow down," said Mary, gesturing to a chair. "What did Jack do?"

A spark of fury lit Anne's eyes as she sat, and suddenly she looked herself. "Jack can bloody well go to hell. We needed all the money he had left to buy the annulment—he *owes* me that, and then last night I find him spending the very last of it—well, where do you think he was?"

Mary pulled up a chair next to her and sat down, making sure they didn't touch. "I'm guessing he wasn't handing it over to James."

"A bloody punch house, with a bloody whore sitting right there on his lap!"

Seeing Anne's sadness turn to righteous anger was reassuring. "Maybe it wasn't what it looked like. Maybe she was just a barmaid resting her feet."

"Me *arse* she was! Resting her tits on his face, more like."

The laughter bubbled up in Mary, irrepressible, and Anne began to cackle too. She dashed the tears from her cheeks. "Come to find out he'd spent his last pennies on her, just the way he spent them when he first was after me. I told him he could bugger himself, and the floozy too, for all I care."

Mary reached out and touched Anne's arm. For a moment she wanted to trail her fingers up to her shoulder, run them along her jaw—she let her hand drop. "He'll come around. He's got to."

Anne's smile faded. "I don't know about that. He shipped out on some privateering mission this morning, and before I told him off last night he swore he'd use the money he comes back with to pay off James. But I don't know, Mary. Now I'm not sure what he'll do."

Jack had shipped out on a privateering mission that morning—it must be the same one that Nat was on. "So then what happened with James, after you left Jack?" Mary asked.

Anne's jaw set. "Well I stomped out of there, boiling mad—and I ran into Jimmy."

"And you laid into him?"

"He was drunk, came right up to me and tried to run a hand up me skirt. I told him he had no right to touch me, that he was no husband of mine and soon I'd have the papers to prove it. You can see where that got me." Her voice went rough again, shoulders curling in as she scrubbed her face with her palms. "I'm so tired, Mary. I haven't slept at all. I didn't know where to find you. And Jack's gone; he doesn't even know what happened."

"I wish I'd been there," Mary said softly, and found that she meant it. "I'm sorry no one was there to protect you."

Anne curled into Mary abruptly, grabbed fistfuls of her skirts, and pressed her face into her shoulder. "I missed you so much," she whispered. She smelled of salt and rust and Mary was sure Anne could hear her heart hammering in her chest. "It's been terrible, not seeing you."

Mary lifted a hand to pull Anne against her—but then, quickly, she drew away. "Here now," Mary said. "Before you get blood on me new dress, let me get some seawater to clean you up." Anne released her and Mary stood up quickly, examining her dress, which appeared to be unsullied. "I've got a clean chemise you can put on. You can sleep here. I'll make sure no one bothers you."

When she returned with a bucket of water Anne was already stripped to her dirty shift and lying on her back on a cot. Mary ripped a strip of fabric from her old, threadbare shirt and wet it, then set about wiping the blood and tears from Anne's face. "You're going to stay here with me from now on," Mary said definitively. "I'll make sure Jimmy doesn't lay hands on you again."

A faint smile appeared on Anne's lips. "Thank you," she said. "I can't tell you what that means to me."

Mary had a flash of inspiration. "I have another idea. This governor is supposedly a Godly man, right? And James is violent with you, and he's never gotten you pregnant, has he?"

"That's right," said Anne, closing her eyes.

"Well, both of those things are grounds for annulment, so long as we can prove it. And just look at your face!"

"It's a desperate idea," said Anne. She sounded exhausted. "But I am a bit desperate."

"You shouldn't need a man to pay for you."

"And yet, Mary"—Anne inhaled sharply as the rag caught the cut in her lip—"experience has led me to assume I do."

Mary dabbed more carefully. "I've got this new dress—" she started.

"Which you look lovely in, by the way," Anne interrupted, opening her eyes. "The cut is just right for you."

Mary smiled despite herself, and continued, "And I'm going to make you one, too, once we can figure out how to afford some fabric. We're going to get cleaned up and respectable looking. And then I'm going to vouch for you, as your friend, to Governor Rogers, and we are going to get that annulment."

Anne watched Mary's face as she gently wiped the cloth against her lips one last time, until the blood was gone. "You'd do that for me?"

"Aye." Mary set the rag in the bucket, where it tinged the water the palest pink.

Anne caught her hand, threaded her fingers through Mary's, and pulled her in, gently but firmly, as she curled away toward the wall. Hesitantly, Mary let herself be pulled—just for a moment. She settled in against Anne's curved back and let Anne guide her arm around her waist. They fit perfectly, Anne's curls tickling

Mary's chin, their knees pressed together. "As me friend," Anne said drowsily. She lifted Mary's hand and pressed her lips to it briefly before she pulled it snug around her waist again. "I hadn't thought of that."

Mary squeezed her eyes shut, breathed in Anne's warm, familiar scent, and decided friendship would be all right.

CHAPTER THIRTY-SIX

NEW PROVIDENCE—1719

"HE TOLD ME HE DIDN'T LIKE THE IDEA OF ME WORKING, CAN YOU IMAGine?" Mary crouched at Anne's feet, pinning her skirt up. Mary had returned her first batch of piecework and somehow convinced Molly to give her some fresh underthings and a bolt of printed calico that she would work off. She was turning the calico into a dress for Anne. "I thought I might be ready to forget about him, but then he put his hand on me thigh, like so."

"Oh, he's mad for you!" Anne said brightly, twisting around to look at her. "One look at you and he doesn't know which end is up. I know the feeling."

Mary flushed. "Hold still, for Christ's sake!" Mary swatted her leg with a scowl. "Every time you move, the hem shifts."

"I never hold still anyway, so what does it matter?" Anne giggled. "No one will get a good enough look to know it's uneven." But she faced forward again and folded her hands demurely.

Mary moved a few pins, then stood and stepped back to consider the shape. "There, I think that's it." Mary had to admit that she'd done a better job than she thought she would. It had taken her the better part of a week to get the angles right; the shoulders, in particular, and the bodice had been tricky. But she'd figured it out. She'd studied the lines of Anne's old dress for a start, but then she'd started thinking about how she could make it better. She imagined Anne's body like wind in a sail, and left room for every gale-force laugh, every blustery curse, her doldrums and pleasant breeziness and seconds of stillness. She imagined the perfect dress for Anne, and then she tried to make it real. And when Anne tried it on it fit wonderfully, only needing a little adjustment. The skirts and sleeves were light and open, breathing with her in the island heat.

Anne whirled around and hugged her. "You're an absolute genius! I've never had so nice a dress!"

Mary laughed and pushed her away. "Well, it's not finished *yet*! I should be done with it soon. Now that I know what I'm doing I'll have to do a bit of tinkering with me own dress as well." *Her* dress. Ugh, her stomach still sank every time she looked down at it. She'd thought she'd get used to it by now. It fit well enough, of course, but when she wore it, it still felt so much more like pretending than being Mark ever had. But maybe there was some way to tailor it, to make it feel right.

Anne watched Mary smooth her hands down her skirts. "Stop looking so pained. You look lovely. Definitely not like a molly, I swear. And that color matches your eyes exactly."

Reade blue. How fitting, that the color of her girl-disguise was the same as the color of her boy-disguise. "Thank you," Mary said, grudgingly.

Anne nudged her. "You should make a pair of britches out of the extra material to wear around the house. I still think nothing suits you quite as well."

Mary flashed Anne a look. Her hair was clean, finally, curls nearly tamed into a braid hanging over one shoulder. She looked guileless. Girlish. She was good at pulling that off.

"The new Mary doesn't wear britches."

"Well, make me a pair then, the new Anne does."

Mary grinned reluctantly. "Don't get ahead of yourself, the dress ain't even done yet. Take it off so I can finish—" Mary cocked her head. Anne's dress fit comfortably enough, but Mary knew how slender Anne's waist was. "Wait, hang on—I think I'll take it in at the waist just a tad. Hold still while I pin—"

"Quite the perfectionist, you are." Anne stepped close and held out her arms. Mary leaned in and pinched the fabric together. Anne smelled so clean, her hair scented with the coconut oil she'd smoothed through to tame the curls—whenever Anne was close, whenever it was quiet between them, Mary's stomach still turned over. She tucked a pin in, then pinched the other side and did the same—but too quickly, and she dropped her pin.

"Can you imagine if this works? If Rogers gives me an annulment, and I don't have to chain meself to Jack?" Anne asked. "What if we could just stay here together, just the two of us?"

Mary glanced up. The swelling was going down on Anne's bruised jaw, but her lip was still fissured and puffy. "You think we could make it on our own?"

"We wouldn't need much," Anne mused. "There's fish and turtles, and it's easy as anything to grow potatoes and yams, that sort of thing. We won't starve. And no one seems to mind us setting up house in here. Maybe we could just stay here forever."

Mary's brow furrowed as she looked away. "Sure, you'd get sick of me eventually."

"That's hard to imagine," Anne said.

Mary fixed her eyes on the floor and dropped to her knees, searching for the dropped pin. She forced her thoughts to Nat. The sweetness of his kiss, his hand on her thigh. He couldn't get back soon enough. "Well, let's get you that annulment first, and then we'll see what happens." She finally spotted the pin and reached to pick it up.

"You like it like this, just the two of us," Anne pressed. "Admit it."

Mary stayed on her knees, eye-level with the waist of Anne's dress as she pinched it again. They'd been together constantly the past few days. In between sewing her piecework and Anne's dress, Mary helped Anne clean most of the filth from the hut with rags soaked in seawater and a makeshift broom. They beat the dust out of the pallets on the beds. They hunted cassava in the jungle and made a pile of it, and Anne had showed her how to properly boil the tubers so they wouldn't paralyze or kill you. Last night they'd sat up for hours, watching giant turtles as big as their own torsos lumber onto the land, scoop sand tenderly with their flippers, and lay piles of eggs big as pheasants right outside their door. Nothing spectacular had happened. But Anne was right, that feeling of being the only two people in the world—Mary *had* loved it.

But it had been just the two of them once before. No. Anne would draw her in, make her feel adored—and then move on without a backward glance. "I'm glad I can be here to make sure you're safe," Mary said shortly, tucking in the second pin.

Anne's hand glanced over Mary's hair. "Come on, Mary," she said softly. "Surely there's more to it than that."

Mary stared at the dress. The hem was even. The waist fit perfectly. Her gaze traveled up, her breath catching as her eyes met Anne's.

Remember, she told herself. This wasn't real—it wasn't *right*—and it never would be, no matter how much she wished it. "There. You can take it off." Her voice was uneven.

Anne held her gaze as she unbuttoned the bodice. Button by button. Mary couldn't look away until the last one was undone. "Here, help me," Anne said, raising her arms.

Mary lifted the hem. She shook it a little, so Anne's chemise would drop down instead of riding up. She gathered the skirt at the waist, then carefully drew it up, over Anne's ribcage, the swell of her breasts—it tangled up around her head and arms—Anne started to twist, and her hip bumped against Mary—

"Stop," Mary ordered, her temperature flaring. "You'll mess up the pins."

Anne went still, and Mary pulled the dress free. Even in the chemise, in the dimness of the hut, there was too much for Mary to see, or to imagine she could see—

Dammit. She wanted Nat. She wanted to be Mary. She wanted to be *done* with this ridiculous desire. She averted her eyes and turned away. "It'll be done tonight," she announced, carefully spreading the dress across the table. "We can call on Rogers in the morning."

Anne sighed shakily—or maybe it was just Mary's own unsteady exhalation. She refused to look at Anne, fussing with the thread and her needle. After a long moment of stillness, Anne picked her filthy red dress up off the bed. The velvet was sun-bleached and salt-stained, crusty in spots, threadbare in others. The bits that saw the most sun had faded to pink, and sparks from various fires had burned holes all around its edges. "Thank God it's almost done," Anne said, her voice irritated. "I think I might burn this old rag right this moment."

"Go ahead," Mary said, bending over her work. "I don't care a bit what you do."

CHAPTER THIRTY-SEVEN

ROTTERDAM—1717

THAT NIGHT, AFTER THE GAMES AND DRINKING, THEY SLOPPED BACK TO their ship and sprawled on the floor in the hold. Nat fell asleep quick and hard.

Mary had finished the game with the boys, saying little. Robbie had given her some sideways looks, but had been too busy making crude remarks to the serving girls to say much to Mary. The food had been good, hot and salty, but she wasn't able to finish it. She'd kept her jaw set, taking great swigs from her mug each time it was refilled. She'd made sure to stare after the yellow-haired maid every time she passed, and hardly looked at Nat at all.

But now that she was alone she hugged her arms around her waist, taking huge, unsteady breaths. Nat snuffled next to her in the dark. She could feel the heat along the side of her body where he lay. The air was close and stifling. His thigh touched hers. A few of his knuckles grazed her hip. She pictured his lips parted in sleep, his lashes thick along his cheek.

All that ale was making her head spin. She rolled away from him, put her hands over her ears, and tried to forget he was there.

She dreamed about him. Restless, warm dreams without words. She didn't have to tell him, he knew what she was. He knew what to do, how to touch her to make her feel like she wasn't such a mess.

She woke up, aching and breathless, to pale early morning light coming through the porthole above them. He was turned away from her, still asleep. She exhaled quietly and reached out, very nearly touching the back of his neck. She let her fingers hover for a moment over his straight black hair where it cow-licked into two almost-curls. His neck was smudged and dirty around the collar of his shirt.

He sighed and flopped onto his back, head rolling toward her. She pulled back her hand. His breath was slow and heavy. She studied his face, its perfect familiarity, all of those memorized freckles and curves.

She wasn't the only one who thought he was beautiful. She saw how girls looked at him. It was the way *she* looked at him, the look that had caught Kit and Robbie's attention.

She'd never get her fill of looking at him.

He had a little crease between his eyebrows, as though he worried about something, and his lashes twitched. His skin looked warm. She leaned in a little closer and inhaled the smell of salt and sleep, and something else she couldn't name.

His breathing shifted and he opened his eyes.

She jerked back, then half-smiled, and gave him a jab with her fist. "Morning, mate."

He blinked at her, unsmiling. Then he clenched his jaw and turned away.

"Nat." She was trembling, but she knew she had to push forward. She had to tell him. "I have to tell you something."

"Please don't," said Nat tightly, sitting up. "I just want everything to keep going between us the way it's always been. I can't—I just want to keep being mates, all right? We can stay mates so long as nothing changes. Do you understand?"

She sat up and reached for his elbow. "But I—"

"Stop, Mark. I don't want to hear it."

Nat got up and walked away without looking back.

CHAPTER THIRTY-EIGHT

New Providence—1719

Mary and Anne were both clean and well dressed. They'd practiced demure faces for each other, laughter dispelling some of their anxiety. Anne squared her shoulders. "Allow me to lead the way," she said, faking a sophisticated accent. "The governor's house is a grand old thing, one of the only buildings on the island that made it through the war. You'll be very impressed."

Mary followed her through the market and down a sandy path that wound up a hill, away from the water. They passed houses made of wattle and daub, with plots of potatoes and yams in the yards, falling into silence as they walked. Anne kept inhaling deeply, then slowly letting out her breath. Her fists clenched and unclenched, knuckles going from white to red and back again. Mary grabbed a hand and threaded her fingers through so Anne would have something to hold onto. "The worst thing he can say is no," she offered.

Anne kept her gaze fixed ahead. "I'm not terribly sure you're right about that."

Tension crawled up Mary's neck. "We can turn around if you like. We can always go tomorrow."

Anne gripped Mary's hand like it was the only thing keeping her upright. "I have to do it before I lose me nerve. I *have* to try. Before I go running back to Jack, or stow away on the next ship that leaves the harbor. This is me home. James shouldn't be able to control me like he does."

Mary let her squeeze the blood from her fingers. Somehow, after just a scant week spent with her, the thought of being without Anne felt empty and dull. But Nat was coming back. It wasn't as though they could go on like this forever.

The jungle opened up ahead, and Mary glimpsed the first grand house she'd seen since arriving in the Caribbean. It was freshly whitewashed, three arches leading into a shadowy, open-air foyer. Two stories rose above that with neat rows of windows. The area around the mansion was freshly cleared, broken foliage and turned earth surrounding the building in a defiantly symmetrical circle. A man in a steward's uniform met them in the foyer, sweating in his high collar and long sleeves.

"We're here to petition the governor," Anne announced.

The man inclined his head. "Of course, ma'am. If you would kindly wait here, I'll inform Mr. Rogers of your arrival."

They waited in fidgeting silence until the man returned and led them through a door, into a hallway that smelled of stewed meat and mildew. The fine curtains were frayed at the edges, and the fixtures on the doors and lamps had the green patina of corrosion. The man knocked on another door and Mary heard a muffled invitation from within. He opened the door and Mary and Anne stepped hesitantly inside.

A broad-shouldered man with gray in his dark brown waves sat behind a grand desk, bent over something and writing intently. As they drew close he put down his quill and looked up, the sideways light through the window revealing a puckered, disfigured cheek. "Ladies. How may I help you?" he asked. His voice was commanding, despite a slight lisp. His skin was drawn and sallow.

"If you please, sir," Anne said, her voice firm, "me name is Anne Bonny."

"Ah," Rogers said, leaning back in his chair. "Bonny's wife. Good man—unlike most of the indolent inhabitants of this god-forsaken island. He's been a great help to me since I arrived."

Mary clenched her teeth to stop her jaw from dropping. Rogers must not know what James was capable of. "I'm Mary Reade," she said evenly. "A dear friend of Anne's. And I have come to vouch for her."

He leaned back in his chair, looking Anne up and down. "And why should you need vouching for, Mrs. Bonny?"

"Anne recently suffered painful injury," Mary said, but when she looked at Anne she realized that much of the bruising was gone. With a cold feeling in her stomach she realized she'd taken too much time making Anne's dress perfect, when she'd just needed to look respectable. "James, the man you claim is so upstanding, is the one who did it to her."

Rogers put down his quill. "Did she not disappear from him these past months?" he asked mildly. "Did she not violate the promise she made to God to stay by his side?"

"I left him because I was in fear," Anne said, her voice trembling. "His abuse started long before I ever thought of leaving him."

"I've heard stories about you, young lady," Rogers said, his tone indulgent. "They say you are a godless woman. An adulteress. That James tried his best to set you on the right path, but that you refused to listen."

"Anne has never borne a child for him," Mary interrupted, trying another tack. "Impotency is grounds for divorce."

"So that's why you're here, is it? You'd like to sue for divorce?"

Anne nodded meekly.

"Who is to say that Anne is not the infertile one?"

Mary glanced at Anne, who shook her head imperceptibly, and Mary choked on her response. If she said Anne had carried

Jack's child when she was still married to James, it would brand her an adulteress. But there was no other proof.

Rogers watched them shift nervously. "My dears." Rogers sighed, steepling his fingers. "Bonny warned me that you might show up with just such a query. He seemed to think a man named Jack Rackham would be accompanying you, Mrs. Bonny. Nonetheless, James advised me that any annulment granted would be against his wishes. And it is his right, as your husband and master, to prevent such a thing from coming to pass if he does not wish it."

Mary felt Anne twitch against her side.

"Sir," Mary said. "Anne's face was bleeding, bruised, and swollen from his hand. His right should be forfeit, whether or not he is impotent. It's not fair that she doesn't have some protection."

"He gave her a bruise on her face, did he? Look at *my* face, young lady. Tell me, does James's chastisement compare in any way?"

Mary's eyes flicked to the puckered flesh of his cheek, guessing it was the result of a musket ball to the face. "What one risks in battle is not what one should have to risk in marriage," she said quietly. "He's supposed to care for her."

"I am a fair-minded man," Rogers continued as if she hadn't spoken, in the same condescending tone. "I will choose not to judge you too harshly for this insolence. Bonny wanted me to have you whipped in the square if you came to me like this, but I am not so harsh."

Rogers smiled indulgently, and Mary felt a surge of dread. She'd seen women and men in the pillory, bleeding, soiled, delirious with dehydration, vulnerable to anyone who would spit on, hit, or fondle them—and for many crimes, that was getting off lightly.

Rogers's smile faded as he stood. "However, if I hear that you do not return, repentant, to your husband—if I hear you are carrying on with Rackham—if I get wind of you continuing to dishonor your marriage vows, I *will* have you whipped, publicly and dishonorably." He leaned forward, fingertips on the desk, giving

Anne a severe look. Anne twitched again, and Mary didn't doubt he would do what he threatened. "Do you understand?"

"I don't think I do," Anne ground out. "How is hitting your wife not dishonoring your vows? How is abusing someone who trusts and loves you not worthy of flogging instead?"

"Anne," Mary hissed. It was clear Rogers wouldn't be convinced. "She understands," she said hastily.

Rogers straightened. He leaned heavily on an ivory-tipped cane and came around the desk. His face up close was grotesque, the blast of a firearm having carved his mouth into an elongated, puckered frown. Mary flinched when he stabbed the cane down in front of her.

"Mary Reade, was it?" he said. "You're new to the island, aren't you?"

Mary fought the urge to look away. "Aye."

"Ah." He tapped his cane against the floor as he considered her. "Do you know, I believe I heard some of my men talking about you."

Fear raced up her spine. "Who would have cause to do that?"

"They were discussing certain—predilections you have."

Mary's throat closed up. "I'm done with all of that, sir." Oh, God. The pamphlet for her hanging would read: *A full and true account of the discovery and apprehending of a notorious sodomite in New Providence, taken in for wearing the dress and affecting the mannerisms of a man.* "I've—ah, repented."

"Have you." The corner of Rogers's mouth turned up. "Tell me, are you a Protestant?"

"Aye," she said quickly. She had every intention of being one from now on.

He tsked. "I haven't seen you at church."

She swallowed. "Like you said, I'm new here."

"And which ship did you say you came in on?" he asked. "Surely you've been here since last Sunday?"

"I—ah—" Her mind went blank. Anne watched with wide eyes.

Rogers sighed. "When I lay in a bunk in the middle of the ocean, unable to speak because of the musket ball buried in my palate, unable to walk, upon death's very door—do you think I whined about it? Do you think I blamed the king or my men or God for my plight?"

She shook her head mutely. It had been a mistake to come, drawing attention to herself. It had been foolish mistake of both of them.

"I had *faith*, Mary," he said gently. "Faith that I would be rewarded by the king, my investors, and God once they all saw the way I bore hardship and tragedy—with humility, with patience. Always asking what God wants of me. I have a greater purpose than my own whims and desires, and I know I will be rewarded for that." He turned and picked something up from his desk. "I expect that once both of you understand that you are part of His plan, you will find the strength to overcome your petty trials."

He held out a folded piece of paper, and Mary took it with shaking hands. SOCIETY FOR PROMOTING CHRISTIAN KNOWLEDGE was printed across the front.

"Do you think I threaten you for *my* sake?" he asked. "My concern is your immortal souls, and the souls of all the misguided people of these islands. I want to make sure you know what God needs of you. I want you to know how great your reward will be if you perform well—and how great the punishment will be if you do not. Do you understand?"

Mary nodded mutely, the pamphlet creasing in her grip.

"Mrs. Bonny?" Rogers prodded.

"Aye," she said tensely. "I understand now, governor."

"I expect to see you at church this Sunday." Rogers walked past them and opened the door, gesturing for them to leave. "Both of you will find the answers you need there."

CHAPTER THIRTY-NINE

NEW PROVIDENCE—1719

"JIMMY GETS THE POWER OF THE LAW, AND I GET THE POWER OF PRAYER," Anne fumed, ripping the pamphlet to shreds and tossing it in the weeds. "I knew it. Me only choice is to go back to James and pray to bloody God he doesn't kill me one day, as is his bloody right."

Now that the fear had worn off, Mary was shaking with anger. "That was unbelievable," said Mary, crumpling her pamphlet into a ball. "I can see now why you wanted to blow the whole place to bits."

"We could still do it," Anne said.

Mary laughed despite herself. "I hear there's plenty of powder in that fort," she said. "We'd have to find a way in—but then, you're very convincing when you put your mind to it."

"I am, aren't I," said Anne, grinning. Then she grabbed Mary's hand and stopped walking. "Except with you." She tugged Mary to face her, and Mary's heart began beating harder. They were out of sight of the governor's house, alone, with the jungle pressing close. "I can't figure out what I have to do to get you to kiss me again."

The impotent anger racing through Mary ignited with the challenge in Anne's gaze. Blood pounded in her ears as she looked back toward the governor's house, but Anne drew her in with the hand she clasped. "Come here, Mary," Anne whispered, and before Mary could hesitate again she chucked the crumpled pamphlet into the jungle and pressed Anne back against the rough trunk of a palm tree. The sound that left Anne's lips as Mary gripped her waist made the whole world go white.

"Dammit," Mary breathed, their mouths almost touching. She stared at the full curve of Anne's lip.

She shouldn't—she should remember—what? Anne breathed her name and leaned forward and caught Mary's lips with hers. Giving in to Anne was dangerous and meaningless and foolhardy—and Mary sank into her. She gathered up layers of chemises and skirts and the skin of Anne's thigh under her hand was a revelation, her mouth gloriously fervent and sweet.

Anne put her hands on Mary's face and pulled away, breathing hard. "There—there could be another way," she said, chest rising and falling. "A way to rid meself of James without having to marry Jack."

Mary struggled to get her mind past the shine of Anne's lips, the smoothness underneath her palm. She let the skirts slip down. "What is it?"

Anne's eyes searched hers. "If Jimmy went to the governor and asked for a divorce himself. But Jimmy won't let me go without getting what he thinks he's due."

"You need Jack for that," Mary said.

"Not if—we could pay him off."

"We haven't any money for that," Mary said slowly. "We never will. The piecework I'm doing will never pay enough, no matter how fast I sew."

"Aye," said Anne. "But what if you dressed as a sailor again, and got a job on the next privateering mission? So long as the war drags on, there'll be more going out and coming back stuffed with

Spanish treasure. A share of that is a sight better than the pennies you're making now!"

"Jesus Christ." Mary let go of Anne and stepped away, shaking. "I'm a bloody fool."

"What—what do you mean?"

"God, I'm so stupid. I can't believe I let you lure me in again."

"No, Mary, that's not it at all!" Anne reached for her, but Mary shoved her hands away. Anne looked panicked—of course she did, now that Mary was on to her. "It would be good for both of us! You're making nothing working for that woman, and anyone can see you hate living like this, wearing your skirts and trying to act like everyone wants you to. What if Mary just disappeared, and Mark slipped off on a mission, with no one the wiser?"

"And risk Rogers finding out and hanging me from the gibbet? Not to mention *completely* scuttling me chances with Nat!" God damn it, how had she let Anne distract her from what she really wanted again?

"The *gibbet*?" Anne asked incredulously. "Don't tell me Rogers scared you that much!"

"I've seen men hanged for much the same," spat Mary. "I'll not risk death just because you turned your charms on me when there was no one else around to save you."

"It's not like that." Anne said quietly.

Mary folded her arms. "Oh, isn't it?"

"I—I'm sorry, Mary," Anne said with a note of desperation. "I shouldn't have asked that of you. I just thought—"

"Forget it," Mary said heatedly. "You can stay with me until Jack and Nat get back, but then you'll have to try your act on Jack instead. See how that works out for you."

"But—that's not what I *want*, Mary."

"I know. You want your freedom. But that's not the way the world works." Mary turned and started stomping down the path.

"You better go to church on Sunday and thank God there's a decent man who still might save you," she threw over her shoulder.

"*Barely* decent." Anne gave a bitter laugh behind her.

"Jack's not so bad!" Mary said with forced enthusiasm, whacking a branch out of her way. "You said so yourself!"

"I really have to settle for that?" Anne asked, sounding defeated.

"You've got no choice," said Mary, walking faster. "Your other options have run out."

CHAPTER FORTY

Rotterdam—1717

The *Queen Catherine* came into view as Mary ran back from the gunsmith, every inch of it shining in the bright sunlight, outfitted with an obsessive perfection that only Dutch money could buy. New cannons peeked from every gun port. The crew had spent the past few days scrubbing it down with holystones, giving it a fresh coat of paint, and checking over every rope and sail. It was ready for the New World, and they were headed straight for Nassau in the morning.

"Did you find the bastard?" Johnny growled as she approached.

"Aye," Mary panted, coming to a stop on the gangboard beside him.

"What's his excuse?"

The gunsmith's English had been terrible. "I think he was saying he never got the order, so I put in another. He was short at the shop, but the extra flint will be here by the end of the day."

Johnny grunted. "All right. See what Abe has need of you for next."

Mary dodged a barrel being rolled up the gangboard. The main deck was crowded with the last bits of supplies being inventoried—barrels of brined meats and water, bags of gunpowder, a few pigs. Her heart leapt when she saw Nat. He sat with Robbie and Kit on the poop deck, close to where Mary had left them a few hours before. They'd since exchanged cards for guns.

Mary had been in misery the three weeks since she'd tried to tell Nat. He had ignored or been short with her at every opportunity—but gradually, he'd gone back to being friendly. She would do whatever it took to stay mates with him. She would cross the sea with her secret still intact, and she would figure out how to tell him once she got to the islands.

"Take a gander at this," said Kit to Mary, waving something as she approached. "Never held a musket before, have you? Here, feel her up and see what you think."

She took the musket from Kit and weighed it in her hand. A pile of them lay in disarray around their feet. Nat squinted at her, running a cloth up and down the well-oiled barrel of a gun.

"You won't believe who I ran into on me way back," she said to him. "That yellow-haired girl from the pub." Nat had told Mary he'd gone back to the tavern, but the girl had been nothing more than friendly with him despite his best efforts. "I told her we was heading out tomorrow, and she wished us luck. Told me she'll think fondly of you, but not so fondly as she'll think of me."

Kit snickered. Nat stayed bent over his gun, fiddling with its flintlock.

Robbie began stacking muskets in the crook of his arm. "We've checked these at least six times over. Grab a few, and I'll show you where to stash them."

Nat stood and lifted an armful of weapons. Mary grabbed a half-dozen bayonets, and they headed toward the hold.

"Don't you want to go visit her one last time before we weigh anchor?" she asked as they crossed the main deck. She fumbled the awkward stack of slick metal bayonets as they almost slid from her grip. "You're not going to let me best you?"

"Best him, did you?" Kit asked over his shoulder as he headed for the stern. "Did Brigitte let you butter her buns after all?"

"You tumble her out back the tavern, or what?" Robbie laughed, stopping at the back of the hold. "Or was it too hard to get your willy up when she lifted her skirts?" He began to set the muskets down carefully, one by one, in a crate by the wall.

"Ugh, Robbie." She choked down her disgust and dropped the bayonets with a clatter beside the crate.

He jabbed her shoulder with the barrel of a musket as he stood. "Aw, hard when that happens, ain't it?" He rubbed the muzzle on her arm, up and down. "Don't worry, molly boy. You'll have Nat all to yourself at night, all the way across the ocean, and I know you won't have any trouble getting it up for him."

Mary couldn't move, frozen by the cold metal stroking her arm.

"Shut it, Robbie." Nat finally spoke, his voice unsure.

"Oh, come off it," Robbie pulled the gun away from Mary and jabbed Nat in the chest with it. "You're the one who was telling us he's been looking goats and monkeys at you when he thinks you're asleep."

She should have never stayed. She should have caught the next boat back to London. She should have turned herself in to the Westminster constable. Anything would be better than this.

"For Christ's sake, Robbie!" Nat shoved the gun. "Would you stop waving that thing around?"

Mary began to inch away.

"Where do you think you're going?" Kit asked, blocking Mary in. "There's some kind of question been raised here, and I think you need to answer it." He flexed his fingers, then crossed his arms and tilted his head expectantly.

She looked at Nat, her throat closing up.

"What the hell is that supposed to mean?" Nat sounded scared. Kit and Robbie outweighed the two of them by a good bit.

Kit looked over his shoulder at Nat. "I don't know, suppose you could tell me?"

"Huh, this should be good." Robbie picked up a musket and put it to his shoulder, peering deliberately down the barrel at Mary. "What do you think, Nat? How's Mark gonna prove he's not a puff?"

Mary ducked toward Nat and bolted.

She'd only taken a few steps when a musket caught her across the ankles and sent her sprawling, her chin and mouth scraping the white-washed decking. She rolled to one side in time to see Robbie kick out at her face as Nat grabbed his arm and yanked him backward. The blow snapped her head back, blinding her. She curled in around the pain blossoming across her face. She heard herself groaning.

"Would you hold it, the both of you!" Nat was yelling. "Mark can pull himself together from here on, right? Can't you, Mark, no harm done?"

She put a hand up to her face and it came away wet with blood. Her nose was bleeding. She rolled onto her back, holding her face, squinting against the pain.

"Sure, sure, but he still can't go till he answers!" Kit's great, square face loomed above her. "Are you a puff or not, Mark? Tell us so we know."

"Yeah, Mark. Tell us." Robbie nudged her ribs with his boot.

Then he paused.

"Now, what's this?"

He leaned over her, narrowing his eyes. He put his hands on his knees, cocking his head to the side. Mary realized with a jolt that her shirt had ridden up, and she yanked it down. Robbie knocked her hand away and reached out to touch the strip of binding that had been exposed.

Mary struggled to sit up, wrenching her shirt down again and scrambling backward until her shoulders hit a beam. Robbie watched her impassively.

Nat said, "Sure that's where Mark was burned when he was a kid. Never did heal up right. That's how long we've been mates, see?"

Robbie nodded slowly, thoughtfully.

Mary took a breath, let it out. "Aye, that's it exactly." She put her hands to the beam behind her and started to stand.

Robbie pounced on Mary, wrenching her down. She punched at his stomach but couldn't match his strength. He got her flat on her back, both of her wrists in one fist, and used the other hand to rip at her shirt until it tore straight down the middle.

He stared at the binding, and at the tiny curve that was plastered down above her ribs. He put a hand to it and she cried out, twisting away from his grasp. He yanked at the fabric with one hand but it was bound too tightly for him to budge.

Not like this not like this not like this—please God he can't find out like this—

Robbie reached down and put a rough hand between her legs as Mary squirmed against him.

Kit and Nat stared down, open-mouthed.

"Christ Almighty," Robbie said, his face reddening as he pressed against her. "He ain't a puff after all. He's a bleeding *girl*."

CHAPTER FORTY-ONE

New Providence—1720

Mary bent closer over her work, squinting at the stitches she'd just done. It was drizzling outside, the rainclouds making the light inside the hut impossibly dim—but her work was still passable. She was getting rather good at it, quick and even.

Stitching cotton for a shirt wasn't so much different from stitching sailcloth for a sail. The weight of the fabric was different, of course, and the thread as well. These stitches needed to be strong, but not strong enough to fight gale-force wind—only strong enough to hold against the excited tugging of a child, perhaps, or a nail catching a cuff, or a hem trod beneath a boot.

Shape was still the most important element. With sails, the shape directed the passage of a ship beneath the wind. It controlled the amount of wind that flowed in and out again. With a dress or britches, the shape changed the flow of a body's movement. A tuck here, a bit of fullness there—like magic, Mary could change a human form. She could make a man's shoulders broader, a girl's chest fuller, an ankle appear a bit more slender. She'd even managed to make herself look like a girl.

Feeling like one, though—that was another matter altogether.

Anne came through the door cursing, dropped the heavy bucket of sweet water she'd hauled from the river, and ran to the steaming pot hanging over the fire. "Didn't occur to you to give it a stir once in a while?" she asked.

Mary belatedly realized that something was burning. "I'm trying to get this last bit of stitching in before Molly packs up for the day."

Anne huffed but didn't respond, the fire hissing as rain dripped from her hair. She'd barely looked at Mary in the few days since they'd been refused by Rogers. Mary bent back over her work, counting each stitch as a moment closer to Nat's return. He was getting nearer every time she pressed the needle through the cloth.

There was a knock on the doorframe and Mary looked up, leaning forward to squint out the window. A piddling rain had forced her indoors for longer than the usual late-afternoon showers. It felt like a London rain, all day, dreary, and gray, but not cold. Never cold. She could hardly remember what cold felt like.

Two men stood outside the door.

"Who is it?" asked Anne, still busy trying to keep the pot of pigeon peas from burning.

Mary's throat closed up. "It's Robbie. And someone's with him. Can't see his face—" Both men wore wide hats, rain dripping off their brims.

Anne peered out the window and her mouth set. "It's James." She turned back to the hearth and gave the pigeon peas a few more vicious swipes with her wooden spoon.

Mary jumped to her feet and tossed her stitches aside. Where had she put their pistol?

Anne set down the wooden spoon, then picked it back up. She held it clenched in her fist like a weapon as she stomped to the door, then thwacked the sailcloth back with it. "What the devil do you want?" she spat, her body blocking the doorway.

"We want a word with you." Robbie peered past Anne, and when his eyes landed on Mary, he looked positively gleeful. "Rogers charged us a while back with clearing out this den of prostitution, but I've reason to suspect you're starting it back up."

Mary kept scanning the room with her eyes. Where had she put the damned pistol?

James stepped close to Anne, eyes narrow. "I should've expected nothing less from you," he said quietly.

Anne didn't flinch, but Mary's mouth went dry at his tone. "We've done no such thing," Mary stammered. "We've just been taking shelter here until we can afford a proper place."

"Nat told me just this afternoon how you was so bold with him before he left, and how you was living in the old whorehouse," Robbie said.

"Nat—he's back?"

Robbie ignored her. "And him, practically engaged to me sister! He seemed to think the way you acted was a harmless bit of fun, but me and James consider prostitution a serious offense." Robbie shouldered his way past Anne, and James slunk into the hut behind him.

"Is that right?" Mary said sharply. "I seem to remember different from when we was back in Rotterdam."

"I've changed," said Robbie smugly. "People change, Mark. I mean—Mary."

"And *I'd* heard from the governor that the two of you showed up together," James said, voice heavy with venom. "When we heard Mary was here, I suspected this might be where you was hiding out as well."

"Get out," Anne ordered, sounding fearless.

"Even if this was your house, and it's not," James snapped, "you're my wife, so's what's yours is mine."

"Very true." Robbie pilfered through Mary's piles of piecework, dropping half-made shirts and britches to the floor. "And you two is suspect, so we're allowed here regardless."

Robbie moved a pile of her sewing, revealing the pistol glinting on the table, and Mary's heart skipped a beat. She watched him pick it up. Consider it.

Keep it in his grip.

"Did you hear that, Annie?" James came close, and abruptly raised his hand, making Anne flinch. Mary could tell Anne hated that she'd betrayed her fear, how her fists clenched. "This upstanding gentleman agrees with me."

Anne turned and lowered herself slowly into a chair. James crouched in front of her, and she winced away. "You thought you'd go to the governor on your own, Annie?" he growled. "Tell him what a terrible man I am, when all I want is to guide you to righteousness?"

"Tell the story any way you like it," Anne said, eyes narrowing. "You know in your heart that's not the truth."

"I thought you was with Jack all this time. Come to find out, he'd shipped out with Burgess." His voice dropped to a hiss. "I thought, my own wife, living alone. No one to comfort her."

"I'm not alone." Anne's eyes flicked up to Mary, and Mary felt her scattered rage gather inside her, into something solid and strong. The pot on the fire was beginning to smoke.

James barely glanced at Mary. "Aye, like a woman in need of the guidance and attention of her husband, you took up with a whore!"

"That's you, Mary," said Robbie. There was a terrible odor, black and acrid, filling the house. "I'm here to charge you with prostitution and take you in. Jimmy can deal with his wife."

Robbie lunged, grabbing Mary's arm and twisting it hard behind her. She yelped as he jerked her arm up, pulling her back against him. The more she struggled, the more he seemed to enjoy restraining her. "You bastard, you can't do this—" she hissed.

Anne jumped up, ran to the door, and flung her arms wide to block Robbie from leaving. "You can't, you've got no proof, it's not *true*!"

Mary felt a surge of warmth as Anne came to her defense. On the hearth, smoke wafted out of the pot of peas as the flames from the fire licked high around it.

"Let them through, Annie," said James.

Anne leapt forward and smacked James hard across the face, the wooden round of her spoon catching him square across his mouth. He jerked back, swearing. "You get out of me house!" she shrieked. "Get out, get out, get out—"

In a flash he had her down on the ground, struggling in the doorway. Blood beaded on his bottom lip.

Robbie spun Mary around and pinned her against the wall, his mouth against her cheek. "You know, I thought I'd mind you less if you'd just put on skirts," he whispered against her skin. "It might do the trick for Nat, but you still look unnatural to me."

James, sweating, held Anne's arms down with his knees. He sat on her stomach as her legs flailed, petticoats riding up.

Mary twisted and spat in Robbie's face.

The handle of the pistol came down hard on her forehead.

Shock stunned her for a moment, time slowed, softened—

Over Robbie's shoulder she watched as James panted over Anne while she held her arms over her face. "You run around on me, you make a fool of me, you defy me in front of me men—I won't *take* no more of it—" He hit her and she made a sound like an animal keening.

He hit her again and she screamed.

James put his hands to the neckline of Anne's lovely dress—

The stitches Mary had so carefully sewn shredded in his grip. He wanted every stitch undone, and her weak work did nothing to stop him. She saw now—Anne needed something strong as sails.

She needed heavy cloth sealed tight with tar so nothing could get through. Something to catch the wind and carry her away.

Mary threw herself against Robbie's grip as he swore, holding her fast as she watched James hit Anne, she was going mad watching it, and then he had Anne's skirts up and he was fumbling with his belt—

Mary twisted her foot behind Robbie's knee and threw her weight toward that side with all her might and suddenly she was falling—shock riding through her bones as she landed on top of him—in that moment his grip loosened and she didn't know what happened next, only that suddenly she was standing over James with a burning brand to his neck. "Get out."

Her voice sounded like someone else's—dark and deranged, capable of murder.

James yelped as the flame at his neck bit into his collar. He flailed off of Anne, and Mary stood between them. Anne struggled to sitting, wrapped around Mary's leg.

Robbie clambered to his feet, swearing, and started for her.

Mary started waving the brand wildly, back and forth. "You get out," she screamed. "You get out or I'll burn this damned house down with you in it!"

She knew she couldn't stop them. Robbie still had her pistol in his hand and could shoot her dead. She'd die, and then Anne would have no one.

There was a burst of light as the sailcloth door lifted. Nat stumbled through and they all froze as he looked around, shock dawning on his face.

"What in—Mary? *Robbie?* What in God's name is going on?"

Mary lowered the brand uncertainly.

Robbie slid the pistol into his belt. He had a smirk on his face, like he thought the whole situation was funny. "You told me Mary was living in a whorehouse," Robbie said. "I had to come down here to make sure she wasn't striking up the trade. I mean, that's why *you* was coming down here, wasn't it? You told me she was waiting for you."

Nat looked from Mary, burning stick in hand—to Anne, hunched at her feet, dress in shreds around her—to James, panting, clutching at the back of his neck, belt undone—and back to Robbie, with that damned smile on his face. Chairs overturned, still-glowing coals scattered across the floor. "Bloody hell, Robbie," Nat swore. "You know as well as I do that's not true. You *know* I was only making a few cracks."

Mary looked down. She couldn't see Anne's face, just her back curling as she rolled onto her side. Anne's shoulders started to shake. She looked small.

"Oh, well then," Robbie said. "If that's the case, I suppose they're free to go."

"Anne's my wife," James ground out, standing.

"Aye," said Nat. He stepped between Anne and James and crossed his arms. "Why don't you go cool off, and think about how you'd like to go about convincing her to come home? I think you've made your displeasure clear enough."

Mary threw him a grateful look as she blew out a shaky breath.

James's panting slowed. He wiped his face and squared his shoulders. "Fine." He fastened his belt. "But I can come back any time I want. It's my right."

"There you go," Nat said. He went back to the door and held the sailcloth door up. James sauntered through with one last glare at Anne.

"Apologies for the *misunderstanding*," Robbie said smugly as he followed James out.

Nat ducked out behind them. Mary knelt beside Anne in the stillness they left, the sparks that showered from the brand winking out into tiny black burns in Anne's dress. She touched the ruined fabric. "I—I thought we'd be safe here together," she whispered. But she'd been wrong. If Nat hadn't shown up—she shuddered, thinking about what had almost come to pass.

Mary stood and pushed through the sailcloth. The rain had let up and the sun, just above the horizon, was coloring the clouds shades of pink and coral. Nat followed Robbie and James up the path. She wanted to call after him, but the side of her head where Robbie had hit her felt hot and tender, and she stayed silent until he was out of sight.

CHAPTER FORTY-TWO

ROTTERDAM—1717

ROBBIE SHOVED HIS HAND BETWEEN MARY'S LEGS AGAIN. SHE WRITHED, but he held her fast as his palm ground rough fabric into her crotch. She watched his shocked expression turn to fascination, then to something else entirely.

She reared back and spat. His head jerked, then his grip slowly released. He sat back on his knees, wiping spittle from his face. Mary put her hands between her legs and rolled away from Nat, squeezing her eyes shut. She couldn't look at him.

"Well, this puts a twist on things, don't it," said Robbie.

"He really a girl?" Kit asked.

"Yeah, he—uh, she most certainly is. You want a feel?" Robbie moved close again, his bulk casting a shadow across her body.

"What the bloody *hell*," said Nat, his voice hoarse.

Mary opened her eyes.

All the lies she'd told. How she'd lain on his pallet with him. Talked about girls. Watched him dress and undress and sleep and make water. How she'd seen all the little moments of his life, and listened to all his thoughts and dreams and fantasies, all disguised as someone she was not.

She couldn't guess at what might be crossing his mind.

"You been holding out on us, mate?" Kit asked.

"Yeah, is this your girl?" Robbie's fingers touched the waist of her britches, rubbing slightly against the bare skin of her hip. "Blimey, that's quite a show the two of you've been putting on."

Mary rolled over and squinted past Robbie's shoulder at Nat. He stared down at her. *Please,* she thought. *Just say yes. I'm in trouble if you don't say yes . . .*

Nat didn't respond, just looked up. She could imagine him trying to put things together in his mind, trying to understand at what point during his entire life his best mate had been taken from him and an impostor put in his place.

"I can see it now," said Robbie. "Strange. I just thought you was a pretty boy." He tugged on her britches, almost playfully.

She slapped his hand away and struggled to sit up. "Nat, please," she said. "It's me, I'm Mark. It's always been me. I just—"

What could she say?

"I was going to tell you," she whispered.

He kept staring upward, as if he couldn't hear her. She slowly got to her feet, wiping the blood from her face.

"Not so fast," Robbie said, stepping in front of her again. "Seems that Nat's as amazed as the rest of us, and don't that change things a bit." He looked her up and down, in a way that no boy had ever looked at her before. Mary's throat tightened as she pulled her shirt across her exposed skin. "If this boy ain't going to claim you," he said, "then I believe you're up for grabs."

"You really didn't know, mate?" Kit asked Nat, shaking his head almost gleefully.

Mary gauged the distance to the ladder up to the deck. If she moved fast, she could probably make her escape from the hold before the boys could catch her.

Nat's head jerked down at that. "Wait," he said, and walked slowly over.

He took her arm and her shirt fell open again. Her breath caught, skin pimpling under his gaze. He looked at her bare, thin chest as if examining her skin for some seam that showed this new skin was the actual disguise, that Mark was still hiding inside her.

He finally saw her, really saw her. Mary held her breath.

His eyes flicked over her face. But he looked at her blankly, as if she were a stranger. He stepped away. "I don't know who you are," he said, his head beginning to shake. "Mark? What . . . I've known Mark since we was babies."

"You know me, Nat," she pleaded. "Please, I need a chance to explain."

"Aha!" said Kit. "I believe she's on her own in this one, after all. What do you say, Robbie?"

Robbie pulled Mary close and grabbed her chin. A smile spread across his lips as he studied her. "A girl parading about as a boy. There's something off about that, don't you think? Something queer."

"Now wait—" Nat put a hand out.

"You had your chance to claim her," said Robbie, his thumb softly stroking the line of her jaw. "It's my turn now."

Mary kicked out with all her might, and made contact with Robbie's middle. He released her with an "Oof!" and doubled over. It was only a moment—he lunged for her again—but she'd already turned and was dashing through the hold, her torn shirt flapping like flimsy wings. She could hear yelling behind her, and the sound of stumbling and crashing over crates and into beams.

Someone was coming down the hold's ladder—Abe and Johnny, their arms full of ammunition. Mary charged past them as their voices raised. She dipped into the head, yanking the little door closed behind her. But it didn't shut fast or lock, and she couldn't hold it forever. There was nowhere on this ship she could hide anymore.

She could hear the growl of Abe's voice in the hold outside.

Then Robbie's, friendly and bright. Footsteps coming closer.

A sob escaped as her hand went to her mouth to block the smell. No seawater churned up through the head while it was docked. The waste that had built up throughout the week would be flushed out once they took to sea, but for now it stank of shit.

Mary lifted the wooden grate. Beneath there lay a soiled, sloping bit of wood, and beyond that, the water. Sparkling, dark, and calm.

She put her hands on either side of the hole, then stepped in so that her feet rested on the shit-stained wood, holding her weight up with her arms. She would fit. It would be tight, and she'd take most of the waste out with her when she went, but she'd slide through. And then . . .

She'd seen people swim before. It couldn't be that hard, could it?

She'd seen people drowned before as well, their bloated bodies washed up on the mud flats around the Thames at low tide.

She swallowed.

The head door thumped open.

Mary let go.

CHAPTER FORTY-THREE

New Providence—1720

When Mary ducked back into the hut, Anne's ruined dress was crumpled on the floor, but she was gone, and Mary was disoriented by the glow of the sunset coming through the window and the darkness of the hut. Then she heard a sound—a stifled sob—coming from a dark corner cot.

Mary crept over quietly. Anne's body curled in on itself like an insect trying to protect its soft bits, only Anne had no hard parts to hide inside. Mary leaned over and touched her. Anne's back shook beneath her hand, curved in so that her spine stood out beneath Mary's fingers in little knobs. Anne pulled away from her touch and Mary heard her body shifting on the palm fronds that lined the bed frame. Then Anne's hand caught hers.

Mary stood awkwardly, at war with herself. She was afraid to offer comfort, afraid of giving in to Anne's tears in the dark, afraid of what that could lead to. Afraid of what she wanted it to lead to.

She was ashamed that she'd consider her own fear above Anne's sadness.

Anne's sniffles quieted and the air became very still.

Mary settled quietly on the bed—just a hip. Her eyes adjusted to the diffused light. Everything was warm and shadowy. Anne's mussed hair, her dark eyes, her bare feet. Mary had never seen anything more beautiful. "If Nat's back," Mary whispered, "that means Jack's back, too."

"I know," Anne said, sitting up slowly. "I've been trying to tell meself . . . that all I have to do is go to him, and get him to find James for me . . ." She leaned forward and her lips touched Mary's cheek, just beside her mouth.

Mary turned her face and their lips met, soft at first and then fiercely, and Mary tasted salt and couldn't tell if it was Anne's tears or her own that were slipping down her cheeks.

This *had* to stop. If anyone knew that this was happening—Mary pulled away, fingers clenching into fists. "We can't," she gasped. "This is madness."

Anne gazed at her, steady and dark, her breath audible and irregular. She leaned forward, chemise slipping from her shoulder, and caught Mary's hand.

Mary had to turn away.

She almost succeeded.

A sound came out of her, frustration and sadness and longing all mixed together, as she gave into Anne's pull. Anne met her lips warmly, put her hands on her waist, and drew her in. James had hit Anne and held her down, and Mary hadn't been able to stop him. Anne's whole body was pressed against hers, their legs tangling. Robbie had pressed her up against the wall. Anne moved against her but Mary couldn't focus, her mind too full of everything. Nat had walked away without looking back. Anne's hand slid down her thigh, and Mary pushed it away.

Anne stopped moving. Her breathing quieted as she stared at Mary.

Mary ran a finger over Anne's perfect collarbones, unable to meet her eyes. "This—whatever this is, we can't do it anymore."

"I know you think the worst of me." Anne's voice quavered. "But there has to be a way—"

"There's not. Don't you remember what just happened? James will be back, and I can't protect you."

"We can get another pistol!"

Mary squeezed her eyes shut and clenched her fists. "I need you to convince Jack to pay off James, Anne. That way I'll know you're taken care of." Her voice almost broke. "I can't be the girl I want to be when I'm with you."

"That girl—she doesn't even compare to who you really are, you know that?" Anne touched her face.

"I—I want to be with Nat." She looked away. "And this, whatever it is—it has to end."

Fresh tears slipped down Anne's cheeks. "Aye. Nat will make a proper woman out of you, won't he."

Hopelessness overwhelmed Mary. She shifted her body and pulled Anne's head against her shoulder. "Shh, please, don't cry. Everything is going to work out fine for us," she whispered into Anne's hair. "Tomorrow I'll go find Nat, and you'll go find Jack, and it'll be what's best for both of us."

Anne pushed away and looked at her, gaze searching.

Mary prayed Anne saw how dry her eyes were, and believed her words were true.

CHAPTER FORTY-FOUR

NEW PROVIDENCE—1720

MARY SLIPPED INTO THE BACK OF THE SMALL, WHITEWASHED CHURCH. She was late, but thankfully a hymn blocked out the sound of the opening door and no one noticed her enter. She'd only just realized that it was Sunday when she woke. She'd shaken Anne awake and tried to convince her to come, but Anne had curled toward the wall and refused.

She was desperate to find Nat and thank him, but when she spotted him sitting off to one side, bloody Robbie was next to him. It was galling that he'd still sit with Robbie after how he'd threatened her, but she should have expected as much. The back pew was empty, and Mary sat down where she had a good view of Nat.

On the other side of Robbie sat a girl with just his shade of hair. When the girl turned her head to smile at Robbie, the line of her jaw mirrored the one that turned toward her. Then she leaned past Robbie and smiled at Nat, and Nat smiled back at her as he repeated each line of the hymn the priest sang.

Let those refuse to sing
Who never knew our God—

It was Robbie's sister. The one Nat had said Robbie wanted him to settle down with.

Mary watched Nat and the girl, cataloging every glance they threw at each other. More on the girl's side than Nat's—but he cast plenty her way. And when their eyes finally met, the smile on both their faces was real, shy and warm.

Mary's insides roiled. Nat had told her he couldn't stop thinking about *her* when he was with Robbie's sister—but as he smiled at the girl, it didn't look like he was thinking about anyone else.

It was hot in the church, the air stiflingly close. Mary was sweating profusely when the hymn ended. Finally Nat glanced around the church, twisting to see behind him, and his gaze landed on Mary. She straightened and lifted a hand—but his eyes slid by without acknowledging her as he turned back around.

Mary stared at the back of the girl's head, stomach burning. Two identical ringlets framed her slender neck, the rest of her hair sleekly pinned up. Mary touched her ragged braid. She could try all she liked, but she had no idea how to begin to emulate that kind of prettiness.

What if she tried as hard as she could, and Nat still rejected her? Would she try to be a good woman because the governor thought she should? Because God wanted her to, when God had never given her a sign He cared?

Mary squeezed her eyes shut. *Here I am, God,* she prayed. *I'm trying to do it right*. She needed to know Heaven was waiting for her, if she just tried hard enough. But no matter how quietly she sat, longing with all her might, there was no sign that He heard her.

The congregation began to murmur, and it echoed loudly off the bare walls. Mary opened her eyes and realized that the service had ended. Her hair was sticking to her neck, her chemise clinging to her armpits and back. She wanted to run to the beach, to cool off where there was water and a wind, but she made herself walk toward the altar as the congregation stood and began to mill about. She needed Nat to meet her eyes.

Nat's gaze landed on Mary as she approached, but he looked away quickly as Robbie's sister said something, her hand on his arm.

"Hallo, Nat," Mary said, trying to keep her voice steady. The front of the church was so hot, so full of bodies pressing close.

"Mary," said Nat stiffly, sweat standing out on his forehead. Mary jumped as he took her hand and kissed it—she still wasn't used people treating her as a lady. "I'm glad to see you made it."

Robbie smiled at her smugly, looking unaffected by the heat. "Livie, this is that mate of Nat's I told you about. The one who used to be a boy."

"Oh, hallo, Mary!" Livie said cheerfully, perspiration lending a lovely glow to her skin. "I must say, I've heard quite a bit about you."

Mary couldn't acknowledge either of them. "Nat," Mary said again. "I was hoping that we could—"

"Not now," Nat said quickly, avoiding her eyes. "I need to catch Rogers before he leaves."

"But—" Mary started, but he was already gone with Robbie.

"Poor dear," said Livie, "that's quite a bruise you've got on your temple. Whatever happened?" She leaned in to take a closer look, nothing but concern in her eyes.

Mary put a hand to her face, struggling to breathe. She couldn't stand the stagnant air in the sanctuary another moment. "Excuse me," she said, trembling, and turned and fled outside.

CHAPTER FORTY-FIVE

New Providence—1720

Mary sat at Molly's stall, hunched despondently over her piece-work. When Mary had returned from church the day before, Anne had still been lying there in her chemise, her skin slick with sweat. Mary had tried to engage with Anne. She'd tried to be friendly, even tried to be flirtatious, but Anne hadn't responded to anything with more than a yes or no. Anne had said she felt sick, and wouldn't eat anything Mary had offered. Her face was swollen and bruised again, worse than Mary's, but she'd refused Mary's offer to take a closer look.

When she'd left the hut that morning, Anne still hadn't gotten out of bed.

Mary looked up at the sound of palmettos shifting and saw Livie approaching Molly's stall through the dappled light beneath the palm trees. Mary's stomach tightened. She wished Molly would hurry back from her house with her pennies. Mary was only minding the stall while Molly fetched payment for her.

"Hallo, Mary!" Livie said cheerfully. "Good to see you again."

"Livie," Mary said stiffy.

"You're looking well, Mary." Livie stopped in front of the stall, a delicate sweat beading her brow, a friendly smile on her lips. "It looks like that bruising is going down quickly."

Mary bent back over her work. "Quick enough, I suppose." It was a gusset for an elbow—a particularly troubling piece of stitching, all angles. Nothing forgiving about it.

"I thought I might find you here. Nat said you worked for the sempstress." Livie cleared her throat as she looked away, running her hands over a bolt of gold chintz. "I've need of a dress, Mary."

Mary set her needle down. "Describe what you've need of," she said, trying to keep the irritation from her voice. The sooner she helped Livie, the sooner she would leave.

"Well." Livie gave her a sly look. "It's to be for a special occasion. Silk, if possible, and I'll want it in a color that suits me."

"We have that organza silk in blue—well, sort of an indigo, really—and a pale green color. The green would look lovely with your hair and eyes. Here, I'll show you—" She got off her stool, feeling a pang as she thought of Anne's ruined dress. She'd dreamed of making her another out of silk, once she'd saved up enough pennies, but she'd barely worked the calico off. She'd have to make Anne's replacement out of cheaper material.

"Blue, that's perfect!" Livie put a theatrical hand to her heart. "My mother always said that blue was the proper color for a wedding dress."

Mary sat back down. "A wedding dress," she said slowly. She knew the answer before she even asked. "Who's the lucky gentleman?"

Livie's eyes widened guilelessly. "Why, Nat, of course! I thought you were close? Surely he told you?"

Of course Nat's drunken touch didn't mean anything. Of course he was going to marry this girl—the kind of girl he'd always wanted to marry.

Not Mary.

She had wanted to marry him. She remembered when she'd wanted that so badly, when she was back in Wapping, still holding tight to her secret. She'd imagined a ring on her finger, a dress. A marriage-house, like Mum, or a chapel for a real wedding. Nat standing by an altar, waiting for her.

But her longing was different now. She could sew it up, take it in here and let it out there, dress it as something else, and alter its shape so others found it suitable—but what she really wanted sprawled deeper and wider and wilder than anything she could name. She didn't want a marriage. Not the kind of marriage Nat wanted, not marriage like it existed within the whitewashed walls of that church.

She'd make Livie a beautiful dress, like the one she made for Anne. The dress that Anne had worn when she threatened Robbie with a wooden spoon in Mary's defense—when she drew Mary in by that palm tree and sighed against her lips—when she'd slowly taken it off, not dropping Mary's gaze.

"Congratulations, Livie," she said, feeling strangely giddy as she stood again. "We'd be happy to make your dress. Come here, I'll show you what I've got."

CHAPTER FORTY-SIX

New Providence—1720

MARY FELT INCREDIBLE.

She tucked her chemise-turned-shirt into the waistband of her new, cornflower blue britches. Britches were *so* much simpler to sew than dresses, and they felt so right! She'd finally made her dress feel like *her*, like she was supposed to be wearing it.

She'd run back from Molly's stall once she'd returned and had spent the past few hours ripping out seams and reassembling her dress in a hunched frenzy. She tore a long stretch of fabric and bound herself tightly, then dressed, shook out her hair, and did her best to queue it in a sailor's pigtail. Anne walked in right as she was finishing.

"Annie! Look, I finally gave in. Turned me dress into a pair of britches." She stood and spread her hands.

Anne stared. She had a freshly plucked chicken in her hand, and Mary momentarily wondered where she'd gotten the bird. They hadn't money for something like that.

And she was wearing a new dress. An ill-fitting one made of cheap linen, but still. Mary started to feel unsure, but she continued. "I realized I was being an arse, and I want to make it up to you," she said. "I—I'm going to Hog's Island, they'll let me join up on the next mission, I just know it, and then *I'll* pay off bloody James." Her gaze fell on a pearl necklace around Anne's throat, just above the bruises James had left there. "Or we'll find passage on a ship with the money I make—you won't need to marry Jack at all, and you'll be rid of James—" She was blathering—ridiculous, transparent. Where did Anne get a *pearl necklace*? Mary wished she'd never started talking.

Anne dropped her gaze. The sun was already visible through the windows. Had so much time passed? Mary sidled up to her like a crab, graceless and over-guarded. "What happened?" she asked carefully.

Anne's spark was gone. She trembled when Mary touched her, skin ashy and damp. "I woke up and you were gone. I went to Hog's Island. I thought I'd just run away, find passage off this island somehow, but James is on to me." Anne didn't look up as she walked by Mary and put the chicken on the table, its head lolling off the side. "He told everyone I'm not to leave, and that he's got the governor behind him. And Jack was out there, helping unload the spoils from Burgess's brig. He was sweet to me, Mary. He gave me this necklace, and money to replace me ruined dress, and I just realized that . . . you're right." She slumped. "He's not so bad."

"What happened?" Mary asked tightly.

"I—I told Jack what happened with James, and he went straight away to talk to him. Jack promised him his earnings from the mission if—if James goes to Rogers and asks for the annulment." Anne groped for her hand and squeezed it. Mary couldn't bring herself to squeeze back. "When he heard what Jimmy did, Mary—Jack cares about me. He's a good man." She took a shuddering breath. "If I marry him, he'll make sure Jimmy never touches me again."

"You're going to marry Jack." Mary felt suddenly lightheaded. She put a hand on the table to steady herself.

"He knows what it's like to be taken advantage of. When he was first taken on as the pirate captain's cabin boy—that man, he did horrible things to him. Jack knows what it's like to be under someone else's power. Whatever else he is—he's never meant to hurt me." She looked up entreatingly. "When he first fell in love with me he saw how James treated me, and it reminded him of what happened to him. And now he's come to his senses. He's done being angry with me."

Mary turned away. She couldn't bear to look at Anne. She took a slow breath, trying to calm her accelerating heart.

Mum had been right. Being a boy was worth any sacrifice. All that freedom, and all she'd had to give up was herself. If she'd been a boy, she could have protected Anne. She would have gone on that privateering mission, come back with that string of pearls. She could marry Anne, she could demand that divorce. Mary had always been poor, she had always been powerless, but this was the first time she couldn't find any way to fight it.

This was the difference between living as a girl, and living as a boy. How could she have been so foolish?

"Once Jimmy talks to Rogers," Anne said hesitantly, "then all we'll need is a witness, and the governor's signature, and I'll be free."

"Free to marry Jack." Mary dropped onto the bed, sitting uselessly. She was useless. What was the use of someone who couldn't work and couldn't protect you and couldn't be herself and couldn't be someone else?

She was no one, she was nothing.

Anne sat beside her. "You said you wanted this." Anne's voice was deathly quiet.

"I know." She should be happy for Anne. There was no place in the world for the two of them together.

"Is it still what you want?" Anne's eyes were bright. Her voice hitched.

You.

I want you.

I want all *of you.*

She'd kept the thoughts buried so far down, they came over her so fast—they almost rushed from her mouth—

She barely kept them in.

She *would not* say them. She'd been this close—and Anne had chosen someone else.

"Aye." Mary's voice was so hard, it surprised her. "I'm done being nothing more to you than a distraction."

Anne pulled away. "What—what do you mean?"

Mary's pulse accelerated. "I should've never talked to you again after the way you treated me after I put me secret out for all to see, back on that island—when you bloody *applauded* when your man undressed me! 'Oooh, mistress Reade, let your bosoms out! Let 'em breathe, sweetheart!' No? That wasn't you?"

"I can't believe you're going on about that," said Anne, drawing away as she stood. "We would've been shot by Jack if you hadn't revealed your bloody precious secret. It was you I was applauding!"

"I risked my life, Anne—for *you!*" Mary jumped to her feet. Standing, she had a good inch or so on Anne. That felt good. "Don't act as if I wasn't just part of some game you was playing to get back at Jack—and me playing right along! 'What's that, Annie dear? Kiss you *where*? Why, it's almost as if you really wanted me!'"

Mary realized she was shouting—so loudly—but she couldn't stop, the anger and sadness a surging wave inside her. It felt like her lungs were collapsing—she couldn't breathe. "And this!" she gasped. "This is just the same. You using me while it's convenient, while Jack is away—then you sail off when you see the tide's about to turn. You're faithless, Anne—I knew it all along, but I was stupid enough to think—" She couldn't finish. She'd thought—what? That they could live happily together forever?

Anne looked like she'd been slapped. Good. Maybe Anne was feeling something real, for once.

"Is—is that really what you think of me?" Anne's voice was small, the room suddenly so quiet after their shouting. The surf crashing outside like it was about to rush in the front door and drown them both. "You really think I care so little."

"It doesn't matter." Mary dropped into a chair. "Marrying Jack's the best way to keep your head above water." She felt herself deflating. "No sense in drowning along with me."

A flash of light came in as the sailcloth lifted. Jack came in, arms full of bread loaves and a round of cheese. "Mary!" he said. "Did Annie tell you the good news?"

"I told her," said Anne loudly. Her cheeks were flushed, eyes bright with tears, her fingers toying with the pearls around her neck. "She's thrilled to get me off her hands."

Mary tried to say something. She tried to speak, to curse or congratulate—

Jack laughed. "Annie, girl!" He pushed past Mary. "Mind your cheek, now!" He lifted Anne into the air—

Mary stumbled to the door.

She ran, feet sliding in sand. She pushed their little boat down to the water—she jumped inside—

She rowed. Big, heaving strokes. She gulped air, arms aching. Her eyes burned. She saw Jack lifting Anne into the air, letting her slowly down—kissing her mouth—Mary wished she'd never kissed her. She wished she'd never met her, that Jack had picked some other ship to attack that day. She wished *Kapitein* Baas had locked her and Paddy in the hold and sailed back to Rotterdam. She wished she'd never set foot in this new world. Then at least she could still imagine there was a place out there for her, instead of knowing there was no place at all.

She heaved past Hog's Island and kept going, her back to the sun.

Gradually she slowed. She looked over her shoulder, at the wide ocean. She looked at New Providence, nestled on the far side of Hog's Island, jungle all around. The sky was pinking. It would be dark soon. She couldn't stay out here—she'd be lost by morning.

She was lost already.

Wherever she went, no one would take her in.

She drifted, anchorless and alone.

CHAPTER FORTY-SEVEN

ROTTERDAM—1717

THE *QUEEN CATHERINE* SAILED ON THE EVENING TIDE, AND MARY watched her go. Alone in the cold, still air. Alone on a strange dock in a strange city, with nothing to her name.

He'd seen her. She'd clung shivering to a barnacled pile beneath the docks for hours, then found a ladder up from below when her panic eased. He'd seen her climbing from the water, clothes clinging to her body, water streaming from her hair. When she looked up, wiping water from her eyes, he was standing by the gunwale. He stared down, dark-eyed and beautiful.

She stood and met his gaze.

She was clean. The blood washed from her face, the filth washed from her body.

She stood and let him see her.

He saw her, and still he sailed away.

CHAPTER FORTY-EIGHT

New Providence—1720

Mary stalked through the empty market square blindly. Gas lamps flickered as a sea breeze caught the flames. The tavern, busy on the far side, grew louder as she approached—probably Burgess's crew was inside, spending their windfall. She could have been there, if she was Mark. She would have been there gladly, drinking with them, if they would let her.

Where did she think she was going? She couldn't walk up the bar and face those lucky men. She couldn't go back to the hut—not if Jack and Anne had left, not if they were still there, not if only Anne was there, with sad looks and soft hands and sweet eyes—

"Mary Reade!" A voice called from the darkness beneath a well-lit tavern window.

She didn't turn. Since she'd become Mary, whenever someone slurred at her from the tavern, it wasn't to say anything she was interested in hearing.

"Mary! Otherwise known as Mark. C'mere you. Me old mate." The voice faded, words running together. Nat? She'd hardly recognized his voice, drunk as he was. She turned and stomped back to the tavern. Maybe she'd convince him to buy her a drink or six with his newfound wealth. Maybe she could forget for the night that no one wanted her.

He was sitting on the sandy street against the tavern's wall, listing to one side. Voices and laughter spilled out of the window above his head. She didn't look in, in case Robbie or Jimmy caught her eye.

She ducked beneath the window and crouched beside Nat. "How are you, mate?"

"Good, good. Just lovely." His head fell back as he looked up at her. He looked sweet and simple, softened by drink. He looked like the boy she'd known—and she looked like the boy he'd known, too, back in her britches.

She patted his hand. "I heard you made a killing with Burgess."

He nodded. "Aye. I've got money enough to build a house for me and Livie now. I'm to marry her, you know." His brow furrowed. "I'm going to be a married man. That's what we're over here celebrating."

She gave him another pat. "Congratulations, mate."

"Mary, Mary, Mary." He cocked his head. "We had some good times together, didn't we? Remember when we used to play at Captain Avery and his mates, down on the docks? An' I was always captain?" He gave her a sloppy shove. "Why'd you let me get away with that, now? God knows I made a terrible captain!"

She smiled, in spite of herself. "You made a fine captain, Nat. Anyway, I was too afraid to be captain meself. Always trying not to be noticed."

He snorted. "Not like now. Mary, Mary, Mary. In your britches. With your hair done up like a sailor, though everyone knows you're a girl. Sure, everyone notices you. They all want to hear your story."

She rolled her eyes. "Do they, now."

He nodded seriously. "People ask, 'Why does she go about like that?' but also, 'Why shouldn't she?' 'S very confusing. People don't like to think so much."

She snorted. If only they knew that she was more confused than anyone.

"Mary, Mary, Mary." He rested his head against the wall. "I still can't quite figure you. I shouldn't like you. You, looking for all the world like a boy jus' as soon as you ditch your skirts."

She felt her skin tingle. "You still like me, even though I'm—even when I look like this."

He smiled and raised his eyebrows.

The buzz of voices behind them got louder, and a couple of women flounced out the door, dragging laughing men behind them. One of them caught Mary's eye and winked as she passed.

Nat whispered, "They ask me, 'D'you think she's ever loved a man?' I never know what to answer to that."

She fought to steady her breathing. "There was a boy I loved, once."

He looked solemn. "It was me, wasn't it."

"Aye."

Nat frowned, his eyes going fuzzy. "I shouldn't kiss you," he said.

Mary exhaled. "No, I suppose you shouldn't."

"I never should've wanted to, when I thought you was a boy."

"Wait, now—" Mary pushed away and looked at him. "You wanted to kiss me when—back in *London?*"

"It felt so wrong having thoughts like that about me best mate. And now of course there's Livie." He leaned forward, staring at her mouth. "It'd be wrong, wouldn't it?"

And he kept leaning forward.

Mary held very still and closed her eyes. When his lips touched hers they were light and sweet. Too sweet—he'd been drinking rum, she could taste it on her mouth when she pulled away.

He'd wanted to kiss her, when he thought she was a boy. He wanted to kiss her now, though she still looked like one.

Mary stood. "Do you have any spirits back at your kip?"

"Aye, I do. But there's plenty to drink here . . ." He trailed off, his mind working slowly. "Oh. Or . . . we could go to me kip, sure. I've got a bit of rum there." He started to his feet.

Mary glanced in the window and saw Robbie looking around.

She grabbed Nat's arm and yanked him out of sight, pressing against the wall next to the window and pulling him to her. She sighed when he groaned and dug his fingers into her waist.

She could make him want her. He wanted her right now, and she'd hardly done a thing.

This was so much easier than Anne. She might not want to marry Nat anymore, but *this* she still wanted.

"Take me home," she whispered.

And just like that, he did.

CHAPTER FORTY-NINE

New Providence—1720

Nat lived up the hill, in more of a tent than anything else—three walls, a lean-to roof, nothing but sailcloth at the front. The fort loomed above. A few men stood sentry, silhouetted against a starry sky, staring out over the battlements for any sign of the Spanish. The moon was huge and bright. Mary could see the spikes of their bayonets, the peaks of their brims, the rock and mortar detail of the wall.

"With the money I've made I can buy real lumber from the northern colonies," Nat said, pulling up the flap of cloth that hung from the roof. "Me own *house*. Who'd have thought a boy from Wapping could come so far?" He gestured past the threshold: a pallet, a crude table and chair, a messy pit with dead coals scattered around. "Soon this mess will be more magnificent than your Granny's place ever was. That's what this land is about. Any man can make it here, no matter what he came from."

Any *man* was right. She held her tongue. "You've done well, Nat," she agreed. "Things are working out for you just splendidly."

"They are, aren't they?" He paused. "It's nice for you to see that, you knowing what we came from."

What about her? She'd come from the same. She could do anything he could. Why did her life look so different? "Where's that rum you promised?"

"Do you ever think about it, where we came from?" he asked, ducking into the hut. "Do you ever think about your mum, where she might be now?"

"I like to think she got out of there," began Mary, then had to stop. All she could think was that she knew how lonely Mum must have been when Mary's da held his arms open to her. She knew how imagining love would be a certain way would make her fall into them—

She knew now that really falling was nothing like the dream of it.

Mary swallowed her sadness. "I'd like to think she found the pluck to leave, once I was gone."

It was dark in the hut, after the sailcloth dropped. Mary pushed the cloth back up and tucked the end beneath the lean-to roof, to let some moonlight in.

"What would me mum say if she could see me in this uniform, eh?" Nat asked. "That's what I like to think of. She always thought I'd end up a good-for-nothing pirate like me da."

Her smile faded fast. "Oh, aye. You call it privateering, you get your signed bloody paper and go off and do the same thing but swear it's something altogether dif—"

"It *is* different!" he growled, grabbing her wrist. "I'm nothing like him, what he was."

"Oh, sure—"

Nat silenced her with his mouth, quick and hard, and pulled her into the darkness.

She tried to be soft, at first, like Anne had told her, but it left her stiff and awkward, Nat's heat deadened by her hesitation. She tried to melt, she tried to be delicate—but she was so *angry* about Anne, about Jack and Nat and their money and how she couldn't go home and how home wasn't here—and next thing she knew she had him up against a wall, she was meeting his heat with equal intensity and that felt good, much better—there was something about their not-softness, him getting hard, her fighting back instead of giving in—

He had her binding off with rushed fingers and quick as he had it off she had him down on the pallet, she had his hands against the table leg with one fist, looping her binding tight around his wrists with the other. It was a heavy table, rough-cut logs for legs. Maybe she was stronger than she'd thought because his struggling only tightened her grip, only made her binding knot tighter against his skin until he was helpless beneath her.

She felt her anger ebb. She paused and leaned back on her haunches, breathing hard.

He looked beautiful. Soft, in shadow. Lashes, a slick lip. Bare chest rising and falling.

"Please," he whispered, longing clear in his voice.

This wasn't how she'd dreamed it would be with Nat. But it felt as heated as her old dreams had been, him begging beneath her. It felt good to stand and drop her clothes because she wanted to, instead of them being lifted from her.

Mary crouched, tucked her fingers into his britches. His hips lifted to let her pull them down, his breath sucked in. She kissed him, and didn't kiss him, as she liked. She ran her hands all over, and he had no hands to touch her. The air grew warmer and warmer, their skin sticky, then wet, their bodies harder and softer at the same time, then harder and softer still—

The smell of him, of them, alcohol and sweat, heat and salt—

He breathed heavily, making soft sounds in his throat. Her hair slipped free of its pigtail and slicked to her shoulders and neck. Her body was wiry and strong and he wanted it. It didn't matter that she was so hopelessly in-between.

She pressed her body into his, hands splayed against his chest, mouth on his neck. He shuddered, his groaning turned to gasps, the muscles in his arms bunching as he arched and strained against his restraints.

The knots held. He never touched her.

He was asleep in moments afterward, his arms still bound above his head, his face tucked against a shoulder.

She sat up for hours, night air drying her skin, and stared at his trusting, sleeping shape. She wanted to feel like this forever.

Finally she stood, pulled her shirt and britches on, and left, leaving her binding tangled around him.

CHAPTER FIFTY

NEW PROVIDENCE—1720

AS SHE SLIPPED OUT NAT'S DOOR, MARY LOOKED UP TOWARD THE BATtlements of the fort and saw a man staring down at her in the early morning light. She knew who it was. She would always remember that silhouette staring down at her.

She imagined him squinting, trying to puzzle out who was leaving Nat's hovel at this hour, wearing britches. She didn't try to hide. She waited until she was sure Robbie knew it was her.

He had taken Nat from her in Rotterdam, but Mary had taken him back. Even when Nat belonged to someone else, even when he married Livie, she'd still have a bit of him.

Robbie disappeared from the battlements. She was sure he'd seen her.

He could wonder what she'd done.

Mary ran down to the water and shed her clothes. She slipped beneath the waves and swam with powerful strokes until she was far out. She floated face up in the early morning light and watched dolphin fins slice the surface a few yards away, everything around her silver and glimmering as the sun began to rise.

Remember when we used to play at Captain Avery and his mates, down on the docks? An' I was always captain? Mum and Granny bossing her around as a child, then the *kapitein*, then Jack. Robbie and James. Even Anne. All of them using her to further their own games, taking the captain's share of the prize while she risked her neck. Always, leaving her with nothing.

Hog's Island shone on the other side of the harbor, its skirt of ships sparkling in the sunlight.

Her arms began to ache, her eyelids growing heavy. The sky was getting brighter. She could see all of Nassau huddled along the shore, the fort hulking above. Guarded and shadowed. Too small for her—too small for Anne—though they'd tried to bind themselves enough to fit.

What if she saw Jack from Anne's perspective—as something like she'd seen Nat last night? Not home, but something close enough. Safe harbor in the storm. Anne, beaten back every time she tried to claim a haven of her own. It was easy to seek refuge in open arms. She thought of a lighthouse, its strong beam of light. A clear path to follow in the confusion of darkness.

She hadn't known, until last night, that it could be so easy to claim what she wanted. Her body went hot—she'd wanted Nat. But it wasn't what she wanted most.

She wanted a ship to sail away in. One of those brigs, anchored at the island. She even knew which one she'd take. But that wasn't all she wanted, either.

She let pure longing rise up like a wave inside her. Anne's dark gaze, the heat of her skin, the quickness of her laugh. Tangled up in her, fitting so perfectly. They'd had so little time, just the two of them, that hadn't been marred by desperation and distrust. Mary could spend every moment with her, explore every inch of her skin, every nuance of her emotions, hear every story and opinion, memorize every motion and expression, and never be done wanting more.

Her strokes grew sloppy, her head bobbing under the surface. It made her so tired to think of what she wanted. Quiet enveloped her underwater, a soothing blue. The ocean was big. Big enough to hold her and hide her, no one down in its depths to deny her. Paddy was down here, somewhere. Perhaps the father she'd never met was down here, too, another hapless tar lost in the confusion of a storm.

She breathed out and sank slowly, watching bubbles spiral to the surface. She looked out at the endless, brilliant blue. This is what the heaven they promised must be like. A place where He will surround you in quiet, beautiful oblivion. He will get rid of your wanting. He will make the struggle go away.

She looked down, where the blue went dark and deep. She was so tired.

But the water was vast and lonely. She didn't want the ocean holding her, or God.

She wanted Anne.

CHAPTER FIFTY-ONE

CARIBBEAN SEA—1719

MARY SQUINTED AT THE LOW RIBBON OF LAND SLOWLY MATERIALIZING against the unimaginably blue water as Paddy finished cinching a knot beside her. The view from the mainsail yard was incredible. A spit of green curved out of a gentle slope of mountains, and the promise of a city—a warm, deep harbor surrounded by alehouses and markets and blessed dry land—lay just beyond that.

Willemstad, Curaçao.

After near three backbreaking, brine-soaked months at sea, she would not sail back to Europe on this ship. Apparently the captain and officers had ways of keeping the crew on board. Padlocks and keys, pistols and bayonets. But Mary knew from experience that there were ways to jump ship that the *kapitein* might not have thought of.

First bell, afternoon watch, clanged from the quarterdeck. She guessed the ship should be passing the tip of the island by third bell, no more than an hour from now.

An hour from now. And after that—might they make port by tonight?

Mary's nerves jumped as she thought of dropping anchor. She looked at Paddy. "What do you think, is *Kapitein* Baas-tard letting us off the *Vissen* tonight?" she asked, legs dangling on either side of the yard.

Paddy shook his head with alarming resignation. "Speaking from me own experience, I'm inclined to doubt it." He didn't care; all he wanted was a way back to Wapping with enough coin at the end of it to woo his Katie. He'd given up on the notion of debarking. "A bit of fresh meat and water is the best we can hope for tonight," he said. "The likes of us won't be seeing the insides of an island alehouse, mark me words. Standard practice, it is."

"I'm getting off this ship tonight, Baas be damned," Mary said, then wished she hadn't. She sounded petulant, defiant, like a child thinking she was entitled to something a wiser sailor knew he'd never get. "I have to get to Nassau."

"So you've told me." He gave her a sad smile and reached up to grab the ratline. "Believe me, son. I hope to God you get your wish."

Mary followed him as he swung himself up the rungs. Paddy knew she planned to jump ship once they reached shore. It hadn't worked for any sailors he'd known. But still, he was willing to entertain the idea that it might just work for her.

It *had* to work. She wouldn't leave the Indies before finding Nat.

She couldn't believe it had been over nine months since she'd seen him last. She'd wasted so much time in Rotterdam, working the docks, holding tight to her secret. Earning next to nothing mending sails and running messages, afraid to return to London. She'd met Paddy at a tavern one particularly maudlin night, and he'd convinced her it was worth it to sail west in October with him on a Dutch trader, the *Zilveren Vissen*.

Paddy turned once he reached the topgallant yard. "I never did tell you how I got me these tattoos, did I?" Paddy gestured to the faint nautical star on his left bicep, one of an almost-matching pair. They were said to protect those who inked them on their bodies from all dangers at sea. "Did I tell you about the time Katie was giving me the second one here—"

She rolled her eyes. "Why yes, I'm afraid you've bored me to tears on a number of occasions." Mary swung herself onto the starboard side of the yard and reached for a handful of sailcloth. Once they climbed past the mainsail yard the wind picked up, and it was good to have an extra grip.

"I swear to you, she hadn't a chance to finish the second tattoo when the press gang busted in."

Mary couldn't believe it; he was truly about to launch into this story again. Paddy settled on the far side of the topgallant yard, a leg hanging on either side. "You can see here where the line ain't quite done—" He pulled his skin tight so that she might see the tattoo he'd shown her a thousand times. Mary did her best to look entirely uninterested, peering around for something more entertaining. Sea birds crowded the rigging all around them, screeching and roosting on the yards. The birds had colonized the *Zilveren Vissen* soon after they entered the islands, and they were disappointingly similar to the gulls back home, all black and gray and white. Not the promised swarms of rainbowed parrots—but they had thrilled her nonetheless. They'd signaled that she was almost *there*, where she'd longed to be ever since Nat had left her on that dock.

"I was yelling over me shoulder about how I'd be back for her, and she was crying, screaming that she'd wait for me—" Paddy shook his head and dropped his arm. "Sure, you don't know what it's like, do you? You're too bloody young."

She turned back to him. "What what's like?"

"Love. Being in love."

"I do, though!" What had carried her halfway around the world?

"No, you don't. Whoever she was, she was a child. Just like you."

"At least she wasn't a loose woman," Mary taunted.

Paddy narrowed his eyes. "Careful now."

"I mean, how can you know it's love with Katie? She lays with other men."

He shrugged. "She may, but it's different with me."

"Sure, that's what you tell yourself."

Paddy rubbed his starred bicep absentmindedly. "Well, it's not any different, mechanically speaking."

Mary smirked. "So what makes you think you're special?"

"See, this is how I know you haven't been in love before." He winked. "It's how I know you haven't lain with a woman, neither."

"Hey now," Mary protested.

"The mechanics—that's part of it. But there's all these other bits to it. And all those bits are different with everyone, and that's what makes it beautiful, and that's what makes it hurt, and that's what makes it feel like there's a point to everything—not the bloody mechanics. You'll know the difference when it happens to you."

"So you never felt anything like that before Katie."

"No, I felt it before Katie. It doesn't happen with just one lass ever, or even just one lass at a time. But it's different with each person, and you only feel it if it's something special. Otherwise—it's just a transaction, and it doesn't worry me none."

The way Mary had longed to touch Nat—the heat of her dreams about him—she knew what she felt for him was special. Her feelings just hadn't been *enough*. Nat didn't feel the same way. She hadn't given him the chance to. "What if you get back and you're too late, you made a mistake, and now she's married to someone else?"

"I can't worry about that." Paddy closed his eyes and lifted his face to the sun. "It feels good to believe I'll make it to her in time. It keeps me going, thinking about how it is when I'm with her.

How I'm going to settle down with her one day. It makes me feel like it's worth it. All this shit."

Sweet Paddy. Nothing had ever gone right for him—but still, he always had hope. He always thought things might just work out. "So it doesn't matter that she might be engaged to some other cove? She's just a nice idea that makes you feel a little less cold at night?"

"Jaysus, no, it matters." He opened his eyes and gave her a piercing look. "Believe me, son. I might not worry about it now, seeing as there's nothing I can do about it. But if I got back and she was promised to some other man? You better believe I would fight like hell for her."

CHAPTER FIFTY-TWO

NEW PROVIDENCE—1720

MARY STOOD OUTSIDE THE HUT, THE AFTERNOON SUN BRIGHT BEHIND her. She'd returned there early in the morning, wet and shivering, but it had been empty. She'd collected her piecework with shaking hands and returned it to Molly. She'd taken her payment and bought hardtack and some fruit. She'd asked around about the new sloop she saw docked in the harbor. Robbie never crossed her path, though she kept an eye out for him.

And now she was back at the hut, dim movement visible through the windows. She stared the mermaid and dolphin sentinels down, willing herself to be brave enough to confront whatever lay inside. They stared back, impassive.

Mary walked to the door, her steps measured. One bare sole in front of the other. She pushed the weathered cloth aside and ducked into the room beyond.

Anne sat on the bed, still wearing that terrible dress, her eyes huge and glittering in the dimness. "You came back," she said. "I was beginning to think I'd never see you again."

"Jack left you here alone?"

"He left me his pistol." Anne shrugged. "And Jimmy wants his money. I don't think he'll be after me now."

"Has Jack made an honest woman out of you yet?" Mary asked, bracing herself.

Anne bowed her head. "He's gone with Jimmy to talk to the governor." Anne's hands, twisting in her lap, looked like a wild animal that she was trying to restrain. When she raised her head, her face was drawn. "I know you think the worst of me," she whispered, "but I never meant to hurt you."

Mary strode across the room, speaking before she could lose her nerve. "I don't think so little of you." She knelt and took Anne's hands. "I think you're incredible."

Anne squeezed her eyes shut. "I wish things could be different between us. But you were right. There's no way this could work."

"I was wrong, Anne." Mary took a deep, shuddering breath. "There is a way." This was so hard. Every fiber of her body screamed—*she'll refuse you again, you'll hurt again*.

But this was it. She needed to be bold. A clear light, when everything raged all around. Otherwise they'd both drown in darkness. "I'm leaving Nassau," Mary said. "And I want you to come with me."

Anne's head snapped up. She put her hands to her throat. "No," she whispered. She sounded strangled. "Don't ask me that. They won't let me off the island, remember? They'll catch the both of us trying to leave."

"I love you so much, Anne," Mary whispered. "I won't live without you." Anne's eyes clenched shut, a tear sliding down her cheek. Mary wiped it away, hand clumsy with nerves. "That's why we have to leave."

"We'll never make it." Anne began to shake. "We might get to Eleuthera in our jolly boat . . . but what would we do once we get there?"

"It doesn't matter. Florida or Africa, there's a whole world we haven't been to, that they won't find us in."

Anne pulled away. "The jolly boat won't get us to Florida."

"You're right. We need a ship of our own."

Anne stared at her. "You can't be serious."

"We've got no choice. There's no safety for you, and no life at all for someone like me. But I sailed across the ocean once." Mary started talking fast, excitement surging through her. "It wouldn't be so hard if we had the right ship. John Ham's ship is docked at Hog's Island as we speak. And I heard it's the fastest ship in the Caribbean. Fast enough to get us far away from here, and quick, to somewhere we can start over."

Anne shook her head, but her eyes began to brighten. "Just the two of us? You really think we could?"

Anne had stood on the deck of the *Zilveren Vissen* with a smoking pistol, a smirk on her lips. She'd raged beside the fire at Isla de Cotorras, stomping her feet and urging rebellion. She'd flaunted Bill's outstretched hand.

Mary squeezed Anne's hands and searched her eyes. "I'm the boy who shot the captain, who outwitted rich ladies and dangerous men her whole life. And you're the girl I met while she was bloody well taking over me ship. The one who stood over a bonfire and screeched at a mob of radicals and vagabonds about how craven they were. If anyone can manage it, I think it's the pair of us."

Anne grabbed Mary around the waist and threw herself back on the bed, and Mary toppled onto her with a surprised *oof*. "I'm in," Anne whispered fiercely against her cheek.

Mary laughed against her neck, and then kissed it, and Anne wrapped her legs around her and slid her hands up Mary's back and into her hair. Mary's mouth opened against her skin, and Anne's fingers tightened in her hair and she made a soft noise and suddenly Mary was fumbling Anne's dress off her with shaking hands, she couldn't wait another second for this—and her chemise was off as well and Anne was so bare and smooth and the way she moved, Mary couldn't keep her mouth off of her—Anne wedged her hands against Mary's shoulders and pushed her away.

Mary sat up and looked at her. She'd never get enough of looking at her. "What?" she whispered hoarsely, afraid that this was it. Anne's eyes were dark and unreadable as she reached up and grasped the front of Mary's shirt, tugging it free of her waistband. Mary faltered, twisting away. She had nothing beneath, no chemise or binding—but slowly she gave in, raising her arms, and let Anne pull the shirt from her.

Mary tried to cover herself but Anne held her hands down and stared at her body. It was different than when men had looked at her. It made Mary hot, instead of cold.

It made her so hot.

Anne pulled her in, her mouth against Mary's bare shoulder, and Mary slid a hand up her thigh and pressed into Anne and she was so soft, and then slick, and Anne hung onto her, hands bunching her shirt, making sounds that made Mary feel like she was going to explode—

Anne's hand slid below the waist of her britches—fingers grazed untouched skin—

Mary gasped as Anne touched her.

This time, she didn't push her away.

CHAPTER FIFTY-THREE

New Providence—1720

"Mary Reade." A man's voice.

Mary jumped to her feet, gasping, as Anne fumbled to sit up.

Robbie stood in the doorway, his bulk silhouetted by an orange sunset.

He smiled, and tapped a set of iron manacles against his thigh. "I've been looking for you."

Robbie let the cloth drop behind him. Mary lunged for her shirt and hastily pulled it on as Anne snatched up her chemise, breath accelerating. Mary faced Robbie, heart hammering, trying to block Anne from view.

Robbie cleared his throat. "I have more than enough evidence to prove that you're a woman of loose morals, Mary—one that poses a threat to our community—and that you need to be taken in, lest you poison those around you."

A dreadful thought occurred to Mary. *Don't say it. Don't tell Anne what I did.* She finished cinching her belt and turned to face him, crossing her arms.

"Is that so, Robbie?" asked Anne from behind her, her voice defiant. "Go ahead, then. Tell us what you have on Mary."

Mary and Robbie both looked at her. Anne sat on the edge of the pallet, still half-undressed, hair loose and wild around her shoulders. She held both their eyes for a moment, then looked pointedly at her lap.

A pistol was clenched in her hands, gleaming dully in the fading light.

Anne looked up again, a slight smile on her face. Robbie had a weapon, of course, tucked into his waistband—but he didn't reach for it. Mary was the only one without a firearm.

"You know why I'm here, Mary," said Robbie.

Mary said nothing.

"I don't," said Anne. "What is this new evidence? We both know all you have is a bunch of nonsense."

"Besides this, the two of you?" Robbie shook his head. "Better you don't know, love. The fewer people who know, the less chance this has of getting back to me sister before I take care of it."

"Your sister?" Anne paused, then looked at Mary. "You and Nat," she said slowly.

If Anne was acting, trying to lull Robbie into thinking his plan to divide them was working—she was doing a convincing job. Mary fought a rising sense of unease.

Robbie crossed his arms. "She went to him when he was celebrating his upcoming union, seduced him, and fornicated shamelessly. She needs to be locked away so she can't bring harm to anyone else." He narrowed his eyes at Anne. "Don't worry, Anne. I won't tell anyone what you've done with her. You'll get your divorce, I promise. I know how badly you want it."

"You and Nat—last night—?" Anne choked.

Robbie tsked. "What is it about you, Mary, that drives everyone mad? I'll confess, I don't understand."

"Listen, Anne, you were to marry Jack—" Mary started toward Anne but stopped when the pistol raised. "Can't you see—"

"I—you just said all those things to me, you just—not a *day* after you lay with him?"

Anne had to be acting.

"That's right," Robbie said, "Let me take her in, and I'll bring her to justice."

Anne's jaw set. She looked mad, capable of anything. She raised the pistol toward Mary. She glanced nervously at Robbie, and Mary felt her heart collapsing. She raised her hands in surrender.

"There you go." Robbie spoke again, his voice so soothing. "Turn her over to me, Anne, and I'll see to it you get your divorce. It's going to be so easy. You'll get what you want."

Anne looked at Mary. "Everything you just said. Everything that just happened." Her voice was small.

"Everything I said was true."

Robbie held out his hands. "Give her over to me and I'll make sure you're protected, Anne."

Anne stared at her, brow furrowed. She studied her for a long, long moment. Mary tried to say it with every bit of herself. *It's you I want.*

"Why do you think it's so easy for everyone else?" Robbie took a step toward Mary. "Why is it so easy for most girls to behave themselves, but it's so bloody hard for you?"

Anne swung the pistol around and discharged it with a yell. Robbie collapsed to the floor, screaming hoarsely. Mary shouted, starting forward—she hadn't thought Anne would *shoot* the bastard; now they were in real trouble. He sat up, teeth clenched fiercely, blood pooling beneath his calf. He lunged when Mary came close, hands groping for his pistol, and she danced away.

Well, since Anne *had* shot him—pity she hadn't got him worse.

Mary charged and kicked his wrist. Miraculously, his pistol went skidding to the corner as Robbie roared and curled around his hand.

She looked at Anne, panting. "I'm sorry I didn't tell you about Nat."

Anne stood and put a hand to Mary's cheek, and Mary felt her blood leap at the warmth of it. "All that matters is what's ahead of us." Her hand trembled against Mary's skin. She leaned closer and put her forehead to Mary's, and Mary closed her eyes and felt Anne's breath, warm on her lips.

Mary scrunched her eyes tight, against the burning beneath her eyelids. "I'd understand, if you changed your mind about leaving with me."

"I want to leave with you more than *anything*." The heat of her hands on Mary's skin warmed her whole body. "And not just because they're going to throw me in gaol if I stay."

Mary laughed. "Aye, I suppose you better come with me after this."

"Let's bloody well get out of this pox-ridden town!" Anne crowed.

Mary was dizzy with the smell of her, the feel of her so close.

Robbie swore and fumbled with a chair, using it to pull himself to his knees.

Mary pulled away. "We have to go!" She looked around frantically. What did they need to take?

"You're done for regardless," Robbie ground out, hanging on to a leg of the table. "You'll never get out of the islands before we catch up with you."

Mary snatched up Robbie's pistol and held it to his head. He flinched away but held her gaze, pure hatred in his eyes.

Mary's hands didn't waver. "I've run from you before. You won't catch me this time, either."

He grinned—or grimaced with pain. She couldn't tell. "The two of you will never make it on your own. We'll be sure to let everyone know that if they help you leave it's a death sentence for them as well. We'll be sure to let *Jack* know, if he's daft enough to try and join you."

Mary looked toward Hog's Island. The sinking sun blazed the horizon red and orange, the whole sky afire—but the sea below was more than dark enough. "Come on, Anne." She lowered the pistol. "I think it's time we made our escape."

CHAPTER FIFTY-FOUR

CARIBBEAN SEA—1719

FAR BELOW, SAILORS SCALING THE POOP DECK LADDER AT A FAIR CLIP caught Mary's eye. Something was amiss in the urgency of their movement. She frowned, leaning forward.

Paddy continued, "I knew the first time, with me Katie—"

"Look." Mary knocked at his arm and pointed to the poop deck. Paddy's brow furrowed when he saw the running and shouting below.

"What do you think has them jumping about like that?" she asked.

Following the gestures of the sailors below, they squinted portside. The *Zilveren Vissen* was passing a small cay as they came within spitting distance of Curaçao. The sun reflected off the smooth sand of its beach to create an intense glare, and it was hard to make out much.

Mary swayed light-headedly and narrowed her eyes against all that dazzle and brilliance, reminded that she hadn't had a meal since morning the day before.

"I don't see nothing." Paddy leaned farther out, shading his eyes.

As Mary strained to see, a vague shadow coming around the cay began to materialize, fading in and out against the glare like a specter. She leaned out and stared past the bow, and then all at once she saw it: the silhouette of another brigantine slipping through the water and fast gaining ground toward them, a black flag dancing in the wind. Her whole body prickled as each hair stood on end, and she clutched the yard beneath her. Before her mind could properly register the sight, she heard the fearsome shout from the crow's nest above.

"Pirates!"

The word pulled a trigger, the crew exploding into frenzied action. Within moments they dragged weaponry out from the forecastle and began distributing it among the frantic swarm of sailors. Mary and Paddy fumbled down the ratline as fast as their trembling limbs would carry them.

Mary stared toward Curaçao. As large and promising as it had loomed moments before, it suddenly seemed terribly far away.

Paddy dashed toward the growing throng surrounding the weapons. Mary trailed after him, watching the approaching brig. That first jolt of panic still coursed through her body, but ideas were forming in her mind. She had no intention of fighting—the pirates could kill the bloody captain and take whatever was in the *Vissen*'s hold, for all she cared. All she wanted was to set foot on land.

The ship intercepting theirs grew larger and darker as it gained on them, becoming solid against the sea. Why should she fight for Baas? She might have joined the crew of her own free will, but she knew about press gangs, how men were stolen from their beds and their families to work a ship.

Mary stumbled into a murky din below deck, the air sharp with gunpowder and sweat. Down the row of cannons and shirtless scrambling bodies, a shaft of light coming through an open gun port illuminated Paddy's grizzled torso. Mary wormed her way through the madness. "Paddy!" He looked up. The light reflected off his eyes unnaturally in the darkness as he strained to adjust the cannon. Mary crouched down and heaved with him.

"Now's me chance to make it off the brig, and you should come with me!" Mary shouted, trusting that the chaos around them and the English she spoke would keep the other tars from overhearing. "You really planning on fighting these pirates, then going all the way back to Flanders with the Baas-tard? On the chance that he might find it in his heart to pay you once you're there, if the both of you make it through today alive?" Metal scraped wood as the four-pounder resisted sliding into place. Paddy clawed up to the gun port and peered through.

"We can't get another shot in, they're following too closely!" Paddy's voice was high and tight, echoing down the line in Dutch as the other sailors registered the same sight. Then the brig lurched again, words turning to garbled shouting as men pitched to the floor.

"They must've jammed the rudder!" Paddy said as a sailor at the foot of the ladder bawled over the racket, *"Alle hens aan dek! Alle hens aan dek!"*

All hands on deck. Mary followed Paddy into the crowd swarming up the stairs. "No one will notice!" she hollered. "Me and you and that wee jolly boat—sure, no one'll miss us in the middle of this! The two of us, starting fresh in the Indies—we'll have a better chance at making our fortune than this!"

He turned sharply, and the press of men pushed her too close to him. "If Baas or one of the officers saw us jumpin' ship mid-battle, it'd be a bullet in the back and no mistake," he hissed into her face. "And I'd not leave the other men besides. It's deserters like you who lose a fight for the rest of us!" He turned and heaved himself up the ladder. A smattering of gunfire echoed above. Feet pounded on the deck, and enemy ammunition thumped as it burrowed into the hull.

Deserters like you. She didn't think of herself as a deserter. She didn't owe this ship or this crew or this captain *anything*.

People wanted to think that everything was black and white. Laws were laws. Family was family. Right was right and wrong was wrong. Boy was boy and girl was girl. Her crew was good and the pirates were evil.

Life had revealed itself to be much more complicated.

The first grappling hooks tore into the stern. She grabbed a musket and had just loaded it when the ship rolled violently and ocean water sprayed across her face, blinding her for a moment. When she wiped her eyes smoke from the muskets had already dimmed the onslaught, but she could see enough to make her stomach drop.

Wild, screaming men with gold earrings, brightly patterned bandanas, and cutlasses in their teeth crawled up the grappling lines. Pirates already on deck cleared the path before them with their bullets, firing flintlocks with both hands. Swordsmen slung themselves on board from the taffrail with swirling blades. They shone with vigor, barefoot and naked to the waist, all shades of sunburned, brown, and even the darkest black. A few dropped from musket fire as they cleared the gunwales, collapsing backward into the sea, but already swordplay and pistol fire along the quarterdeck gave them the clear advantage.

Bolting to the forward end of the ship, Mary crammed herself between the forecastle and a barrel, so that the forecastle ladder blocked her from view. She peered at the fight through its rungs, giddy with nerves. No one was coming this way, pirate or sailor. Bending low, she scurried over to the jolly boat and lay the musket at her feet. She untied the tarpaulin and rolled it back, letting it slide to the deck. She'd need to winch those ropes to let it down into the water. She just might make it.

Mary looked back toward the fighting again, to check that she still went unnoticed—and what she saw changed everything.

CHAPTER FIFTY-FIVE

NEW PROVIDENCE—1720

THE NIGHT AIR WAS HOT. IT WAS INFERNALLY HOT AND SO STILL, THE bugs and animals making an obscene racket in the jungle behind the hut as they crept toward the water in darkness. Mary kept peering over her shoulder, at the hut where they had left Robbie trussed and bleeding beneath the table, but no one emerged.

Her fingers found the sun-splintered edge of their jolly boat, then Anne's hand on the other side. She held it for a moment. Anne's eyes were dark and bottomless and beautiful. Anne was here. She would push the boat to the water with Mary. She would row to Hog's Island. She would sail across the world with her.

She leaned forward and Anne did too and Mary kissed her and it was a shout, it was a cheer, a celebration.

Then they silently slid the boat into the weak foaming waves lapping the sand—no wind to rile the water—and under the cover of a thousand crickets and the light of a thousand stars they slipped away.

They stayed silent all the way to Hog's Island. The water was deathly quiet, after the noise of the jungle on Nassau, broken only by the gurgle of paddles slipping in and out of the water, and the creak of the boat. The air cooled a bit over the water. Mary wished for the cover of clouds—but then she wouldn't be able to see Anne in front of her, moonlight pearling the hollow of her throat.

The knock of water against the hull echoed loud as they maneuvered the boat beneath the docks at Hog's Island. Mary stood up and put her hands to the planks above. They could pull themselves up from here, she was sure. They held their breath in the darkness, listening hard.

Then—men's voices murmured above them. The rattle of dice tossed across wood.

Mary sat down again, liquid beginning to pool around her ankles as the jolly boat let on water. She pushed off of a piling with her paddle, and they tried another dock.

The third dock down was the charm. No words or footsteps. No cigar ash feathering down, signaling someone above. No stench of alcohol or pipe tobacco, just the dank smell of ship. Mary had missed it. She'd been ashore too long. She wanted to hug a slimy piling, mush her face in the stink.

Pulling herself up proved a bit of a challenge. The footing of ankle-deep water in the unsteady bottom of the jolly boat was no help, nor the sharp edges of the beams above her, cutting her palms. But she managed, barely; then she lay flat to the dock and hung her torso down, pulling Anne up and into her arms.

They lay on the dock for a moment, breathless, the soggy bottom of Anne's dress sticking to Mary's legs. Mary's breath caught in her throat when she looked over at her.

Everything was different. *I am different*. She had shaken loose from her moorings. She could go anywhere from here.

Mary wished they could lie there forever, staring up at the stars.

They crept along the docks until they saw their vessel, its prow glowing in the moonlight. It was in such gleaming condition that it stood out clearly among the other boats and brigs, light catching on its bright spars and beams and railings. John Ham's sloop. John "Catch Him if You Can" Ham—the famous privateer, made so by the quickness of his little ship. Small enough to man with just a few people, if it were needed. Big enough to carry them across the ocean. Fast enough to get them there before they died of starvation or thirst, if they were lucky.

"There it is," Mary whispered. "That's our ship."

Anne nodded, a slow smile spreading across her lips. She'd come back to life, Mary could see it. She had been crushed, living in New Providence. She needed more room. She needed a whole ocean.

It was a handsome sloop, with six guns, its lines sleek and well-maintained. Its name was the *William*. Asking around, Mary had learned that John Ham was on shore, receiving commission for his latest raid on the Spanish. It was tethered to the dock by a sturdy line and bowline knot that was easily untied. No plank to board it with, but there was a plank on the ship next to it, and how easy it was to slide it off one ship and lay it against another, with the two of them to move it. It thunked against the railing of the ship, and Mary held her breath. Surely if someone was aboard, they would have heard that. Ham might be at the governor's mansion, but he could have left someone to guard his precious ship.

But no one came.

They crept up the plank. Their bare feet hit the *William*'s deck. They pulled the line in, and then the plank. They set about hoisting the sails.

Just a bit; just enough to get them moving.

The *Delicia*, the governor's flagship, stood guard at the entrance of the harbor between Nassau, Hog's Island, and open water. In a jolly boat, they'd been too slight to warrant notice. On their way out, though, in John Ham's precious sloop—

Mary had a plan.

On the docks of Hog's Island, no man looked up from his dice long enough to see the sail inch up along a mast. No man set down his bottle long enough to notice that Ham's ship had come unmoored. No man looked past the glowing end of his pipe to see the silhouettes of two women creeping along the railing, hands held fast.

CHAPTER FIFTY-SIX

CARIBBEAN SEA—1720

"STATE YOUR BUSINESS," THE WATCHMAN ON THE *DELICIA* HOLLERED pompously.

"John Ham here, sir," said Mary easily, a broad-brimmed hat from the captain's quarters hiding her face. "Was settling in for the night and damn it all, my anchor line broke and I discovered myself adrift."

"Horrid bad luck," remarked the watchman. "Losing an anchor like that. What do ye need—a tether for the night?"

Anne squeezed her hand excitedly, crouched next to the gunwale so she wouldn't be seen.

"No need, I've men enough to keep it in place for the night with sailpower—I'll wait till morning to go find a new anchor."

"Aye. Makes sense, that," said the watchman.

Anne clapped a hand over her mouth, eyes wide with delight.

"We'll stand outside the harbor for the night. Be back in the morning."

"'Night then," said the watchman.

They hardly breathed as they passed the *Delicia*, rounded the corner of Hog's Island, and hoisted the sails. They certainly didn't whoop until they were well out of earshot.

They were on board the fastest ship in the Bahamas.

It mattered not if you were on the run, if no one could catch you.

This ship was different. This ship was fast; Mary felt it hum beneath her feet as the sails unfurled, she heard it sigh when the wind picked up. She realized she'd only ever been on stiff, awkward vessels before now. Resisting the water, when water invited so much give and take. She'd liked sailing before, but this was different. This ship was small and light and unafraid. This ship was built to hug the wind, to skim the water—it felt like flying.

She was sailing as Mary Reade, and she would man a cannon. She would mend a sail. Whatever happened, she'd live and die as herself—not poor dead Mark, not some pretend girl she thought she should be.

Mary's lungs filled with warm air and it felt like her heart was heating up inside her. She was running away, but this time Anne was with her. It wasn't a home she was running from, but another would-be prison.

Home was coming with her this time.

CHAPTER FIFTY-SEVEN

Caribbean Sea—1719

It was then, as Mary looked into the battle fog with the stench of blood and sulfur in her nose, that she saw a strange and incredible vision hurtling over the gunwales.

Eyes wild, the fantastic creature had two men down before Mary could scarcely register the sight of her. A girl. Unmistakably a girl, like her, but dressed in battered velvet and lace worn in a steady salt spray and the West Indian sun. Her curly red hair tangled atop her head in an outrageous mess. She sweated, beaming as if she'd impressed herself by ascending the grappling line in skirts.

Cutlass, flintlock, one two, and the man before the girl went down. The girl's cunning black eyes swept the deck.

Nothing about the girl made sense.

Mary had never seen anything so exhilarating.

ACKNOWLEDGMENTS

SO MANY BRILLIANT, KIND, AND THOUGHTFUL PEOPLE HAVE CONTRIBUTED to this book since I was first inspired to write it.

Thank you to Joy Neaves and Tommy Hayes, and everyone in that workshop at Warren Wilson College and my classes at the Great Smokies Writing Program who read my first pages and encouraged me to actually write the dang thing, and to apply to the MFA program at Vermont College of Fine Arts.

Thank you to my entire, enthusiastic VCFA family. What an incredible and supportive community! In particular, a thousand thanks to my advisors, Martine Leavitt, Susan Fletcher, and Rita Williams-Garcia, for teaching me so much while I got the story down—and to Julie Larios, for giving me such a fun break from it! Thank you to An Na, for being a wonderful friend and mentor after VCFA.

Thank you to my extra-special super team at VCFA, the Secret Gardeners! I love you all. A special thanks to Cordelia Jensen, for giving me so much advice and letting me peek behind the curtains of the publishing process before I was there myself. And the most grateful love and appreciation for Nora Carpenter and Rachel Hylton, my SG Asheville buddies when our time at VCFA was done. You guys were there, cheering and commiserating and beta-reading through every dang step. You both are the literal BEST.

Thank you to Mom and Dad, for letting me read all the books I wanted when I was growing up, and for thinking that everything I ever wrote was amazing. Thank you to all of my awesome friends! Thank you to G Tates, for being the best pen pal ever and not telling me I was insane when I sent you poorly written chapters composed on a typewriter by snail mail because I thought it was romantic. Special thanks to Caroline and David, for reading an early draft of the manuscript I gave you after I'd had a few cocktails (even though I was adamant about not letting *any* of my friends read it) and then telling me it was amazing every time I was feeling discouraged. Thank you to Hannah, for being my inside operative at Malaprops Bookstore. Thank you to Al for believing in me and my stories even when I didn't, and for all the impassioned conversations about gender and the world and history and queerness that influenced this book.

Thank you to the French Broad Chocolate Lounge, Dobra Teahouse, and the Battery Park Book Exchange and Champagne Bar for all the sugar, caffeine, and wine it took to keep me going. Thank you to Sharyn November for your enthusiasm, and for some particularly impactful feedback. Thank you to Heather Demetrios and the Pneuma Creative community. Thank you to Raki Kopernik, for being my rad new writing group since I moved to Minneapolis!

An extra-special thank you to Linda Epstein, my passionate and enthusiastic agent, for falling in love with Mary's story and then never giving up on her, or me. I couldn't ask for a better advocate. And thank you for having such amazing taste, so that I'm part of the most talented and fun crew of clients ever!

Thank you to the Sky Pony team, especially Sammy Yuen for an adventurous and romantic cover that makes me squee every time I see it, and Kat Enright for that awesome scene suggestion!

And finally, thank you to Rachel Stark, my perfect, badass editor. Working with you has been a dream come true, and somehow this story has become exactly the book I wanted to write. I can never thank you enough.